CEMETERY MURDERS

A mystery by
Jean Marcy

New Victoria Publishers

Published by New Victoria Publishers, Inc., a feminist literary and cultural organization, PO Box 27, Norwich, VT 05055-0027

Printed and bound in Canada
1   2   3   4   5   2001   2000   1999   1998   1 997

Acknowledgements:

We wish to acknowledge the people who own and manage a few of the small businesses that give St. Louis its unique coloration, places Meg, Pat, and we like to hang out—the still thriving Pho Grand and South City Diner and Duff's, the ever-special Left Bank Books, and the late and certainly lamented Paul's Books and Blue Moon Coffeehouse.

We thank every mystery writer we've ever read, most especially the women, just for being there to inspire and refresh.

We thank all our friends for the love that sustains us. We especially thank the Susans for their indefatigable listening. They with Karen and Joanne, Tina and David, Margarette and Terry, Marilyn, and Thoraya offered encouragement and enthusiasm during our journey.

Not least, we thank ReBecca Béguin at New Vic for shepherding these lambs toward the fold. Without her editorial help we'd still be stuck in draft seventeen.

Library of Congress Cataloging-in-Publication Data
Marcy, Jean.
        Cemetery murders : a mystery / by Jean Marcy.
              p.   cm.
        ISBN 0-934678-83-9
        I. Title.
      PS3563.A6435C4   1997
      813'.54--dc 21   96–45120
                                                                        CIP

For Grace

Chapter One

On the Sunday morning after Thanksgiving, I looked over my newspaper at my friend and neighbor Patrick Healy. His lanky frame was slumped in my overstuffed chair. He was grinning at the front page of the *St. Louis Post Dispatch*.

"Queer St. Louis held a die-in at the Department of Family Services office because Medicaid won't pay for home nurses for AIDS patients," he said. "Here, take a look, Meg."

I put down the section of the paper I was reading and held out my hand. Patrick handed me the paper and pulled himself out of the chair. As he went into the kitchen to start our breakfast, I looked at the photo he had pointed to with its caption. My eye then skipped to a single column below the fold.

THIRD HOMELESS VICTIM DUMPED AT CALVARY

The article sketched the details of the latest murder by strangulation of a homeless woman. Like the others, this body had been found in a St. Louis cemetery, propped in a mausoleum doorway. This time it was Calvary, the huge old Catholic cemetery on the North Side. The article quoted Detective Sarah Lindstrom of the Homicide Division: "The victim has not yet been identified, but it appears she was also a homeless person. We are following up on several leads at this time." Unfortunately, there was no picture of Lindstrom.

Lindstrom and I had first met a decade earlier when I was still in the Army. A party of us gals and guys—we'd all called ourselves gay then—had rented a place in Texas on San Padre Island and were spending a lot of time on the beach in the sunshine and in the moonlight. Lindstrom was with another volleyball party. I was immediately attracted to her athletic grace and infrequent but lovely smiles. On her part, she'd looked interested until she learned I was from the St. Louis area. Then a complete freeze-out.

Two years after that vacation, out of the Army and back in Belleville, just across the river from St. Louis, I learned that Lindstrom was with the St. Louis Police Department and on the fast track. She was said to be smart and ambitious. She was also said to be the closeted partner of a successful corporate lawyer. They lived the high life. About two years ago, I heard they were what Jerry

Burger describes as 'Splitsville' in his society columns. The Norwegian cop didn't attend any community events or hang out in any of the usual places. In the gay gossip circuits Lindstrom was seen from the outside, her inner life only imagined. She was not popular, but certainly admired. She was tall, trim, well-tailored with broad shoulders and a chiseled chin. From a distance she looked perfect, and she managed to keep most folks seeing her from that perspective. What really made her tick was a mystery. Maybe her standoffishness would grow tiresome, but she had piqued my curiosity. I wanted to pique hers.

Six months ago I'd had my chance.

I'd headed for a warehouse where we had set up security because neither Walter, the uncle I work for at Miller Security, nor I had a good feeling about the guard, Russ Riker. I'd only seen him once, but he had been ogling Colleen, our receptionist-secretary, in a way that made both Colleen and me nervous. His references had checked out though, and he'd told Walter that he'd quit working for his father because the old man was too controlling.

It was a lovely May night. I'd had one or two beers at Attitudes. By the time I remembered I was supposed to check on Riker, it was after twelve. I nearly skipped it because my pillow was calling to me. But Walter had asked me just before I left work not to forget. Reputation is everything in the security business. So I headed south on Broadway and passed Busch Stadium.

Calley's Carry Away, a rent-to-own business, was a new contract for us. Emil Calley had wanted younger security guys—types who would be able to lend an occasional hand at getting furniture on or off the truck. He had also been in a hurry so we didn't have Riker bonded yet. A new employee, a new contract, all this made Walter nervous.

I was thinking I would sleep in the next morning to make up for this little babysitting chore when I saw the cruiser outside Calley's Carry Away. All thoughts of my pillow vanished as I pulled my Plymouth Horizon in behind the white St. Louis Police vehicle, and rolled down my window. The smooth hum of the police car engine contrasted with the Plymouth's occasional hiccoughs. No other noises seemed out of place on this St. Louis night, except for the faint crackle of the scanner.

When I got out of the car, I saw the flashlight moving towards me. The male officer looked short against the chain-link fence surrounding the warehouse, and he was alone. Either he had just arrived or the problem wasn't a big one. I approached the double-gate—wide enough to admit Calley's blue delivery vans. The flashlight passed the gate and played over the high warehouse windows. This red brick building was much older than Calley's business—I had no idea what commodities had previously passed through it. I figured I'd better make my presence known before the flashlight found me and the cop assumed the worst.

"Hey—hello there. Had some trouble?"

The flashlight snapped to my face. I blinked and held up my palm. "I'm Meg Darcy from Miller. We manage the security on this building."

A dry laugh came from behind the flashlight. "Not something I'd be bragging about."

"What kind of trouble are we in?"

"Your guy a young man? Short, dark hair?"

I tried to remember Riker's looks. "Yeah, he's twenty-something. Slightly built."

The cop pushed open the gate with his heavy black shoe. I still couldn't see his face, my eyes unable to adjust after having the flashlight shine in them.

"Come on in. Don't touch anything or go anywhere except I tell you it's okay." He paused as he peered at me. "You want to see him?"

"Is he hurt? Have you called for help?"

"Yes, I've called, but he's beyond help." He modified his tone just enough to be respectful.

"He's dead?"

"Gave his life for a few VCRs, I'd say. Homicide will be here in a few minutes. If you want a peek, it'll have to be now." I nodded and followed him to the north end of the building. There, half in and half outside the gray metal doorway was Riker's body.

"He pressed the alarm button before they got to him. I just got here about three minutes ago."

I peered into the semi-lit warehouse. "Any chance they're still in there?"

"I doubt it—left as soon as they shot him, I'm sure. You better go back to your car anyway. Homicide catches you here, I'll be in for an ass chewing."

I wanted to do something for Riker. I hadn't really known him, but he belonged to us, and it seemed callous to walk away. I noticed Riker hadn't had time to sew his Miller Security patch to the shoulder of his white shirt. The cop yanked my arm.

We walked back to the main gate. Just before we reached it, a beige Crown Victoria pulled up to the Horizon's back bumper, effectively blocking my car in. The door popped open, and a blond head appeared over the hardtop. Lindstrom.

She walked to the gate in her purposeful stride. She hadn't yet recognized me in the shadows. My pulse speeded up. The her blue eyes held mine a long two seconds before she acknowledged the uniformed cop. "Evening, Mallory. You call Meg Darcy here for back up?"

"No…," he stuttered. "…She just drove up a minute ago. I didn't call nobody but headquarters."

"I wandered in on my own, Lindstrom. We just took on this client. I was checking on our security guard because he is new." Was new.

The crime scene van pulled up and double-parked next to my car, making my departure even more impossible.

"Well, since you're here, stay awhile, and I'll get some information from you later," Lindstrom said. "Stay here." She indicated the spot where I was standing, and nodded to Mallory, signaling her readiness to see the victim.

I stood and watched the crime scene techs unload flood lights, and a man with two cameras around his neck light a cigarette. Evidently the ban on smoking had reached inside his own truck. Another tech said something to him, and they dragged their equipment toward the warehouse.

The photographer grinned at me on the way in. I waited about three minutes and then followed. Staying near the building, I stopped about fifty feet from Riker. The photographer was snapping pictures, his companion holding lights. Mallory and Lindstrom were in the warehouse looking for evidence. The photographer finished, and then his companion took out tape measure and chalk, and began measuring. I bit my lip. This wasn't my first dead body, but this was the first death by violence I'd seen. Walter would take it hard. I hoped it wouldn't send him on a downward spiral.

"I told you to stay by the gate."

I nearly jumped out of my skin; then I was irritated at her for the patronizing tone. I said blandly, "Sorry. I thought you meant for me to stay on the property. I was just watching your men at work."

Lindstrom flipped to a new page in her notebook. "His name?"

"Russ Riker."

"Address?"

"He's a brand new employee, his first night on the job. Walter hired him. We have all his personal information on his application at the office."

Lindstrom gave me a hard look I couldn't interpret. "All right. We'll go to your office. Call Walter and tell him to meet us there in twenty minutes."

Her tone made me think she was ordering Mallory, but when

he didn't move, I bolted for my car. On the way I prayed that Walter was home *and sober*. I didn't want to give him this news on the phone, but didn't see any way to avoid it. Rummaging around my back seat, I finally found the cheap cellular phone he'd given me. The phone rang twelve times before finally rousing him.

"Walter, this is Meg over at Calley's."

He grunted.

"Problem here, Walter. It looks like Riker interrupted a burglary." I paused. "He's been shot. Dead." I waited a moment for him to absorb it, then said, "The cops want you to come down to the office so that we can give them his information."

"Okay, I'll head right over."

I waited for some reassurance from him, that he'd be okay, that we'd be okay, that we didn't just send a young man to his death for four dollars and fifty-five cents an hour. Walter groaned There was a long pause." Then he yelled, "Meg!"

I nearly dropped my cell phone.

"Meg, you still there?"

"Yes, I'm here."

"Did the shooting happen inside or outside?"

"He's in the doorway actually, so I'm not sure. Feet inside, torso out. So maybe he was shot while inside and then fell outward."

"There are two cameras inside the warehouse, Meg. One on the north side of the building and one on the front, facing east on Broadway."

"I thought Calley said he couldn't afford cameras."

"I installed them just as a trial run. Figured he'd change his mind. Figured with all those easily transportable goods we'd catch some goon taking home a PC or VCR soon but not this soon."

I reminded him to meet Lindstrom and me at the office, and pushed the End button before walking back to the north end of the building. The photographer passed me as he returned to his van, sucking hard on his cigarette.

The gray metal door was still open, Riker's body still across the threshold, and the other tech stood about ten feet away from the body, guarding the scene until the medical examiner arrived. I couldn't slip by the tech and didn't see any way to create a diversion so I walked by him, smiled, and stepped across Riker into the warehouse as if I had a right. The tech merely watched.

Inside was lighter than outside. About a third of the long florescent lamps suspended from steel rafters were lit. I looked up into the corner of the building. Walter would have needed to place the camera by an outlet or light fixture. Eyeing the length of one of the huge steel beams away from the brick wall, I then skipped to the next.

There it was, a small black camera, its red light reassuringly steady. Perhaps at least part of the crime had happened in its line of sight. For a second I debated trying to get the film without Lindstrom's knowledge. But if we were to prosecute, the chain of evidence couldn't start with me.

I looked around for a ladder. The camera was too high for the aluminum one back at the office so there had to be one here. But before I could find one, Lindstrom found me, arriving without Mallory.

Her blue eyes sparked. "What are you doing here? You're contaminating the damn crime scene. Can't you follow a simple order?"

"Save it, Lindstrom. We need a ladder to get the film out of that security camera."

"Camera? You forgot to mention a camera?"

"I didn't know. Walter installed one there at the end of the building. We may have something on it."

"Darcy, are you jerking me around or are you stupid? Were you going to get a ladder and take the film without telling me?"

I could feel my fist tighten and my shoulder pull back for the punch, but I glared instead. "No, I wasn't going to take the damn film. I was going to find a ladder so you could take the damn film, and if it shows anything, you can find the stupid son of a bitch who killed Riker. Then you can take the film and shove it, for all I care."

With that I walked away on my search, seething. Minutes later when I found a ladder, I wasn't any calmer. Returning, I found Mallory and showed him where the camera hung, let him do the climbing.

By the time he had the film in hand, the medical examiner had arrived, and twenty minutes later Riker was in a bag on his way to the Clark Street morgue.

I was cold and angry, those earlier beers sour in my stomach, as I leaned with my back against the chain link fence.

Lindstrom walked up to me, stood close, the video cassette in her hand, checking her watch. "Where's the office?"

"On Gravois, almost to the city limits." I reeled off the address.

"Isn't there a Quick Pick near there?" Her eyes bore into mine for a fraction of a second before she averted her gaze.

"Yeah, one block past the office."

"I'll stop there for coffee and then be in." As she turned away she brushed my arm with the back of her hand, nearly but not quite by accident.

I didn't tell her that Walter would have a pot waiting for us. Let her drink gas station coffee. West on Russell and southwest on Gravois, I tried to think calmly about Lindstrom and her signals to me that night. Right from the beginning she had been unhappy I was there. Did she think I was going to blow her cover? Act queer in front of her subordinates? The woman was attractive physically but such a horse's ass. My thoughts veered between violence and an urge to excuse her. She was a homicide detective, after all. She had to be tough, proving herself twice as good at every step. Even if it had to be with me. And she was so delicious. I could almost taste her skin.

When I turned into the side street at the office, her unmarked car slid by toward QT. Walter's Oldsmobile was in the small lot behind the office, and all the lights were on in the building. If it hadn't been for Walter and that video tape, I'd have gone home and pulled the covers over my head. Instead I locked the Plymouth and opened the back door of Miller Security.

Walter and I chatted a few minutes. His beefy face was ruddier than usual, but he was sober. I filled him in on exactly how I found Riker, and our removal of the tape. I omitted saying what a jerk Lindstrom had been. Let him draw his own conclusions when the Ice Queen turned her scowl on him.

Over coffee we looked at Riker's unremarkable application form. His last employer was listed as his father's salvage business, home address on Pestalozzi, his interests were in part-time or full-time work, preferably nights.

Lindstrom found us sitting in the office talking about going to see Russ Riker's father the next day to offer our condolences. After I made minimal introductions, Lindstrom sat on the captain's chair to my right as we both faced Walter in his chair behind his cluttered metal desk.

As she began to question him I noticed that while not deferential, Lindstrom didn't fire off at him as though he was a half-wit, as she had with me. I took the opportunity to go make copies of his application and references, and also of the help wanted ad we had put out for the job. Before I was done, I heard them going into the store room. I walked in to find Walter turning on our VCR as she stood holding the tape out to him. How had he talked her into watching it here?

As the tape spun out, I recognized a stack of boxed TVs and the corner of one marked as a washing machine. We could see half the doorway where we had found Riker. We watched boxes and the door for long minute as I became aware of Lindstrom's faint perfume until finally Walter hit the fast forward button. A figure came into view and Walter snapped back to Play.

A figure foreshortened by the camera angle had no face, just a dark head, dressed in dark jacket and pants, not Riker, who wore a light shirt and blue work pants as Walter required. The figure moved in and out of view, then another figure moved in—carrying a box out the door! Shit. Not good news. The two figures came back and took out more boxes. Suddenly Riker appeared empty handed, followed by dark jacket, pausing just inside long enough for the camera to get his face.

"Freeze!" I blurted to Walter. Out of the corner of my eye Lindstrom flinched. I moved closer to rewind and replay, pausing. The face was familiar, but from where? Thin nose, acne scarred.

"You know him?" Lindstrom was all business, but curious.

"Walter, isn't that Tom Swann's brother-in-law? The one who was ripping him off after Swann gave him a job and all?"

Walter peered at the grainy image. "Huh, could be."

I pressed Play again. "That's him. Billy Dodd. He was stealing dirt bikes from Swann a couple of years ago. Swann didn't prosecute, just fired him."

"You were doing security for this Swann?" Lindstrom asked.

"No. He called us in after he noticed bikes missing. We staked out his place a few nights, didn't see anything. Later I caught Billy driving a load of bikes to Jeff City. He'd already sold a load but we recovered some."

She nodded her head towards the TV. "How about the other one?"

Again we studied the tape. The third figure didn't reappear. Unexpectedly an arm flew by the camera, and Riker fell to the floor hitting with his head and shoulder. He scrambled up and out of camera view. A long look at the boxes. Then Riker walked quickly to the door, hesitated, looked over his shoulder. Dodd came into view and it looked like Riker was shouting at him with agitated gestures. Then Dodd grabbed his arm and Riker punched back. Dodd doubled over and Riker turned to the door. Without warning, he fell backwards, his arm striking the door frame.

"They shot him!" Walter shouted.

The third figure ran into view, pulling Dodd to his feet, and they both scuttled out the door, Dodd stepping on Riker's arm as he fled.

Lindstrom was writing in her notebook, and addressed her question to Walter. "You have an address on Dodd?"

"Only through Swann's Cycles on Rock Hill." Walter rewound the tape. "Should I call Russ's dad?"

"No, the department will do that. And don't mention this tape

12

to anyone," she said, gesturing for him to hand it over. Taking that and the photocopies I handed her, she was gone without further instructions and barely a good night.

I sighed in exasperation. "She treats me like an idiot!"

Walter peered at me. "I don't think so. Why would she let us see the tape with her then?"

"She wanted an ID from us. And she got it!"

Neither of us mentioned what it felt like watching as Riker was shot.

"You going to be okay, Meg?"

"Nothing a good night's sleep won't cure," I grumbled. And a weekend with a gorgeous, funny woman who admired my smarts.

Two days later, Monday, Lindstrom swaggered into Miller Security. Walter was in but she had Colleen buzz me, and then lead her into my office.

I'd had time to simmer down but I wanted to stay cool another way. So for one thing, I remained seated, looked her over, and tapped my pen on my desk. "How can I help you, Lindstrom?"

She hadn't lost any of her looks, nor any attitude. Uninvited, she sat down, hitching up her expensive slacks and crossing her long legs. Her linen jacket was crisp, so was her tone. "We've got it wrapped up, Darcy. I'll buy you a drink some time, but I thought you'd like to know now."

"You found Dodd? He talked?"

"He sang sweetly."

"How'd you find him?"

"Through Swann." No cat ever looked more smug over cream. "Turns out Emil Calley put them up to it. He has been fencing stolen goods. Slipping hot goods in with his rentals. To cover up and because Miller Security had installed a camera, Riker was supposed to act like he was trying to stop them in full view. Dodd was supposed to beat him up but hit him too hard. Riker got angry and started yelling and punching at Dodd. That's when Charlie, Dodd's older brother, who hadn't got the message that a camera had been installed, got nervous and fired his gun."

She stopped there as if waiting for applause. I didn't oblige her. "Go on."

"Calley set him up to be hired by Miller Security. He was going for an insurance scam on 'stolen goods.' Had to have legitimate security."

I felt the heat climbing to me cheek. "And thought we wouldn't catch on?"

She changed the subject. "Too bad we can't pin the murder on Calley, but we have the Dodd brother anyway."

"Thanks to brilliant police work."

She smiled, missing the irony. "Well, sometimes taxpayers get their money's worth." She glided up from her chair. "Most of it will be in *The Post*, but I just wanted you to know."

The smile looked like a smirk to me. No nod to Walter's tape. No thanks to my identifying Billy Dodd.

Then, incredibly, she leaned over my desk, offering a handshake. I scrambled to my feet, leaned over to grasp her hand, off balance several ways. Touching her hand jolted me. She held on longer than necessary, saying, "I'm not sure we can keep Miller Security's name out of the case."

I shrugged as I let go. "As long as they spell it right." Teasing, of course.

She relinquished my hand but kept my eyes. "You've always got a comeback, haven't you, Darcy?"

With that she walked out, leaving me precisely without one. She had done it to me again—made me feel like an idiot. And regrettably, that was the only chance I'd had to work with her. I still wanted to vindicate myself. Badly.

Rustling the front section of the paper as I put it down, I called into my small kitchen, "Hey, Patrick. Do you remember Lindstrom?"

"How could I forget the Norwegian Ice Queen?"

I followed the smell of coffee and watched Patrick chop green onions and whisk eggs. Harvey Milk, my white cat, twined a figure eight around my legs, so I picked him up. He hates to be hugged, so that's a good way to shoo him off. "She's on the cemetery murders."

"Oooooh, perfect for her social skills," he said. I laughed, and happily Patrick did not turn to see my blush. I located the toaster, made toast, and set plates and silverware on the small red-topped table that Patrick and I had rescued on trash day last year.

"Too bad Lindstrom doesn't use her investigative talents on you, Meg. Suppose she had half the persistence of your pal Ann Yates." He shot me a look.

He was just testing the waters. He suspected I carried a torch for Lindstrom, but he had decided she was the wrong woman for me.

"Ann isn't coming on to me."

"I know a courtship when I see it."

"I've known flirty straight women; Ann isn't like that."

He gave the irritatingly knowing laugh of an old friend. "If she isn't the one putting the moves on, why are you hanging back?"

Fair question. Maybe a therapist would be interested in sorting it out. My last two years had rung too many changes. Susan had announced our relationship had gone stale. A surprise to me, but I'd been too proud to admit it or fight for us. We'd had an amiable divorce with a sour taste developing only afterwards. At the same time, Barb Talbot, my best friend from my Army days, went to the Pacific Northwest to chase her rainbows. Then Chris, my closest friend from Belleville, had followed her husband to Virginia. Abandonment themes figured in my dreams.

Then there was Detective Sarah Lindstrom. My feelings about her sharpened my loneliness. I didn't know Lindstrom well enough to like her. What I felt resembled lust. On the one or two occasions I'd seen her since Riker's, she'd shot me a look that suggested she'd like to know me better, if circumstances changed. But I didn't know which circumstances I was supposed to change.

By contrast, Ann Yates' overtures were openly flattering. They did resemble a courtship, but I was certain what she wanted to woo from me was friendship. We had met while stuffing envelopes to combat Missouri's anti-gay initiative. I'd sat next to her, drawn by her warm smile and striking auburn hair. It was one of those situations in which people form quick if somewhat superficial bonds. Lots of laughter and speeches at the opponent's expense. Ann took it all in, her serious face dominated by wide-set hazel eyes.

I told her that I was a thirty-three year old, unattached lesbian, working for Miller Security, my uncle's private investigation firm. I mentioned my mother, Betty. I told her a little about my friend Patrick and a lot about my cat Harvey Milk.

She was thirty-three, too, but straight. She won a point when she didn't pass that information on defensively in the first sentence. She was engaged to a man named Philip, but she was refreshingly sparse with details about him. Natural reticence or good manners or even indifference. I couldn't guess.

A St. Louis native, she'd gone to school in University City, then Washington University, and graduated from Wash. U's law school. She'd practiced corporate law a few years, then started teaching pre-law courses at the University of Missouri—St. Louis, or UM-SUL to the locals. "I make a better teacher than I ever did a lawyer," she said with a charming smile.

In that very first conversation, it was clear that we lived in different worlds in the same city. Her folks lived in Ladue, St. Louis' top-drawer suburb. I lived on the South Side in a kaleidoscope, a changing neighborhood where businesses jostled old homes and the city's first automatic teller machine murder netted twenty dollars. So I was wary when Ann Yates kept calling. We did lunch and took in a movie; once we went to an art exhibit. Sometimes we just bummed through flea markets. But Patrick was right. I was hanging back, and it wasn't just the class barrier. Maybe because I would rather have been doing these things with Lindstrom.

"Grab the coffee." Patrick was splitting the omelette onto two plates. From his, he scooped off a small corner into Harvey's bowl. We settled to the breakfast that has become our Sunday custom—if neither of us is entertaining a sleep-over date. Patrick and I have seen quite a bit of each other over the last hundred Sundays.

"So," he said as he buttered a bite of English muffin, "what's the latest on the Yates-Darcy affair?"

"Some affair. This Friday she took me with her to visit her aunt in a nursing home."

"Thrilling. The rich are so deft at entertaining."

"Well, it was interesting, anyway. And a little sad."

"If it was a nursing home, it was a lot sad."

"Yeah, but this was a bit different. Ann's Aunt M—that's what they call her—is only in her sixties, but she's got Alzheimer's."

He shook his head sympathetically.

"Ann is really good with her. She talks to her as though Aunt M makes sense. She connects emotionally even though her words are all garbled."

I could see Patrick's face soften. He basically believes in the goodness of the human race, and he now probably thought Ann was the perfect wife for me. Rich and loving. No matter her predilection for the male of the species. I decided to ignore him.

"Aunt M is Ann's favorite relative. She was Ann's childhood idol."

"Get to the good part. Did you kiss her?"

"This is the good part. Aunt M was, is a lesbian. She lived with the same woman for nearly thirty years until death did them part. And she was pretty up front and open about it, at least to the family."

"Being out to your family is the hardest part."

"Of course, she didn't have to worry about her job. Aunt M was pretty well-heeled, and her partner was a travel writer. They traveled all over the world. Maybe that's Ann's interest in me. She thinks lesbians are adventurers."

"Or maybe she's looking for an aunt substitute."

I shot him a look. "Her mother and a cousin, also fond of Aunt M, were visiting the nursing home, too."

Patrick leaned forward. "That's a good sign. Being introduced to the family."

"Her mother is a doctor, a radiologist at Barnes, and her cousin is a stockbroker."

"Is she cute?"

"Ann's mother?"

"The stockbroker."

"Greg is good-looking."

Patrick grinned. "Maybe you could introduce us. We'd double date."

"Not your type."

"Because?"

"Too fond of money."

"I like money."

"Though I have to admit he was good with Aunt M, too. Like Ann, he just chatted away with her as though they were having a real conversation. And he didn't faint when he saw Ann with a lesbian."

"She introduced you to her family as her friend, the lesbian?"

"No, but I just got the sense he spotted me. Instead of a smirk he gave me a manly handshake."

Patrick didn't look impressed. "So was the nursing home really grim?"

"The smell gets to me—disinfectant on top of…" I shrugged. "Whatever it's on top of. But I saw some good things, too. There was a young aide there, a guy named Rudy. He looked like a post-adolescent addict—stringy blond hair, bad complexion, glassy eyes. But he really had a touch with the old ladies. Ann says he takes the time to walk Aunt M every day.

Patrick's own eyes were starting to glaze over. "So what happened after the nursing home?"

"We went to Pho Grand and had dinner and talked about Ann's family history."

"The John Brooks Brewing Company."

"That was her grandfather. Aunt M is his daughter, so is Ann's mom."

"Think about it, Meg. Ann Yates is going to be able to buy more expensive trinkets than any detective can."

"I pay my own rent."

"I meant you can marry for love, but you can love a rich woman as well as a poor one."

"I don't think it is going to happen with Ann, Patrick. She doesn't set my hormones in motion."

"Better than the Ice Queen is all I'm saying."

I decided to eat the last English muffin rather than throw it at him. Restraint is occasionally the better part of friendship. While he cleared the table, I ambled over to the windows that faced the park.

17

A blustery wind was swaying the bare limbs of trees. It looked strong enough to discourage me from our usual after-brunch stroll. I thought about the homeless who didn't have such comfortable choices, about the three homeless women who had been murdered and dumped in local cemeteries. I thought about Aunt M, warm and fed but trapped in the broken maze of her own mind and I shuddered.

Chapter Two

I beat my uncle Walter to the office that foggy Thursday morning the week after Thanksgiving. When he comes in late, his bleary eyes and stooped shuffle tell the story. Most of the time Walter stays within his limits with booze, but sometimes his demons sneak up on him and he drinks a fifth before bed. Periodically I get the urge to talk to Walter about his drinking or about my dad, Walter's step-brother. But Walter always manages to forestall any subjects that require feelings. I'm fond of him and grateful. Grateful for everything he's done for me. Grateful, too, that I do get to work with him and even more grateful that I don't have to live with him.

Colleen, our receptionist-clerk-secretary, greeted me silently with a cup of hot coffee, the files I had requested and the list of calls I needed to make. For the first six months she worked for us Walter said Colleen was only temporary. He insisted we didn't need a receptionist; he was only helping her with some work until she could find a permanent job. She was the daughter of an official in the International Brotherhood of Electrical Workers. Walter had done some work for the union, and he and Colleen's father had become friends.

Only gradually did it become clear to me that Colleen was here to stay. She was self-assured for a twenty-four-year-old and attractive. She was unfailingly punctual and smart and didn't suffer fools well even when the fools had cash to offer Miller Security.

"Thanks. Walter call in yet?" I asked as I took a sip of the coffee.

"Not yet." She didn't meet my eyes, maybe out of her loyalty to the man who'd given her a job.

I've thought about her occasional reserve with me. I've not yet figured if it's because I'm a lesbian, a woman PI or some other Colleen reason. But I consider her a challenge to the Darcy charm.

"Great coffee," I said as I sauntered back to my office.

A moment later, Colleen buzzed, "You've got a call on line one. A woman, Ann Yates; she sounds upset."

"Thanks, Colleen." I picked up the line.

"Hi, Ann, what's going on?" I asked my friend.

"They've let Aunt M wander off. Can you help us find her? She's been gone all night. The idiots here at the nursing home didn't call us until this morning. Please come, Meg."

Aunt M with her memory already badly eroded, would never find her way back to the nursing home on her own. In fact, I was a bit surprised that she'd had the strength and sustained purpose to wander away at all. No wonder Ann sounded so frightened.

"Where are you, the nursing home or your mom's?"

"At Gateway. We're all looking for her. I just don't know what to do. This idiot Rolfing just keeps telling us not to panic. He doesn't have a clue."

"Okay, Ann. I'm on my way. Has anyone notified the police?"

"Yes, my cousin Greg did that a couple of hours ago."

"All right, I'm leaving now. I'll see you in twenty minutes."

I explained the situation to Colleen and asked her to fill in Walter if he inquired about my whereabouts, which I doubted; in his probable condition, he'd have enough trouble keeping track of his own. I told Colleen I'd probably be back after lunch. How far could an old lady wander?

The dense fog I'd driven to work in wasn't clearing, and rush hour traffic was clotting the streets. It took an extra twenty minutes for me to grope my way to the nursing home.

Gateway Nursing Home looked like all the nursing homes I'd ever visited—red brick building hugging the ground, surrounded by small, tidy shrubs. Every entrance had a wheelchair ramp. The quiet drive leading up to it and the firs and bare maple trees surrounding it gave it some distinction. The entrance way led into a formal lounge that looked like the lobby for an inexpensive hotel. The sofa, chairs, and tables were new but not impressive. The lighting was soft. Two family groups occupied the furniture; neither had a patient with them. Either they were just gearing up to go in or recovering from an encounter.

I walked through the lobby and into the long tiled hall that led to the center of the nursing home. Here began all the sights, sounds, and smells I wanted to avoid. I was already taking shallow breaths. On each side of the corridor old people—all old women I think— were lined up in chairs. As I passed, a babble arose. Some called, "Help me." Others said, "Let me go." I just kept moving, avoiding eye contact.

The nurses' station was a hub for four corridors. More patients, including some men, were lined up along the high counter in front. One or two hunched over metal trays, nodding over applesauce and instant mashed potatoes. The sour smell of old bodies was stronger here. Nurses and orderlies moved about the hub and paid me no attention.

I found Ann in what had been Aunt M's favorite lounge. It was faintly recreational with two sturdy card tables and more institutional couches. The picture window looked out on the asphalt parking lot where Aunt M had liked to watch visitors coming and going.

Ann was talking with a short, thick woman in a pantsuit and nursing shoes. Ann turned and said, "Oh, Meg. Thank God you're here. This is my cousin Arlene. Arlene, this is Meg, my friend, the private detective."

"Hello, Meg. I'm Arlene Dorman, the assistant administrator." She made steady eye contact and gave me a firm handshake.

"Hi, Arlene, pleased to meet you." Another cousin? She didn't say Arlene was Greg's sister.

Arlene said that Aunt M had first been missed at bedcheck last night, about eleven. The aide doing bedcheck had searched all the lounges, the cafeteria, and all the bathrooms. She had then notified the nurse on duty and three aides had been dispatched to search every corner of the nursing home. When that was done, Dr. Rolfing, the chief administrator, was called. He sent two aides to search the grounds and arrived himself at six that morning. At seven he had called Deborah and Sam Yates, Ann's parents.

I had several complaints about the way this had been handled so far, but I didn't voice them to Arlene. She clearly was caught between third and home with the catcher bearing down on her. Both family and the nursing home expected her unwavering loyalty.

We walked back to the main nurses' station where the wheelchair brigade was still lined up down the hall and aides were gathering lunch trays. Behind the counter, the tension was more obvious; faces were set in grim lines, and everyone spoke in subdued tones. Arlene excused herself to go back to work. Ann and I walked down to the small entryway lounge.

"So, what's been happening besides the foot search?"

"Greg notified the police, and they said they'd radio a description of Aunt M and instructions to be on the lookout for her to all their cars. One officer is cruising the area, specifically looking for her."

"How many are out on foot?"

"Mom and Dad and Greg and Philip and Rudy, her favorite aide, and Mom's best friend Shirley. Oh, and another aide. I was out earlier, but we're taking turns staying here in case someone calls in that they've found her."

"Do they have a picture of her that they're showing people in the neighborhood?"

"No, no one thought of that. I'll drive home and get one as soon as Mom checks back in."

"Yeah, we need to get a photo and have several copies made at one of those one-hour photo places. Every searcher needs to have one, and we can get some posters made with her picture as well. And we ought to call the *Post-Dispatch*."

"Oh, God, don't you think we'll find her before tomorrow's paper comes out?"

"Yes, I think we will. But if we haven't, it'll be important to pull out all the stops. I have a friend who works for the *Post*; she'll tell me how to get Aunt M's picture in and a short article."

Just then a tall, slender man entered the lounge. He walked like the boss. He came directly to Ann and laid a hand on her shoulder. Ann introduced me to Dr. Rolfing, the administrator of Gateway. She told him my suggestions.

"I'd hold off on the newspaper for now. We'll find her before tomorrow's paper is out. It will just bring a flood of false sightings that we don't have the resources to track down anyway," Dr. Rolfing said.

"I'm sure we'll find her before tomorrow morning, but if we don't, we sure don't want to have to wait until Saturday's edition. If we find her, we'll just call the paper and have them kill the story," I said.

"Ms. Darcy, I'm sure your intentions are good, but let us handle this matter. Alzheimer's patients are our specialty. We know exactly what we're doing here."

I was about to tell Rolfing exactly where to stick his expertise, which amounted to no more than wanting to keep Gateway's name out of the paper, when Ann grabbed my arm and pulled me out of the lounge, mumbling an insincere excuse.

"See what I mean. That snake doesn't give a rat's ass about finding Aunt M," Ann said as we marched down the hallway. We nearly ran into Greg and Ann's mother in the main corridor.

Ann got her looks from her mother. Dr. Yates was about five feet seven inches with auburn hair and hazel eyes, like Ann's. She was immaculately kept and her posture was as erect as a drill instructor's. With her fur-collared coat she looked more like a Ladue matron than a radiologist from Barnes. Greg had the same hazel eyes, but his were set in a broader face, and his hair was brown. He was tall and his legs long, but it was Dr. Yates who set the pace with quick strides—no doubt her usual pace in Barnes' myriad of mile-long corridors.

"Have you heard anything, honey?" Deborah Yates asked her daughter.

"No, but Mom, Meg's got some good ideas for the search. We're going to get a good picture of Aunt M from your house and get copies made to show neighbors, and then we're going to get some posters made to hang up in the area. Meg is going to get an article put in the *Post-Dispatch*. Just in case we don't find her by tomorrow, people can be on the lookout for her."

Greg was nodding vigorously. "Those are great ideas. We need all the help we can get. That way if someone sees her, they'll know where to call."

Just then Rolfing came up behind us. "Dr. Yates, let's go into my office and talk about our next step. I've called in extra aides for the afternoon shift to augment our search party." Ann shot a look at her mother, and Deborah looked from her daughter to the administrator and back again.

"I'll be glad to talk to you, Dr. Rolfing, but while we're talking, Ann and Meg will be getting some pictures copied for posters." Deborah took a step forward and took Rolfing's arm as if she were leading him to her office. Ann nodded at her mother and started for the door.

"Greg, check back here in about two hours. I hope we'll have pictures and posters by then," Ann said.

"Okay, Ann. Good luck." The cousins hugged, and we were on our way in Ann's bright red Saab.

The Yates home in wealthy Ladue was not the biggest, nor the most ostentatious on the block, but it wasn't shabby. The front door was oak with slender panes of frosted glass on each side. It was a two-story Georgian brick with dark green shutters. The front foyer had a terra-cotta tiled floor and an antique table. There was an ornate wooden umbrella stand with two umbrellas and a beautifully carved walking stick. Ann saw me staring at the walking stick.

"That was a present to Dad from Aunt M and Linda. It was carved in India. They spent a winter there when I was little. They both loved to travel." We headed back to the large carpeted staircase. "Mom keeps all the picture albums together in a closet. I'm sure there are some good shots of Aunt M."

We entered a large bedroom that had windows on two sides. The bed was covered with a white duvet. Head and foot board were simple but old and lovely. The carpet was peach, soft and thick. There was a small cherry writing desk to the left of the bed and an off-white couch against the opposite wall. To the right of the couch was a closet door. Ann walked through it and emerged a minute later with several large albums in her arms. She sat on the couch and I joined her. We flipped through what seemed like hundreds of pictures of Ann. She was indeed the treasured only child. Finally we found a photo of Aunt M taken fewer than five years ago that was clear and a good likeness. I found the telephone book and located a place that agreed to make copies of the picture while we waited. They also had the capability to make eight and one half by eleven posters in a rainbow of colors.

On the way to the copy shop Ann seemed more hopeful. She chatted about the adventures of Aunt M and Linda. They had been on four continents and in fifteen countries. Linda had made her living as a travel writer, contributing to dozens of "how to be a tourist" books, as Ann referred to them, and publishing two collections of Linda's own essays about travel. The pair had always lived together as far as Ann knew and made no secret of sharing a bedroom. Even as a child Ann had been clear about their relationship, although she had never heard Aunt M say the word *lesbian*. Ann said she had once talked to her mother about it.

"I asked Mom if Aunt M had ever said she was a homosexual. Mom said no, but Aunt M had often talked about loving Linda.

"I missed Aunt M when she traveled. She was so different from Mom and Dad. They were pretty wrapped up in their own lives. I would have given anything for a brother or a sister."

"Weren't you and Greg close?"

"Greg and I spent quite a bit of time together. But not enough to develop that daily kind of closeness. We were always too competitive to be very supportive of one another." She made a face. "He always wanted to win all the marbles."

"He seems like a nice guy."

"He is. But somehow we still aren't close. Our values are different for one thing. His love for the almighty buck makes him pretty conservative politically. He used to manage my portfolio, but when I insisted it be invested in socially responsible stocks, he freaked. Said as my financial advisor he couldn't allow that. So I took my money to another company. We didn't speak for a while after that, but we got over it, especially when I accepted power of attorney for Aunt M, but asked him to manage her finances—I just didn't have the time. But that's...was simple, seeing to her bills because her investments have been locked in a trust. Well, till now."

"Does he manage your parents' money?"

"No, Mom's used the same guy for a million years. She just never switched to Greg."

"He does pretty well as a stock broker?"

"Yes, he travels a lot and buys all the newest toys. Maybe he's reacting to his dad, too. His father, Aunt M and my mother's brother, had a kind of conversion late in his life and spent all his time and money helping the homeless. In fact, he left a big portion of his money to a couple of shelters in the city."

"How does Arlene fit in?" I asked, figuring that I had added up the family members correctly so far.

"Poor Arlene, you mean. Her name is rarely spoken in our house without the modifier." Ann laughed. "You see, the really big money in the family was made by John Brooks, my grandfather. He had some family money and turned it into a fortune with the John Brooks Brewing Company. Etta was his sister. She married someone Grandpa didn't approve of, and he cut her off without a cent. Etta and the ne'er-do-well had only one child, Vivian. Arlene is her daughter. Mom took a notion about ten years ago to find Etta's child. She found Arlene, but Vivian was already dead. Breast cancer. Mom started inviting Arlene to family gatherings and such. Arlene's never taken the initiative, but she comes when Mom invites her." She paused, seeming to search for words. "She acts like someone who doesn't belong."

"The poor relation, huh?"

"Yes, I guess. Arlene really helped when we had to find a nursing home for Aunt M, though. She told us all the inside details to look for and recommended two nursing homes, Gateway and a place run by the diocese. We finally decided on Gateway. You could tell she was really pleased. I'll say this for her, she makes sure Aunt M has the best care."

I have to admit that I was sympathizing with poor Arlene. I had more in common with the poor relation than with Ann—including, I suspected, a sexual preference. I wanted to ask if Arlene were out to the family. But I thought if she weren't, it might be sticky.

When we arrived at the copy shop, I explained I'd called earlier. A young man in a terrible haircut had an orange tag identifying him as Todd, the Ass't. Manager. He promised he'd start on our order immediately. We ordered ten copies of the snapshot and one hundred posters. He said it would take about two hours, so we found a pay phone, and I called Jill at the *Post-Dispatch*. She promised to get the photo and a short piece in tomorrow's edition if I dropped off the picture and all the relevant facts as soon as possible.

We found a coffee shop nearby where we could wait. Ann recounted the story of Aunt M's illness. One year Aunt M had been her usual self, perhaps a little forgetful. The next year Aunt M was practically a stranger, and Linda and the family were discussing a nursing home.

We finished our coffees and headed back to the copy shop. Our order was on the counter with a yellow post-it note that read YEATS. Todd at least knew his poetry.

The fog lingered and gave an already strange day a surreal

edge. Anyone could get lost and confused on a day like today. I heard a sharp siren pierce the cotton wadding of fog. I cracked the window and wiped the driver's side windshield for Ann. Nothing helped visibility. We headed downtown for the *Post* building on Tucker. Ann circled the block as I dropped the picture and two paragraphs of facts about Aunt M and her disappearance with the receptionist.

Back at Gateway the panic had slipped down a notch or two. Like any group that has an on-going crisis, the staff had begun to respond as if the crisis situation were normal. Ann and I found her mother in Aunt M's room. Ann had all of her prettiness from her mother. But now Dr. Yates' features were distorted and sagging with her worry. She had aged years since I'd first met her.

"Dr. Rolfing asked if we would agree to wait until five tonight before talking to the newspaper," she said.

"Sorry, too late, Mom. Meg already talked to a reporter there, and we dropped the stuff off on the way here."

"That's just as well. It's done now. I imagine at five he would have wanted us to wait more."

I chimed in, "At five, Jill may not have been able to get it in for me."

"Yes," Dr. Yates said vaguely.

"Mom, we need to get some of these posters up while we have daylight and get copies of the pictures out to the searchers."

Dr. Yates didn't respond, so I did. "Ann, let's leave the photos here. The searchers are coming in every hour or so. Each searcher can pick one up from here. You and I will go hang posters, and we'll leave some here for Greg to find the next time he checks in. Tell him to do every corner south and east of Gateway, and we'll do everything north and west."

Just then Dr. Yates put her face in her hands and began to sob. Ann sat beside her and put her arms around her. This didn't look like anything a private detective could help with so I stepped out into the hall. Fifteen minutes later, Greg found me on the front stoop breathing in the foggy cold. He was dressed for searching in faded jeans, a cable knit sweater, and scuffed tennis shoes. All of it was casual but expensive. We decided we'd do posters together, and we'd check back with Ann and her mom later.

He went in and borrowed scotch tape and a stapler from the nurses' station. He insisted on driving and I folded myself into his gray BMW. The smell of leather was seductive. When we reached the nearest strip mall, we both got out and asked several shops to put posters in their windows. It took us the rest of the afternoon to do the whole area.

Greg talked about spelunking. He had taken up the hobby two years ago and now spent most of his vacation time in caves. He said he had done caves in several parts of the U.S. and was looking forward to a trip to France in the spring to explore some caverns. When I asked him about how dangerous spelunking really was, he laughed. "It's as dangerous as you want it to be." Then he told several stories in which he starred as the shrewd trader saving clients from their own financial ignorance.

At the end of the afternoon I had to agree with Ann that his values were different from hers. I noticed that while she had spent almost our whole time together talking about Aunt M., Greg had not mentioned her name.

I left Gateway at eleven-thirty that night. The Yates family had organized a fresh search team. Greg was staying on to coordinate the continuing search.

Ann walked me to the front lobby. I put my arms around her, and she leaned into me, just resting for a moment. No perfume tonight but her hair smelled sweet.

"We'll find her," I said. My tone was soft, but I'd chosen the words for their oracle-like ambivalence. I wasn't sure everything would be okay. The fog scared me. I thought Aunt M might well walk into the path of an oncoming car.

I stepped out into the night. The fog was as dense as it had been when I'd arrived that morning, wrapping the nursing home in eerie silence. The parking lot lights were blurry, yellow puffballs of light above me, but not helpful illumination of my path. I found my old Plymouth and drove home slowly, still straining my eyes for the sight of a lost and confused Aunt M.

Chapter Three

The next day—a bleak Friday—I woke at eight-thirty and rushed to get to work on time. I didn't make it, and Colleen gave me a look.

"Smirking doesn't become you," I said as I marched past her to the coffee pot. The brew still smelled fresh, and I perked up.

Colleen reached out to push down my shirt label. I don't wear brands whose labels are supposed to show.

I took coffee into my office and sat behind my battered gray desk. My desk at Miller Security is a little neater than the one at home because at work Harvey, the feline menace, doesn't come in to run through the folders, scattering papers. I ran my finger over the R.J. that a previous owner had scratched into the metal. Another day, another dollar.

I had a moment's thought about calling Ann. I'd noticed the fog was still pretty dense and the temperature chill. The longer Aunt M was missing, the more likely she'd come to harm. I had a flash of anger at Rolfing for his obstructionism.

Before I acted on the impulse to call Ann, I got a phone call from a client, then another, and soon I was sucked into my day. I was thinking about the breakfast I'd missed when Colleen said I had a call from Ann Yates.

I glanced at my watch: eleven-thirty. Damn! She'd think me heartless for not calling sooner. Maybe I was.

"Ann!" I said, putting a lot of enthusiasm into it.

"Meg, they found her. Yesterday—"She burst out crying, then fought to regain composure. "Yesterday when we were just getting the search started, they found her in a cemetery. Meg, she was *murdered*!"

Immediately I thought of the three homeless women who'd been strangled, then transported to cemeteries. "When did they notify you?"

"About an hour and a half ago. I was at Mom and Dad's. They had Mom go down to identify her." Her voice wavered again, but she steadied it. "Daddy went with her. They just got back."

"Where did they find her?"

"In Memorial Park. The horrible part is a cemetery attendant found her early yesterday, about ten in the morning. While we did all that searching, she was already dead." She was crying again. I understood. Aunt M dead while we searched was a bitter image that would pain Ann for years.

"Ann, I'm so sorry," I said and waited for her to regain some composure, then repeated it.

"Damn, Meg, I'm sorry to be having a breakdown in your ear."

"Where are you now? I'll come over," I said, the words out before I'd considered.

"Would you? Listen, I'm at Mom's now. But meet me at the Parkmoor. Do you know where that is?"

I replied that I did know.

She didn't explain why the change of venue, but I didn't argue. I asked Colleen to reschedule an afternoon appointment and headed north to Clayton Road.

The Parkmoor isn't the sort of place that I would have picked as a hangout for Ann Yates. It has no ambience, no green ferns, no black beans stuffed into ravioli. Instead, it has a big city diner's impersonality with unexciting but edible fare at moderate prices. On the other hand, it has one of the city's more cosmopolitan clientele. Here you see people of all races, religions and cultures. For me it's a place to come when the movie is over at the Esquire or the Hi-Pointe or when I'm visiting someone at St. Mary's Hospital.

She was there already, sitting at one of the two-person booths in the middle row. To my right was a long counter. To the left, a row of booths for four. Beyond those the big windows were all steamy, making the restaurant seem cozy.

I have a good, all-purpose hug to cover awkward dialogue, but since Ann was sitting, I slid in across from her, grasped her hands and squeezed gently instead.

She squeezed back. "Thanks for coming."

I nodded.

"I wanted a chance to talk to you without getting my family involved. We could have met at my apartment, but when we finish, I want to get back to Mom's. This is closer."

"This really is okay," I said. I preferred a place that discouraged a big emotional scene, and I was grateful not to be offering condolences to her whole family.

I wasn't sure what direction Ann was headed. Grief takes people in different ways. I just prepared myself to nod and pat and listen.

A young white man of dour expression came and took our orders. Ann asked for tuna on wheat, and I ordered soup and a barbecue sandwich.

"Mom thinks she may sue Rolfing for negligence." She said it as though seeking my response.

I sidestepped. "Rolfing owns Gateway Rest Home?"

"Yes. And he certainly hasn't accepted responsibility for allowing Aunt M to wander off."

"Rolfing hasn't been a stand-up guy, but I'm not sure a lawsuit will get you what you want. It's too bad the law doesn't just allow for a swift kick in the pants now and then." Ann shrugged and I changed the subject. "Do you have any clearer idea of how Aunt M got out?"

She shook her head. "The police found her wearing a flannel nightgown and her new house shoes. But the curious thing is that she had on a smelly old coat—not hers. Where did she get it, Meg?"

This was interesting. Had her killer provided her with a coat? If so, why? I shrugged, not wanting to show what I was thinking. Instead, I asked, "How did the cops identify her?"

"They didn't right away. They figured she was a homeless woman like the others."

The waiter came back and deftly arranged our orders in front of us. "Anything else?" he asked sternly. The wonderful fumes from warm food tickled my nose.

"Just keep the coffee coming, please," I said with a smile. It didn't warm his heart, but he kept his grimace under control. I gave Ann a prompting look.

"At the pathologist's they noticed Aunt M was clean—except for that coat. That tipped them off that maybe she wasn't a homeless woman after all. They checked the missing person's reports. I'm really glad Greg had called the police right away instead of postponing it as Rolfing wanted us to do."

She paused and I nodded, caught with a hot spoonful of soup in my mouth.

"Mom says the police think Aunt M was killed by the same person who killed the others. She talked with Detective Lindstrom, who's in charge."

"Really?" I said with too much interest, my cheeks hot, then quickly slurped my soup.

Luckily Ann didn't notice. "You know, I feel Aunt M is getting lost in all this—who she really was. That'll get worse, won't it?"

"Yes, yes. And you and your family will get more attention than you want." I figured she needed plenty of bracing for what was likely to be crude and overwhelming attention. As it was, this story was beginning to pick up national news coverage. Aunt M's case would increase that. Homeless women were expendable. But suppose a wealthy family's nearest and dearest could wander out of a nursing home and be the victim of a serial killer? It was easy to see the media spin on that.

Ann seemed to be seeing it, too. She was staring disenchantedly at her tuna sandwich. I reached over and gave one hand another squeeze. "This is hard."

She looked at me, the tears welling up quickly. She grimaced, squeezed my hand, excused herself, and dashed to the ladies' room. I'd handled that well.

I finished my soup and bolted the barbecue—quite tasty—so I wouldn't be struggling with an awkward sandwich when she returned. I finished my coffee and poured her cup into mine so that she'd get a hot refill, too. Our waiter had just poured those when Ann returned, having washed away the tears but still showing the strain.

"I'm sorry. I've never cried so much in my whole life."

"Why shouldn't you? She's worth it," I said. "The sooner you can cry, the better."

She nodded vaguely. Maybe we'd gone to the same therapist.

She took a visible deep breath and looked at me in her old way. She was Ann Yates, instructor of law, backer of causes, interesting friend. "Meg, not enough attention is paid to these women. They're society's discards."

I wasn't clear who she meant by 'they'—the murdered women, homeless women in general, or all elderly women. All were pretty eligible. So I waited until she told me. "Nobody cares that four old women have been murdered and treated so cruelly. It makes sensational headlines. But no one really cares. Not like when little girls go missing."

I agreed only partially. The closer our identification with victims, the more indignant we become. Lots of white people got more upset about white little girls than black little girls gone missing or any number of black boys shot dead. So some people probably cared more about these women than for murdered black children. On the other hand, climbing from my pulpit, I realized I had my own share of guilt about neglecting the homeless. But I nodded to encourage her.

"The story will make the front pages as long as it's gory, but no one will keep the pressure on the police to find out who killed them," she went on.

A good listener doesn't interrupt to debate every point, so I didn't rise to defend Sarah Lindstrom. I was tempted to agree with Ann's cynicism, but I thought the police would stay pretty hot on this one, especially now that a 'well-to-do' woman had been killed.

Ann got my attention back when she said, "So I want to hire you to investigate these murders, Meg." She was looking at me calmly as though she had reached a logical conclusion.

I took a moment so I wouldn't sputter. Then I said, quite deliberately, "Ann, I'm not equipped to do this kind of investigation. First of all, it's way beyond the scope of Miller Security. Secondly, he police are the pros. They have the resources. And thirdly, I know Sarah Lindstrom. Believe me, she'll stay on it. She's a bloodhound." Unconsciously I had started ticking off points on one hand with the index finger of the other.

She grabbed both hands and eased them onto the table, deftly avoiding Parkmoor's china. "I want you to do what you can. To devote time to pestering them, to make sure they're on track. I want you to be Aunt M's advocate—my advocate. I'll have plenty of money to pay for it now."

Was that gallows humor in her last words? I bit. "What do you mean?"

"Only that Greg and I will inherit her money." She watched my reaction which surely looked like she'd drawn a blank even though my mind was spinning, and added, "It's quite a sum."

"In ball park figures?"

"Enough to pay you," she said with a little coyness. Then she looked sorry as she heard how that made her sound.

"Are you the only two?"

"Yes. Maybe some minor bequests to charities."

"How long have you known this?"

"Since before Linda died. She could see the disease starting— Aunt M's I mean. Linda steered her toward making a will." Ann stirred her coffee. "In some ways Aunt M was quite conservative. I guess I think of her as being more of a hell-raiser because she was a fairly open lesbian when it was quite rare. But family meant something to her. She'd always cheered Greg and me on. We were like her kids in a way. She was a wonderful, eccentric aunt."

"Which one of you did she really love more?" I asked on a hunch. Lots of non-feminist lesbians, especially the older generations, really identified with the boys.

"Oh, me," she said without hesitation.

I wondered if Greg would agree. "But she split the money equally?"

"Sure—money isn't everything, just an important thing."

I wasn't sure why, but it sounded like the first snobbish thing she'd said to me.

The waiter came and refilled our coffee. "Anything else I can get you?" he asked pointedly. We shook our heads, and he retreated.

She pressed, "So—will you do it?"

"It wouldn't be professional. I'd be taking money for something I know I couldn't really deliver."

She looked annoyed. "I don't expect you to catch this maniac personally. But I know something about how the legal system works. Victims get shoved aside. Nobody has enough time to make all the calls necessary to find out what's going on. I'd just be paying you to track the case." She was using her professorial voice.

Unfortunately, I'm an annoying student. "A waste of my time and your money."

"Look. Let's compromise. Let me give you a retainer. You set aside an hour or so a day to make calls, stay on top of what the cops are doing. If in a week we feel you're just spinning your wheels, you quit. How's that?"

"Have you considered a career in labor negotiations?" I said. Sometimes you know you're stepping into the pile and still can't avoid it.

Her face lit. Triumph or gratitude? I read it as the latter.

I hadn't told her anything personal about Sarah Lindstrom, so I squirmed a little when she said, "You know the detective?"

I hedged. "I gave her information on a case once."

"Good, that'll make it easier."

"Well, maybe," I said.

I told her it would help if her mother put in writing that I was going to be the family's liaison with the police. She said she'd have her mother do that right away. I left the waiter a generous tip. Ann left her tuna sandwich.

Chapter Four

Back at the office, Colleen was busily sorting files and muttering over misfiled pieces. I'm wise enough to leave the files entirely to Colleen, but Walter forgets.

"Walter in?" I asked.

"Yep." She belies the chatty receptionist stereotype.

I walked back to his office. Walter was indeed there, his size elevens hoisted on his desk, his rumpled gray slacks pushed up so pudgy, fish-white shins showed above olive green socks. Walter's handle on sartorial splendor is always tentative. He is a chunky man but not yet soft despite his frequent marinations in beer and rye. We never say the 'A' word. He grew up in a generation that saw twelve step meetings as an admission of weakness and not, like mine, as a way of belonging. He'll never admit he's an alcoholic.

Walter is a good investigator. He is attentive to detail. Despite being a world-class practitioner of the art of denial about his own feelings, he's quick and accurate about other people's emotions and motivations. He'd taught me well almost in spite of himself; it certainly wasn't his idea to take me into his small security and investigation firm. He'd done his share to help my mother, Betty, after his step-brother left us when I was ten. He'd helped with money and been a good, if sporadic, uncle to my brother and sister and me. He'd never taken a single drink at our house, or for that matter, in my presence.

While I was in college, I worked for him parttime, serving summonses for extra money. I came out to him the summer I turned twenty. He hadn't had much to say and had coped by ignoring my sexuality altogether. But he never talked about his own sex life either. More importantly, he consistently treated me with respect.

Walter didn't really think the private investigation business was a good career choice for a woman. I'm sure when he first agreed to hire me full time, he thought I'd get tired of it within the year. By the time that didn't happen, he'd gotten used to me. He needed a good operative, and I was already trained. He told Betty once that I was as good as any of the male operatives in St. Louis. I'm sure he meant for her to tell me. That's the way we do employee evaluations at Miller Security.

"I was wondering where you were," he said, even though I'd left a message with Colleen.

When I explained I had a new case for us and the details, he brightened. "Sounds like we'll be paid for work the St. Louis police are doing." Several parts of that appealed to him. He has cop friends, but in the aggregate the police are 'the Department,' which is Guv'ment—a devil whose nose is for tweaking. Besides, though Walter frequently denounced the concept of a free lunch, he always longed to partake in it.

I didn't argue about it. I ambled back to my office, found a blank contract, filled in some spaces by hand, and addressed the envelope to Ann. Friendship makes getting the terms down in writing even more necessary.

I decided to start right away. I looked up the Clark Street station number. It took me three minutes to get Lindstrom to the phone. I just kept repeating, "I want to talk to her about the Mary Margaret Brooks case."

Finally Lindstrom said, "Hello." She doesn't really have a Norwegian accent to go with her Nordic looks, but she speaks abruptly with a slight something that sounds like an accent.

"Darcy here," I said, matching brusque for brusque.

"Ah, you," she said.

"I'd like to talk to you about the case you're handling—the homeless women."

"Would you?" She sounded amused.

"Yes. I would."

"Perhaps you've solved it for me?"

"No, not yet," I said. "My clients are Mary Margaret Brooks' family. Her niece in particular."

She was silent while thinking about that. Usually my clients are kept confidential, but, as I'd explained to Ann, in this case it would be essential for the police to know I had the family behind me.

"Ah, you're going to do our work for us," Lindstrom finally said, flipping to the other side of Walter's coin.

I gave an audibly patient sigh. "Not at all. The family just wants to stay in touch with how the case is going." I knew Lindstrom would resent monitoring—so would I. I tried to minimize it.

She was silent again. Then she said, "Not well. That's how the case is going." Her tone was matter-of-fact, maybe a little tart. But I was surprised she'd admit such a thing. Unusual candor in a cop.

"That's off the record?"

"Off, on, whatever." She sent an impatient puff down the line. "Yes, off. For now. Read between the lines in the *Post*."

"Could we talk? I'll come there."

"I'm busy."

"Lunch. Dinner. You have to eat."

"On the run. No time."

"Look. I know these case must be making you crazy. I think I can take some heat off you just by keeping the Yates family informed. They're intelligent people. I think they'll be reasonable. I just need the broad strokes." I hoped visions of victims' rights danced in her head.

"I know you, Darcy. You'll end up wanting every little detail." She sounded superior but not exactly hostile.

"I want whatever you'll give me," I said with a candor of my own. I had little to bargain with here, and honesty is a policy.

Her silence this time was so long that I had time to replay my words, hear their possible innuendo, and start blushing like a teenager. An unintentional corny come-on is the worst.

Finally, after I'd twisted in the wind long enough to think I had been disconnected, she said, "You intend to be a pest about this, don't you?" This time I tried the silent treatment. It didn't take long. "Meet me at four in Memorial Park Cemetery. I'm going out there for another look around. I'm hoping inspiration will come with a second look."

"Will I be able to get in?"

"I'll tell the patrolman." She hung up. A busy woman.

The fog was all gone by the time I left the office to head to Memorial Park Cemetery where Aunt M's body had been discovered. Early rush hour traffic was leaving the city, and it was dusky enough that some cars were already using their headlights. As I'd guessed, there was a patrol car at the entrance gates of the cemetery to check on who was coming in. Locking the barn after the horse my cynical self said, but I knew it was actually keeping out ghoulish spectators.

I identified myself and the young, rosy-cheeked cop handed me a cemetery map with the route traced neatly in red magic marker. Detective Lindstrom's handiwork he said. Like most cemeteries this one had winding loops of blacktop and was an invitation to get lost. I have a pretty good directional sense, but cemeteries and really large department stores confound me. I drove slowly, trying to translate the map.

This was a fairly modern cemetery. Its monuments were short and squat with rounded shoulders, two to three feet high. It lacked the towering and baroque markers of earlier times. But it did have headstones that stood up, not the flat kind you mow over.

By the time I saw two patrol cars and a light sedan clustered on a hilltop, the wintry twilight was blurring figures. How close would you have to be to see someone unload a body? And how many people hang out in cemeteries on a winter's day to notice?

I parked my Plymouth behind the second patrol car. Three young uniformed cops, two white males, one a black female, were stationed around the yellow crimes-scene tape. A short white man in civvies stood next to Lindstrom. I was surprised she had brought such a large team back to the crime scene, but I supposed such a big case led to double-checking.

St. Louis's winter weather is a roller coaster. I've heard thunder crack while snow is falling. By mid-afternoon the temperature had climbed to the mid-fifties, but it was falling rapidly now as evening crept in. The short man had on an open overcoat and a golfer's cap. One patrolman was in long shirt sleeves, and the other two in winter jackets. Lindstrom was in rust cords with a yellow Oxford collar peeking from the crew neck of a Norwegian sweater in browns and beiges. She had the sweater pushed up on her forearms. Just looking at her pushed up my pulse rate.

I approached cautiously, not wanting to spoil anything. She saw and ignored me for a few minutes. She and one patrolman were taping and stepping off distances. I assumed my patient expression. When she finished her count, she motioned me forward and introduced me to the short man in civvies, Ted Neely, her partner. He was at least a decade older, but it seemed clear that she was in charge. He stuck out a small hand and gave me a firm handshake and a cordial greeting.

"This is the monument the perp used to prop her up," Lindstrom said, pointing to a modest headstone about three feet high in a combination of gray and mauve. The name Wheeler was cleanly cut into the stone. Lloyd and Velma. She had died first by ten years. "It's about ten feet from the asphalt. So were the two at Valhalla and Calvary. The Schwenger woman was maybe fifteen feet from the asphalt in Bellefountaine."

"The murderer came in the main gate?"

"With the other three he did, but he must have carried the Brooks woman in. The cemetery was closed before she disappeared. He could have come through the fence over at Calvary, but we think he didn't. No sign of tracks."

"All in daylight?"

"The first three were in this kind of light," Neely injected. "Dusk or dawn, or foggy." The twilight now was gathering shadows rapidly. I was losing all the fine details. The small print under Wheeler was blurring. The headstone was on a knoll and surrounded by waist-high shrubs and tall fir trees.

Lindstrom, as if reading my mind, said, "But still a bold act."

"You're pretty sure it was a he?"

Neely nodded. "But not impossible for a woman. Sarah tested it. She threw me over her shoulder and toted me down a hallway." He didn't look embarrassed, but she did. She stared into the middle distance. He continued. "Aunt M was fairly slender, easier to carry than the other three."

"Plus serials are almost always a man's crime," she said, taking the lead back.

Neely nodded again. He wasn't handsome, but he had a clean-shaven, pleasant face, thin, with clear eyes and five o'clock shadow hollowing his cheeks. His aftershave was piney. He looked grim. "Cocky bastard," he said.

"Fits the profile of a certain type of serial killer," Lindstrom said.

"Yeah, the cocky bastard type," he said, not cowed by her.

She didn't seem to resent it. She looked at me. "So, what's your take on it?"

I stared back, hoping the rush of heat I felt when she looked at me didn't flush my cheeks.

"Well?" she prodded.

"Were the women sexually assaulted?" I asked.

"No," said Lindstrom.

"This cemetery was certainly conveniently located, wasn't it?" I said. It was only minutes from Gateway Rest Home. The other cemeteries were cross-town. "Are you sure Aunt M's isn't a copy cat murder?"

They exchanged a quick look. Had I said something smart?

Neely looked at his watch. "I need to get back. I'll leave you the car and have Hodstedler drive me in."

Lindstrom nodded. "Tell Palowsky and Travis we'll send a new shift at six." I wondered if she always used him as a buffer to the troops, hiding even her concern for the lower ranks. Neely would be popular, an easy guy to work for. He spoke quietly to the black woman, then left with a white patrolman. Hodstedler turned out to be the man in shirt sleeves.

"Let's go sit in my car," Lindstrom said to me. She led the way. It was a modest four-door. Inside it was neatly kept, but it smelled of french fries and onions. Definitely a department vehicle. Lindstrom slid behind the wheel, then turned to lean against the door. "Now tell me, Darcy. Exactly why are you taking this case?"

"I told you, Lindstrom. I'm representing the family."

"Why?"

"For money." I resented the implication I heard in her question.

How could I possibly help? Maybe it was my own question. "And for friendship."

"Oh?"

"Ann Yates, the niece, is a friend. Aunt M—your Mary Margaret Brooks—was a favorite aunt. Ann is pretty upset. I think she just wants to spend some money to do something."

"How close a friend?"

"Is that relevant?" I watched her for the wince but she busied herself with her notebook as though she hadn't asked anything personal at all. Then I said flatly, "Just a friend." I thought about adding that Ann was straight, but decided I wouldn't stoop to it.

All the metal surfaces of the car were turning cold now that the sun had gone down. We were steaming up the windows. The inside of a car on a dark winter night is an intimate space. I wondered if Lindstrom had ever necked in a cemetery as a teenager. If Lindstrom had ever been a teenager.

"Don't you have a coat?" I asked irritably.

She twisted around and fished into the backseat and picked up a corduroy blazer and slid into it. Despite the confined space, she made it look easy.

She started the car and turned on the heater. "We've formed a joint task force with the Vinita Park police, but we'll be carrying most of the load—don't quote me. Most of what I can tell you has been in the papers or on TV. You know we want to withhold some information so we can sort out fake confessions from a real one."

"Have you really had some false ones?"

"Sure. This kind of crime activates the nuts."

"How have the women been murdered?"

"Like the paper says. Garroted, small rope or cord." She wasn't going to be more precise.

"The Brooks woman like the others?"

"Yes."

"Why homeless women?"

"They're accessible? Vulnerable?"

"What incredible luck—for the murderer I mean. Did he just run into her strolling down the street? It was pretty far from his hunting turf."

She shrugged. "Maybe she got a ride downtown. We're trying to get that point across on TV. Did anyone pick her up, give her a ride, even see her?"

"The same M.O.?" I repeated. Maybe she'd spare a little more change this time.

"The same."

"What about the coat? Ann said she was wearing an old coat

that didn't belong to her."

"I was hoping you could tell me. It's definitely old, smelly, off a rag heap."

"Could her killer have given it to her?"

Lindstrom shifted in her seat and turned the heater down to a lower hum. "Maybe. This case has more questions than answers. Believe me, lots of people want the answers besides you."

I could imagine the pressure on her. I thought about a comforting remark but couldn't think of any she wouldn't see through. It was completely dark. I thought about how easy it would be just to reach across the seat and touch her. Well, easy was not the right word.

She flipped on the overhead light, reached around into the back seat, rummaged around. She opened an attache case, pulled out a folder, took out some papers. "We've done everything. We have all kinds of charts down at headquarters to visualize patterns: times, locations. Did Schwenger, Lubbie, Bellis have any ties?" She handed me three sheets. "Here are copies of the cemetery maps with the locations of the bodies marked. You can keep them in case you want to look at the sites later. Maybe you'll get an inspiration."

I was surprised. "Thanks," I said feebly, folding the papers carefully and putting them into my jacket.

She was flipping through the folder. I spotted color photographs.

"May I?" I said and reached for the top one.

She didn't stop me. "That's the third. Rita Bellis," she said. "She was found in Calvary."

The dead woman leaned against the mausoleum. Her legs jutted out stiffly; she was angled so that her back rested against the stone corner and the ornate doorway grill. She was dressed in layers against the cold: old-fashioned buckled galoshes, the tail of a faded plaid robe sticking out from under the cumbersome blue coat in nubby wool, a red sweatshirt showing at the vee of the coat. The bulky coat and other layers padded her, disguising her size and shape. She wore a man's old-fashioned felt hat mashed down over a knitted blue ski cap. Her face was a distended pudge. Around her neck was a bright print scarf. She wore no gloves on her swollen fingers; her hands were streaked with dirt. They lay inert against her stomach.

I swallowed hard, trying not to dwell on the life snuffed out.

"The cemetery work crew found her in the early morning the day after Thanksgiving," Lindstrom said. "Since the second body was found, cemeteries have been doing morning bed checks." She reached for the picture. Our fingers brushed, and I felt the tingle down to my toes, though it wasn't my toes which grabbed my attention. "This mausoleum where Bellis was found isn't visible from Broadway on one side or West Florissant on the other."

"Are you stationing cops in the cemeteries?"

"I can't tell you that. But our resources are stretched pretty thin. I think some cemeteries are asking their daytime crews to put in overtime at night."

I nodded. Taxpayers want to fight crime on the cheap. "What about where he picked up these homeless women? Do you know those locations?"

She was silent long enough to tell me she was editing her answer. "We're investigating."

"Is this guy likely to keep going?"

She didn't answer that question. Instead, she said, "Darcy, if you do poke your nose around, be careful. I think this guy is smart—whether he's a monster or not. A lot of serial killers are bottom feeders. They drift around the country, killing randomly, but they don't have prior connections to their victims. Makes 'em hard to find and saves 'em from their stupidity." She gestured with her hands. Good hands, I noticed again, the muscular sort you imagine around basketballs. "This guy may be different. He's working in a tight space. I think he'd be dangerous if cornered."

"To more than homeless women?"

She nodded. She clicked off the dome light. "What is the Yates family like—a happy family?"

I sighed. Our tête-á-tête was about to end. I wasn't here for a fair trade. Some people would think that as long as I said only good things about clients I wasn't breaking their confidentiality. But information is a sword that cuts all directions. I had already compromised by asking permission to make public who my clients were.

I tried a finesse. I gave her a brief version of the public record stuff on Ann Yates and her mother and father. I did not mention cousins Greg or Arlene or fiance Philip or Dr. Rolfing.

She saw it for what it was. "You've spent a lifetime at poker, haven't you?"

"Just the Army years," I said. Then, impulsively, I decided to throw her a curve. "Maybe Dr. Yates didn't tell you—Aunt M was a lesbian. Her lover of thirty-plus years died the same month Aunt M was put into the nursing home."

An interesting silence. But she wasn't flumoxed. "Darcy, you aren't going to argue that this is a series of gay bashings?" Her voice breathed new life into the phrase 'heaped scorn.'

Lindstrom is not only apolitical, she is hostile to politics. Maybe she gets enough within the department.

I saw her look at her wrist. A busy woman who didn't bother being surreptitious about checking her watch. Better get out before she threw me out. I had a strong sense of her presence in the narrow confines of the car; sensory messages came across—breath, body heat, cologne. I could kiss and run. No, with two of St. Louis's finest stamping their feet in the cold outside the car, I couldn't.

"Thanks for the information," I said, opening the door, spotlighting her under the dome light.

She shrugged. It was nothing.

"I do have one more question."

"Only one?" She cocked an eyebrow.

I was standing outside, leaning in. "Did you really carry Neely down a hallway?"

I relished her startled look. I think it as a rare day when I catch Lindstrom off guard. I waved goodbye.

I stopped at a pay phone to call Nina. She ran Ruth House, a shelter for homeless women and children downtown. Socially, it was a bit awkward. The last time I'd seen Nina, I'd been helping her lover, my best friend, Barb Talbot, move out of Nina's apartment. But Nina would know about anything having to do with homelessness in St. Louis. I deposited thirty cents and flinched as the icy metal phone cord hit my wrist. Nina professed to be glad to hear from me and suggested we meet at the Blue Moon as she had a committee meeting there later that evening.

The Blue Moon Coffee House has become an integral part of St. Louis's lesbian community in a short time. Its location on Gravois is perfect for me and not inconvenient for the gay South Grand crowd. The inviting smell of brewing coffee welcomes customers. Its tables and chairs are an eclectic mix of several yard sales, the tables reborn with rainbow colors and gay-friendly slogans. The walls display the work of local artists and the hallway toward the patio and basement offer all the brochures, pamphlets, gay and lesbian newspapers and 'zines that the community offers.

Several organizations hold committee meetings here, but its main attraction is that Blue Moon is the kind of place where you can nurse one cup of coffee all evening, a place where friends gather to play cards or Rummikub.

I beat Nina there and got a cup of chocolate macadamia nut, the decaf flavor of the day.

Nina came in a few moments later. She is a short, attractive, cinnamon-skinned black woman. She's a couple of years older than Barb and I, and seems to have a much stronger sense of the purpose of her life. She accepted the job of director of Ruth House when it was a hit-and-miss affair run out of the basement of her Southern Baptist Church. She searched for and found enough funding outside the church to make the shelter independent and as soon as it was financially feasible moved it into separate quarters. Every year she expands the services Ruth House offers, job training, special arrangements for medical services and day care for the homeless children. I watched her greet nearly every woman in the place before ordering a veggie burger and salad and soda from the proprietors.

When she came and put her food on the table, she squinted at me. "So you're investigating the homeless murders, huh?"

"Not really, more like keeping up with developments. Maybe I'll be enough of an irritant to the cops, to get them going."

Nina snorted. "We...you know, if the victims were citizens of Ladue or Town and Country, we wouldn't need an irritant to get some progress."

Hearing Nina's cynicism, I was tempted to argue. Instead I waited for her to start her dinner and told her the story of Aunt M and her disappearance and subsequent discovery in Memorial Park Cemetery. She merely raised her eyebrows when I mentioned that Aunt M was one of the heirs of the John Brooks Brewing Company. I told her I needed any information she could give me to help me begin sorting out whether the cases were truly related.

"The first two victims were former clients at Ruth House. Sophie Schwenger was a resident about a month ago. I thought she would make it on her own. Her son dumped her in an apartment she couldn't afford when he got a job in Arizona. She came to the shelter in September when the landlord finally got her evicted. All she could really afford on her pension was a sleeping room. We helped her get it lined up. I don't know why she was on the streets again in November. She didn't call us.

"Lubbie has been in and out of all the area shelters. She's crazy, poor thing, but not crazy enough to qualify for the State Hospital. She's one of the ones really abandoned by the reform of the mental health code. It makes me so mad that someone just killed her. She was harmless."

"Any connection between Lubbie and Sophie?" I asked.

"None that I know of. Sophie was originally from Tower Grove. No one knows where Lubbie was from."

"What was Lubbie's real name?"

"I don't know. We could never get her to stay long enough to get our hands on her S.S.I. check so we could get her a place. She was in a group home for a while last year. They would know."

I wrote down the name of the company that administered the group home. "How about places where I could go to talk to homeless women?"

"You're always welcome at Ruth House and there is New Life Evangelistic Center, Christ Church Cathedral, The Salvation Army, and the battered women's shelters." Nina pulled her calendar out of her bag. It was held together with a thick rubber band and was stuffed with innumerable slips of paper and post-it notes. She flipped to the back and read numbers for the shelters. She added the address of downtown's soup kitchen.

"How do you think he is picking the women, Nina?"

"Well, Lubbie was a loner. She could hardly bear living in close proximity to others—mostly why she never stayed in shelters for long. She didn't make sense all the time, but she was wary. I can't see her willingly trotting off with someone she didn't know. Sophie was more naive. She might have trusted someone with a good story."

"Is it possible that the killer is someone who works in a shelter or somehow is supposed to be helping the homeless?"

"Anything is possible, I guess. But I can't imagine it's like a pedophile looking for a job in a day care. If your intent is to kill, not misuse, why would you want daily contact with your victims? We're telling the women not to panhandle. That has always been the rule at Ruth House, but I'm really stressing it these days." Nina chewed thoughtfully. "Maybe he's posing as a homeless man. The women might be less wary with someone they thought was homeless."

"What if he were offering them money? Money for sex or maybe he just offers to give them money for food."

"Possible. Lubbie certainly understood money even when she wasn't connecting with consensus reality in other ways."

"How about Sophie?"

"Anyone poor enough to be on the streets is always trying to figure out how to get some money. Money buys independence and safety. For Lubbie it would have bought some place to be alone, for Sophie somewhere she could live comfortably with others. But surely an offer of a few bucks wouldn't have impressed your heiress," she said, referring to Aunt M.

"But she wasn't able to think clearly. If she could, she wouldn't have been out of the nursing home. Anything I should know about interviewing street people?"

"They're like the rest of us, concerned mostly with what is going on in their own lives at the moment. An offer of cigarettes or a couple bucks is a good way to start. Authority folks, cops, social workers are to be avoided or told what they want to hear so they will go away."

"Thanks, Nina. You've been a help."

"No problem. I'm glad you're doing this, Meg. Someone needs to let the cops know that lives in Hyde Park are as important as those in West County. Anything you can do towards greater safety on the streets would be great."

Back at my apartment on the south side of the city, I pulled on long underwear and two pairs of socks. I chose my oldest pair of jeans and two sweatshirts, the dirty one on top. An old pair of army boots completed my outfit. I ran my hand through my short hair and thought I needed a hat. Unfortunately, all I could find was my prized St. Louis Cards ball cap. I wasn't willing to risk it. So I decided I'd stop at Schnuck's and pick up a cheap knit cap. I found a navy blue cap, but not before the manager sent a bagger to follow me around the store. So much for not judging by appearance.

I started at Christ Church Cathedral at Locust and Thirteenth, downtown, one of the shelters Nina mentioned. Christ Church Cathedral is a beautiful old Episcopalian Church with massive proportions in light-colored stone which houses a large shelter in the basement. It is only three blocks from the upscale mall, St. Louis Centre. I parked a couple blocks away and just walked around the neighborhood for about twenty minutes to get a sense of things. My sense of things was that it was too cold to be out following the homeless around. It did occur to me that if our murderer had mistaken Aunt M for a homeless woman, he might make that mistake again. I saw a white woman standing on the sidewalk outside the shelter smoking the stub end of a cigarette. I sidled up to her.

"Did you hear they found another woman in a cemetery?"

"Who the hell are you?" she snarled.

"My name's Meg."

"Who are you?" she insisted. "Are you trying to act like you're homeless or something?"

So much for my theatrical skills.

"I just wanted to blend in, sort of. I'm a private investigator. A fourth victim has been found. Her family hired me. But I've also talked with Nina who runs the shelter near here about what can be done to provide security—"

"I need some cigarettes."

I sighed and asked where. We walked together to a small liquor store and she picked out two bags of chips and asked for two packs of Kools. Both she and the young clerk looked expectantly at me. I paid and we headed back toward the shelter.

"What's your name?"

"Pam. That family must have money, huh?"

"Yes, actually the victim was wealthy."

"Why did she get it then? I thought he was just after us."

"She wandered out of a nursing home. She had Alzheimer's. Where do you think he's finding women to kill?"

"I figure he works in a shelter or maybe down at the DFS."

"How's he getting the women to go with him, though? Would you let even a shelter worker take you off somewhere?"

"No, but there's some isn't smart as me. Some just hit the streets this month. I been out here going on three years. I know better. No asshole's gonna shoot me and dump me at the cemetery." She pounded one of the packs of Kools against her wrist repeatedly. What had started as tamping the loose tobacco back into the cigarettes had obviously become some kind of compulsion. She tapped and tapped and tapped. By the time she opened the pack and carefully pulled out a cigarette, there was a quarter inch of empty paper at the end of the barrel. I waited while she searched her pockets for a lighter and didn't find one. I had no matches, so she ducked into the shelter for a minute to borrow one. She came back out with her cigarette lit.

We stood on the huge stone steps of the church and looked out at the west bound traffic on Thirteenth Street.

"Have you seen anything unusual, or heard any talk about the murders?"

She pushed her dishwater blond hair out of her eyes. "I seen all kinds of unusual. We don't talk about it. We don't like to think about it. Too damn much scary shit around here anyway. I need some money."

"I'll only give you money for real information. Did you know Sophie Schwenger, Lubbie, or Rita Bellis?"

"Everybody knows Lubbie. She's as crazy as the day is long."

"When was the last time you saw her?"

"Last month I saw her at the Currency Exchange cashing her check. There was a woman with her. Fancy coat and shoes. She and Lubbie drove off in a fancy red number."

"Do you know who the woman was?"

"I don't . Lubbie didn't have any family that I ever knew of."

"What kind of car?"

"Low to the ground. Bright red."

"Was it a Saab?"

Pam scoffed. "You think I'd spend time looking at it—like I'm in the market?"

"Sorry. Anything else you can tell me?"

"I thought it was pretty funny at the time. Lubbie going off with somebody like that. But then after they said she was murdered, I tried to tell the police."

"What happened?"

"He said he'd write it down, but he didn't. He just got back in his car and drove off. He didn't even ask my name."

"You called the cops?"

"No! I stopped one outside the library."

"The main library?"

"Yeah, over on Olive."

"Which Currency Exchange did you see Lubbie and this woman at?"

"The one on Grand. Across from the Veteran's Hospital."

"Did you hear the woman say anything to Lubbie?"

"Just told her to hurry up when Lubbie was fooling with her papers. Lubbie acted like she didn't know me. But that might have just been Lubbie. Sometimes she's pretty off in her own world—not exactly paying attention to what's happening here on earth."

"What did the woman look like?"

"Rich white bitch."

"Age? Hair color?"

"Kinda tall, reddish hair, sort of long."

"Anything else you remember about her?"

"No, just she seemed in a hurry to get out of there." Pam tossed her cigarette butt onto the step and ground it out with her foot.

"What day and time did this happen?"

"My check comes around the first of the month. It was a Monday."

I counted backwards. "Monday, November second?"

"Yeah, that's it. I caught the eleven-forty-five bus. Got there about twelve-fifteen."

"How can I get in touch with you again?"

"I get mail at my sister's on Natural Bridge."

"Do you generally stay here at the Cathedral?"

"Sometimes. Sometimes I live with my sister. But she and I don't get along all that well. So I don't live there all the time. She just wants my money."

I wrote down her sister's address and gave Pam my card and ten dollars.

I drove to the Currency Exchange on Grand across from John Cochran Veterans' Hospital. At this late hour I could see from the street that the exchange was closed. That would have to wait until tomorrow.

Grand was gridlocked with Barry Manilow fans. He was at the Fox tonight. So I cut down Compton and missed the high culture of Grand Center, Powell Symphony Hall, the Fox, and St. Louis University. Could the woman with Lubbie possibly have been Ann? If so, it seemed too coincidental that Lubbie had been killed shortly after that and then Ann's Aunt M had also been murdered. I tried to remember Ann's tear-streaked face as she asked me to be a liaison with the police.

Clients frequently don't tell PIs everything about themselves, but then they don't often use us to cover serial murder either. Chances were the woman in the red luxury sport sedan with Lubbie wasn't Ann but a family member or a social worker of some kind.

Would a social worker drive a luxury sport sedan to take a homeless woman to cash a check? It didn't seem likely. A sport sedan sounded more like someone who didn't spend her days and weeks among the down and out. On the other hand, there were lots of red sport sedans in St. Louis. Hundreds. Pretty bad odds that it was Ann's red Saab. Ann just wasn't the serial murder type. With that thought I took myself home to bed where Lindstrom intruded into my sleep and smiled invitingly.

Chapter Five

The next morning I pounded on Patrick's door and waited to hear sounds of his stirring. I knew he had a rare Saturday off, and he'd still be sleeping at eight-thirty in the morning. I had woken up at six-forty-seven, unable to shut my eyes again. My mind raced. I kept thinking about the bodies of four old women left in cemeteries. One of them a well-loved aunt. All of them, perhaps, well-loved at some time in their lives. Why, why, kill these old women? Surely they were the most harmless among us? I needed to go to the Currency Exchange, and I wanted to see the other cemeteries. Maybe seeing where Sophie Schwenger, Lubbie, and the third victim, Rita Bellis, had been placed would help me focus. And someone at Currency Exchange would no doubt tell me the woman in the red luxury car was Lubbie's social worker or rich cousin. Not that I had changed my mind about this case; I still didn't think I'd be able to solve it. But I needed to reassure myself that Ann wasn't involved somehow in the murders.

I heard no Patrick noises, so I banged again, and yelled, "Hey, Patrick, it's me, get up."

Presently I heard the shuffle of his old corduroy slippers. The dead bolt shot back, and Patrick's unshaven face peered out.

"Meg, it's my day off. It's eight-thirty!"

I walked in uninvited. I figured if I had to pitch this field trip standing out in the hall before Patrick had a cup of coffee I was doomed. I kissed his cheek without comment and set to brewing a pot of his favorite hazelnut decaf. He glared at me and went into the bathroom. Presently I heard the sound of toothbrush hitting teeth. Halfway there I thought. By the time the coffee was done Patrick was back in the kitchen, still in his robe but with his eyes open. I set our cups on the kitchen table and smiled at him.

"Good morning, Patrick. How did you sleep?"

"Fine, Meg. Cut to the chase. Why did you wake me up?"

"The police found Ann's Aunt M yesterday."

"I heard it on the news last night. I checked your door, but it sounded like you were already asleep. How's Ann and her family?"

"Devastated. Alzheimer's is a special kind of horror. But I think the family was almost resigned to it. To have her murdered this way is a shock. They all feel guilty. Like they didn't protect her."

"Maybe now there will be more pressure to get the cemetery murders solved."

"Yes, I imagine so. Some of it from me. Ann's hired me to keep tabs on the investigation, be liaison for the family to the police."

"That means dealing with the Ice Queen. Brr."

"I've already met with Lindstrom once. She wasn't too bad really."

"So you were going to explain to me in your own inimitable way why you woke me up this early on a Saturday."

"I want to see the cemeteries, Patrick. I know there won't be anything left there; the police will have gathered up anything of importance. I just need to see where the bodies were put. Maybe there will be something—"

Patrick's shoulders slumped. "You mean you want me to spend a cold, damp December day tromping around in cemeteries?"

"You don't have to. I just thought you might want to see the less glamorous side of detecting." After a couple more whines about his first Saturday off in a month, he got dressed. He extracted a promise of lunch at Duff's for his trouble.

"We have to make a stop at Currency Exchange first," I said.

"Currency Exchange? What currency?"

"One of those check-cashing places. For AFDC checks. People get their food stamps there."

"Isn't that a dangerous place to go?"

"Yes. We expect poor people to do it all the time." I saw his look and climbed down. "Post offices are dangerous, too. Saddle up, kid."

Patrick said he'd wait in the car. I heard him lock my door as I walked away. The pitted asphalt of the parking lot alongside the Exchange was strewn with trash and broken glass. The interior of the cinderblock building was as bad. The tile floor was filthy and the only decorations were a running billboard sign for the Missouri Lottery and stenciled signs with instructions for cashing checks, picking up food stamps, and paying utility bills. I was advised by one sign that only one person at a time could be at the counter and that I needed three forms of ID, including a picture, to cash a check. The bottom of the chest-high counter was wood that had been painted brown in a futile attempt to cover the dozens of scuff marks. The Burns Security guard on the lobby side of the counter looked bored. As there was no customer at the counter, I stepped up and peered through two thicknesses of bullet-proof glass to an equally bored young black woman.

"Hello, my name is Meg Darcy." I whipped out my card from Miller Security and dropped it in the metal tray that opened on both sides of the glass. "I'd like to talk to you a moment if I could."

She peered at the card. "Okay."

"Could I come back there for a moment?" I pointed to a spot beside her, behind the glass.

"Nope. Employees only back here."

The Burns Security guy looked more interested now. At least he had stopped staring out the barred side window and started staring at me.

"Look, I'm a private detective. I'm not here to rob you. I'm unarmed." I patted where my shoulder holster would be if I had been wearing it.

"Sorry. Can't do it. You want to talk to the manager?"

"Yes. Thanks."

The clerk walked down her side of the counter and disappeared through a door. A minute later a tall, heavy, black woman came into view. She had my business card in her hand.

"Good morning, Ms. Darcy. My name is Helen Robinson. What can I help you with?"

"I'd like to talk to you about a woman who cashed her check here last month. Could we talk privately?"

"We could meet outside."

The parking lot didn't appeal to me. I settled for the current arrangement. "That's okay. This will only take a minute. We can talk here."

She motioned me down to the last window which was marked *Money Orders*. Just to the right of the window was a yellow strip marked in feet and inches to assess the height of the expected goon with a gun. The top of Helen's hair just hit the six-foot mark.

"The woman I need to know about was called Lubbie. She was homeless and she cashed her check here on Monday, November 2."

"I knew Lubbie. In fact, we were busy that day so I was working the counter. I waited on her. I was so sad when I read in the papers that she was murdered."

"What was Lubbie's real name?"

"It was Joyce something. Let me see. Something common." I waited while she consulted her memory. A middle-aged white man in dirty clothes came in and bought three dollars worth of scratch-off lottery tickets from the clerk. "It started with a 'B' I think, but I just can't remember."

"Do you remember if she was with anyone?"

"Yes, she was with a woman who brings her sometimes."

"Was the woman named Ann?"

"I don't know her name. She's brought Lubbie a couple of times, and she brings another woman in almost every month."

"What other woman?"

"She's a white woman, too. I think maybe they are related. The woman she brings all the time is schizophrenic. Sometimes she's really out of it."

"So the woman who came with Lubbie usually brings in a woman who is schizophrenic?"

"Yes."

"Is she a social worker?"

"I don't think so. She dresses too well to be a social worker. If she is, she has a rich husband."

"What does she look like?"

"About your height. Reddish-brown hair to her shoulders. Brown suede coat and a white scarf."

"Did she ever say anything to give you any clue to her identity?"

Helen paused and thought a moment. I looked out the square window in the cinderblock wall. Patrick was squirming around in his seat to see if I was coming out yet.

"I always believed she was the schizophrenic woman's family somehow. But I can't tell you why I think that exactly. She acts like she cares more about the schizophrenic woman than about Lubbie."

"Do you know the schizophrenic woman's name?"

"No, but let me ask. Someone might."

She returned to say no one in the office remembered the schizophrenic woman's name, but everyone agreed the woman who brought her was a family member.

"Did you notice what kind of car she drove?"

"No, sorry. There aren't any windows back here. I generally don't even know it's raining till I step out in it."

I gave her another card and asked her to give it to the well-dressed woman the next time she was in and thanked her for her help. I wanted to shake her hand, but because of the security glass, I had to settle for a wave.

When I got back in the car, I found Patrick rifling through the jumble in my back seat.

"What are you looking for?"

"Something to relieve the boredom. I thought you'd never come out of there."

"Boredom is a self-inflicted wound, Patrick."

"Why do you carry around phone books, a camera, clothes? And what is this thing?"

"My picklocks. Put them back. All that is important PI stuff, Patrick."

He rolled his eyes. "What did you tell your mother about the collections under your bed? And you need to take those cassette tapes inside. It's not good for them to get so cold in the car." He plucked one tape out of the tangle. "God forbid we lose this old Holly Near stuff."

I grabbed it out of his hand. "That is a classic. Besides, anyone who listens to Frank Sinatra has no room to sneer." I started the Plymouth and pointed her north onto Grand.

"There is a possibility that Ann is trying to pull some kind of scam on me, Patrick."

"Tell me."

"A woman of her description and driving a red luxury car like Ann's Saab brought one of the homeless victims in to cash a check last month. The crazy one they called Lubbie."

"You think Ann is stealing welfare checks from the homeless?"

"I doubt it, but she didn't mention knowing another of the victims to me."

"Maybe the woman isn't Ann."

"Certain kinds of things are rarely coincidences."

Patrick snorted. "That must have been a chapter in the PI bible I forgot to read."

Our first cemetery stop was Bellefountaine, pronounced Bell Fountain, where Sophie Schwenger, the first victim, had been found. On the way I thought about what Nina had told me about Sophie's descent to the streets and her naivete. We stopped at the cemetery office where Patrick picked up stapled information sheets. I took out the maps Lindstrom had given me. She had told me that Sophie Schwenger had been placed inside a Greek temple-like mausoleum. It took us a while to find it. Cemetery roads, I noted again, are not built or marked for the tourist trade. Finally, Patrick saw it off to our right, and we drove as close as we could and got out of the car. I wondered what burial arrangements would be made for Sophie, Lubbie, and Rita Bellis. Did cities still have potter's fields?

The monument Sophie had been propped against was swank all right. Seven columns on each of its two sides, four on each end. No walls, an open temple.

Patrick was consulting the cemetery's information sheets. "Thomas Hart Benton's buried here."

"Thomas who?"

"The Missouri Senator—back when—the first one."

"Oh, sure."

"William Rogers Clark—half of Lewis and Clark. Adolphus Busch—the beer business—you know him." Patrick's voice was rising with glee.

"Intimately."

53

He ignored me. "The Danforths are here. Sara Teasdale."

"Don't swoon, Patrick."

But I smiled at him as he wandered off to inspect other grave sites while reciting, "'Spend all you have for loveliness / Buy it and never count the cost.'"

I brushed away some brown oak leaves and prickly balls from the sweet gums and sat on the top stone step of the Greek temple. I looked at the gray of the sky and the gray of the stones and monuments and tried to think why someone would kill these women. Aunt M didn't fit the pattern. The killer would have to know she wasn't homeless by the way she was dressed. Had he tried to make her look like a homeless woman with that old coat? Or had someone taken pity on Aunt M and given her the coat when she was out wandering? Why would you give a woman wandering lost and incoherent a coat and not try to find out where she belonged? Could she have possibly found one of the city shelters Wednesday night? They might have given her a coat.

Patrick interrupted these musings by calling me over to look at a family plot that included three infant children. We stared at the small stones in silence. One of them didn't even have a name. The baby was born on October 7, 1912, and died October 9, 1912. A birth defect? A flu epidemic? We would never know.

We drove next door to Calvary Cemetery. Calvary and Bellefountaine are both very large and wealthy cemeteries that sit side by side; from the outside they are often mistaken for one huge cemetery though a narrow street cuts through them. Calvary is a Catholic cemetery, more ornate in its angels and crosses than neighboring Protestant Bellefountaine, but both are heavily populated by those who were born in the middle of the nineteenth century and died in the early 1900s. Here and there in Calvary were clusters of clergy—priests, brothers, and nuns lay under modest markers; small headstones for the men, small metal crosses for the women. Around the hilly slopes ran a dark green, metal picket fence. Large sections of the fence were down. A four-wheeler could drive through. But Lindstrom had said the police thought the perp kept to main gates.

St. Louis cemeteries closed at five. By five-ten these winter days it would be completely dark. The timing was tight—to bring the body in at dusk and position it, then drive out. To risk being seen unloading the body? Lots of risk. More to the point, Aunt M had disappeared during the night so that pattern didn't fit for her murder. The murderer couldn't have used a main gate then.

The temporary resting place of the third victim, Rita Bellis, had been a large mausoleum in pink granite, built to look like a church. It had three stone steps leading to the front door. Inside we could see stained glass windows on the other three sides. There was a small altar and some words carved in the stone which we couldn't read. It was quite a fancy place for one's final rest. Was the killer trying to make some comment about the disparity between the poorest of the poor and the 'haves' in our city? Social comment through murder?

"I just don't get it, Patrick. It doesn't make sense."

"I'm glad about that."

"Why kill homeless women? Unless the killer is a homeless person or a shelter worker, he's having to go to some trouble to find the victims."

The watery winter sunshine managed a lukewarm touch on our shoulders, but if we stepped under one of the spruce trees, the shade brought a chill reminder of winter. The ground was damp and spongy in the patches clear of snow. The air smelled fresh. It was good to be outside, but I wasn't stumbling over clues.

Patrick was leafing through the information sheets we'd picked up at Calvary's office. "Did you know Dred Scott is buried here? General Sherman—you know, the one who burned Atlanta?"

I nodded.

"Tennessee Williams!" He looked at me.

"Okay, we'll drive by on our way out."

"A.J. Cervantes."

"The mayor they named the Convention Center after?"

"The same." He read on. "Dr. Tom Dooley." Another grin. He might have been meeting the fellow for lunch.

"Who?"

"Oh, Meg, learn our history. He was the Navy doctor famous for providing medical services to the refugees from North Vietnam before the U.S. got involved in the war there. The Navy was ecstatic about the good PR till they found out he was gay. He died young. Cancer, I think."

I kept my promise and on the way out we stopped to pay homage to both Tennessee and Tom.

Lastly we toured through Valhalla where Lubbie's body had been found. Obviously, it was a place for the secular crowd, a bank of vaults at one end for urns. The killer would have had to use the main entrance as the post-and-chain fence was in perfect order as were the drab November lawns. The only other way to have brought the body in would have been on foot after the gates were closed.

"Well, this cemetery haunting has just taken me to the heights, but I'm ready for lunch," Patrick said.

We reconvened at Duff's, our favorite Central West End restaurant whenever we are flush. We prefer the old section where dark wood wainscotting and framed mirrors and a pressed tin ceiling seem both cozy and classy. The food is terrific and worth every pricey penny. The wait persons usually wear tee-shirts, giving customers permission to go casual, though a dress-up crowd shows up, too. I've heard that one of the chefs cooked for the Grateful Dead when that group toured.

On nights we have dinner at Duff's we often press our noses to the display windows next door where Rothschild's exhibits its latest antiques. Or we stroll across the street to browse in Left Bank Books or look for CDs at West End Wax. Patrick and I have spent many Saturday nights in such wild celebration. Balaban's sits on the third corner of Euclid and McPherson. It's an even pricier restaurant. The fourth corner's establishment keeps changing hands. Once, long ago, it was a gay bar upstairs, lesbian bar downstairs. Now straight yuppies rush into a neighborhood gays and lesbians revived.

Today for lunch we warmed ourselves over Duff's French onion soup and sandwiches. Patrick recapped his date with a friend of a friend Friday night. It sounded suspiciously like a blind date to me, but he denied it. He thought he might go out with the fellow again, but didn't have much hope for true love's emerging from this relationship.

That reminded him of my love life. "How's Detective Lindstrom? Is this case giving you opportunities to see her?"

"Not for long. I don't think I'll be on this case more than another day or two."

"You've got it solved?" He leaned forward. "Did you find the missing clue this morning while we were tramping around?"

"No. If Ann did pick up Lubbie, I'm going to have to take that information straight to Lindstrom and get as far away from this case as I can." My shoulder muscles pulled tight. "I need to find out if that was Ann."

"You'll figure it out, Meg." He has an endearing faith that I'm a great detective. And I am—in my league.

Patrick had a pal date with some guys that evening, so we split up after lunch. Despite his complaining, he'd enjoyed our trek through the cemeteries more than I had. To him it was a lark. To me it was frustration.

I settled onto my couch, petted Harvey till he snoozed, and reached for the phone.

I tried calling Ann and got her machine. I tried calling her parents' home, but they were unlisted. I called Lindstrom and reached her quickly. But she curtly dismissed me with the brief comment that she had nothing to tell me. "Keep reading the paper," she said sardonically. Before I could ask if she were unhappy with her press clippings, she'd hung up.

That confirmed my notion that Lindstrom's brief burst of forth-comingness had been a one-time aberration. Not that she had spilled any new information. The cemetery maps had been a wonderfully clever distraction to keep me tromping around grave sites and out of her hair.

I was at the wrong end of the telescope. Although it was possible that someone might get lucky and see the killer dumping a body into a cemetery, the best bet was probably going to be catching him at the other end. Someone must have seen something when the killer kidnapped or killed or loaded up the bodies from the downtown areas where the homeless huddled around dark doorways. The police were better equipped for discovering that. Lindstrom didn't need my nudging to remind her to keep looking. Although the news coverage was different from the saturation coverage during the child abduction/murders of '93, it was still heating up and not giving St. Louis the image that attracts visitors. Reporters and politicians alike would provide all the pushing Lindstrom would need.

I had the fidgets. I was just getting ready to wrap myself up for a brisk walk through Tower Grove Park when Ann returned my call. She said Philip had just cancelled a date; why not meet at Chuy's in Dogtown?

Perfect. I needed to figure out how I would ask Ann about her connection to Lubbie. I had time for a hot shower and a change of jeans. I put down some tuna for Harvey.

Chuy's has the ambience of a college town pizza parlor, but it serves up Tex-Mex food that's tasty and reasonably priced. It's good enough to get praise from Joe Pollock, the *Post's* restaurant critic.

For once I beat Ann to a meeting. I was sipping a draft beer and starting on chips and salsa—the latter just a tad too strong on tomatoes and short on spice.

I watched Ann park her car, then dart across the street. She was wearing a suede jacket, three-quarters length, and a white silk scarf around her neck. Exactly as Helen, the Currency Exchange supervisor, had described. She was also wearing a brighter smile than I'd seen the last two days. She looked as though she'd had a night's rest and a respite from crying.

We got through the initial social exchanges and ordering. Ann said there were reporters camped outside her parents' home in Ladue, but she'd reached her limit today when a reporter had burst into her classroom during a lecture. I suggested that the family release a prepared statement and maybe agree to a press conference as a tactic to limit the press's intrusiveness.

"Did you know any of the victims besides Aunt M?"

"No," she answered quickly and without apparent guile in her clear hazel eyes. "Why do you ask?"

"A homeless woman told me that a woman in a fancy red car took Lubbie somewhere last month."

Ann's eyes narrowed. "Meg, what are you saying?"

"I'm not saying anything except that I need for you to tell me everything and if you aren't on the level about this I'll have to drop the case."

She rubbed her hands over her face. "I have never met Lubbie or the other two women in my entire life. I have never taken any homeless women anywhere."

One of the things I'd liked about Ann was her directness. She had always seemed so honest, so free from ordinary kinds of eva-siveness. "What were you doing on Monday, November 2?"

"You can't honestly think I'm murdering these women?"

"Tracking down loose ends and strange coincidences is my job. It doesn't mean you murdered anyone."

"Monday is my heaviest teaching day. I'm at UMSL from eight a.m. until seven-thirty at night. I'm in the classroom from eight-thirty till noon, from one-thirty to three-thirty and from four to seven p.m."

"What did you do for lunch that day?"

"Christ, I don't remember. What did you do for lunch on November 2?" Ann toyed with her enchilada, then pushed the plate away. "Meg, I'm sorry, it's pretty hard for me to fathom your sus-picions. But I want you to follow up on everything. I won't rest until we've found Aunt M's killer." She sighed. "Are you coming to Aunt M's memorial service?"

I hadn't thought to, and she read my blank look.

"Don't detectives do that?"

I shrugged. "If they think the killer might show up."

"Well. Just consider the possibility I'm not her killer."

"Yes, I'll come." I finished the last bite of my fajita and poured the last of our pitcher of beer into our glasses. She gave me the par-ticulars.

We didn't linger as long as we usually did. Chuy's was filling up with families and boy-girl couples. Neither of us was able to manage small talk. We said good night, and I drove back to Arsenal. I was tired of thinking about the cemetery murders. I was ready for an evening of petting Harvey and reading a good book.

There are those who argue that our sophistication robs us of helpful rituals. Aunt M's memorial service, held on a bleak Monday five days after her disappearance, seemed as pointless as possible without its star. All form, no substance. The city coroner's office was impossibly backed up and so the police could not release her body. I arrived embarrassingly early so that I could be seated in the last row of the fifty folding chairs, thinly padded, that faced the small, freestanding lectern.

I waited a long time before the first mourners drifted in to pay homage to the late Mary Margaret Brooks. The trickle pretty much stayed a trickle, too. Other than family members, they were mostly women in their sixties and seventies, arriving in twos and threes, only two men among them, dressed in drab winter colors. Neighbors and friends of Mary Margaret and Linda? They all seemed to huddle in seats on one side of the room to my left. Lindstrom and Neely arrived and sat at the opposite end of my row. Neely nodded at me cordially, but Lindstrom looked through me as though recognition would tip her hand. She was stylish in a gray flannel slacks suit that must have cost half a month's salary. Well, half a month of my salary.

About ten minutes before the main event the family arrived and took their reserved seats in the front. Dr. Yates entered, sandwiched between her husband and Ann's fiance, Philip Seaton. Ann and her cousin Greg followed behind. Ann's father wore a look of impatience. Ann had said that he and Aunt M got on well, but he showed no sign of that now. Maybe the whole empty ceremony annoyed him.

Deborah Yates, however, looked as I remembered her. Very classy, very sophisticated, but today also very strained under that veneer as though letting go of her sister, even symbolically, hurt. Throughout the ceremony Philip Seaton was attentive to her as though she and not her daughter were the object of his affections. He was a smooth-haired blond with a long nose and a sharp chin, but he moved with grace, and his tight body would be an object of envy at the exclusive gym he no doubt belonged to. Dr. Yates looked appreciative, too, of his support. Certainly her husband, who stayed restless, wasn't proving a bulwark against grief.

Ann Yates and Greg Brooks were similarly allied. Side by side, they might have been brother and sister or husband and wife. Handsome, smartly attired, powdered, cologned, slender and sleek. They looked less the tail end of the yuppie generation than the epitome of it.

Perhaps they were not as complacent as they looked. Ann certainly tried to lead a less sheltered life. During the service they exchanged few words, yet seemed at ease with one another.

After the Brooks/Yates family was settled, Poor Arlene arrived. She didn't bother greeting the others, just sat discreetly in the third row. I noted she came alone and wondered briefly if she had no one, or had someone she didn't dare bring.

A few more mourners, including Dr. Rolfing, came in and stopped by the family to offer condolences. All the exchanges were somber, dignified, although I noticed Ann did not shake Rolfing's hand. Five minutes after the stated starting time a young Episcopalian priest stepped to the lectern, flanked by two elegant sprays of gladioli. He was a handsome lad, the sort whose looks overpower other impressions. He had a good speaking voice too, rich and well-modulated. He was candid about not knowing Aunt M. The family sat, stiff-necked and blank-faced, while he addressed the key points of salvation.

My mind slipped to Aunt M's disappearance. How had she gotten out of the nursing home without being seen? If she'd gone out the emergency exit nearest her room, an alarm should have sounded. If she'd walked to the front entrance, surely someone would have spotted her. If Ann were involved, she could have led Aunt M out, but surely at least one of the staff at Gateway would have seen her.

Every now and then I checked on Neely and Lindstrom, who were checking on the audience before them. Once I caught Lindstrom shifting restlessly. Neely caught my eye just then and gave me a big wink. From the safety of our last row I grinned at him. The handsome priest labored on. It was obvious that the love of the sound of his own voice had attracted him to his profession.

He kept us in school a long time. I wondered if he felt discouraged to give such a heartfelt oration to such a starched audience.

Upon our release we made small clusters in the parking lot. The temperature was heading downward, and folks didn't linger long. Arlene spoke briefly to Deborah Yates, and they hugged awkwardly. Ann and Greg strolled over to me; we exchanged funeral formulae. Over their shoulders I saw Philip helping Dr. Yates into a sedan. The cousins excused themselves, and I promised to call Ann soon. I meant to report on the investigation, but to say the words directly seemed vaguely indecent in this setting. I watched Greg help Ann into his gray BMW and drive away.

As I started my Plymouth, I reflected. Nothing seemed amiss. I wondered what Lindstrom and Neely had made of it, but they had melted into thin air.

If her killer had made an appearance at Aunt M's memorial service, he was in deep disguise.

Chapter Six

I headed back to the office and got on the phone to Nina at Ruth House.

"Hi, Nina, I have a couple questions. Do you have a minute?"

"Sure, Meg. What do you need?"

"I'm looking for a homeless woman. She's white, a schizophrenic. She cashes her S.S.I. check at the Currency Exchange on North Grand."

"Oh, lord. There are probably a dozen women who fit that description."

"This one has a rich relative that sometimes helps her."

"Now you've gone too far. None of my clients seem to have relatives that help them, rich or otherwise. Let me see." I could hear her take a sip of coffee. She mumbled to herself for a moment.

"Mildred would fit, but I'm pretty sure her family is all poor. She told me last year that her father 'borrowed' every penny she got from her check. About two months ago we had a woman stay just a couple of nights. Her name was Leanne, but she didn't mention any rich relatives to us."

"What is her last name?"

"I'll need to go look in our files. Hang on a minute."

It took her a full five, so I booted up the Macintosh and made some rough notes in the file. Then I played a quick game of solitaire and was in the middle of the second game when Nina picked up again.

"Sorry I was gone so long. There is always somebody who thinks she needs to talk to me 'right now'," Nina said. "Her name was Leanne Hightower and the number she listed for her emergency contact is not a working number. Most of them don't want us to be able to contact anyone."

"Any other information on her?"

"Just that she was on Haldol and Prozac."

"Where did she get her prescriptions?"

"Don't know. We don't take that kind of information unless there is a problem. If she weren't taking her medicine or had run out, I'd know."

"Thanks, Nina. You've been a big help."

I sat and considered a minute. Malcolm Bliss seemed the most obvious choice. The old hospital was St. Louis's repository for the unfortunates who had a grasp on neither reality nor funds to make their illness easier in the psychiatric ward of a more luxurious hospital. I pulled the fat Greater St. Louis Yellow Pages out of my drawer and found Malcolm Bliss. I cleared my throat and pinched my voice a bit.

"Social services, please," I said to the operator.

"Social services, how may I help you?"

"Hello, my name is Jennifer Streetor. I'm a social worker at Regional. We have a problem here I hope you can help with. A patient came to the emergency room. She needs some stitching up and isn't coherent enough to give permission. She can't or won't tell us her next of kin. We thought she might have been a patient of yours at one time."

"Just a moment, please. I'll connect you to the social worker on duty."

Presently a wonderful, sexy, female voice come on the line. "Hi, this is Marty, how can I help?"

I went through my story again for Marty and she put me on hold to consult with her computer.

"Yes, Leanne Hightower is a clinic patient. It says here her emergency contact is Maureen Hightower."

"That sounds like it. Can you give me her number?"

She read it to me. "The address is on Oakleigh." She spelled it out.

"Thanks, Marty. You've been a big help."

"Don't you want to know what meds she's on?"

"Oh, yes. The doctor will want to know that."

"It says here ten milligrams of Haldol and four milligrams of Prozac daily."

I thanked Marty and assured her I would call her when Leanne was released from Regional. I hoped Leanne wouldn't wander into the clinic at Malcolm Bliss that afternoon.

I dialed the number for Maureen Hightower and got her machine. I left my name and number and added that my message was about Leanne. I shuffled some papers but realized that Aunt M's internment had just about done me in. It was dark. Time to head home.

On the way, I stopped at the dry cleaners to pick up some pants I'd had hemmed. Then to the grocery store for something to eat. Schnuck's deli department does dinner for me several times a week. When I pulled into my alley, I saw that a car was in my spot.

It wasn't Patrick's MG, but a blue Toyota. Lindstrom was sitting in the driver's seat. I pulled into my downstairs neighbor's usual spot and gathered my stuff. What on earth was Lindstrom doing here? Had she come to tell me I'd better stop interfering in her case? By the time I had everything in my arms, she was opening my door for me. I looked up. She really was tall, at least five feet ten inches.

"Hello, Darcy. Want me to carry something up for you?"

"No, thanks, I think I've got it. Here you can unlock the door, though." I handed her my keys and pointed to the brass-colored one that unlocked the door to my apartment. When I finished stowing the dry-cleaning in the closet and supper in the fridge, she was sitting at my small kitchen table looking perfectly at home. And I felt like a cat thumped down in a stranger's territory. Was this a social visit? Should I offer her something to drink, or just steel myself for a lecture? "So, is this a social drop-in or a police tactic to catch me unaware?"

"I just wanted to have an informal conversation with you, Darcy."

I pondered this. To my knowledge, we'd never had a formal conversation with one another. I had a brief image of her towering over me, a single, unshaded bulb behind her blond head. "Okay, I'll converse. Would you like a soda or something?"

"Coffee, if you have it."

I took a couple minutes finding a filter and rinsing out the pot. She watched me carefully, but seemed willing to wait to begin our informal conversation until she had my full attention. In the meantime, Harvey decided to forgo the finish of his late-afternoon nap to join us and petition for some kibble. I tossed a half-cup of the dry stuff into his bowl and he looked at me disdainfully and leapt up on the table to inspect our visitor. I shooed him off, trying for the surprised look of one who never allows her cat on the kitchen table. Finally the coffee was brewing, and I sat and looked at Lindstrom.

"You've been working on this case," she said. It was a statement. Did she have spies everywhere?

"Yes." The less said the better until I knew what she was looking for.

"Found out anything?"

"Not much, really. I'm wondering how Aunt M got out or if there was any real motive for killing her."

"Why would you be searching for a motive for her in particular?"

"Her death is the one that concerns my client."

"I thought you were just a liaison, not investigating a crime."

"I'm not really investigating, just asking a few questions.

Checking out to make sure the reason for Aunt M's death wasn't closer to home than a random serial killing."

"Found anything to support that theory?"

"No."

"Do you know what you'll do with it if you do?"

"Sort of depends on what I find, I guess."

"No, it doesn't. Information germane to an investigation, especially a murder investigation, must be turned over to me immediately. I find out it hasn't and you won't have your license for long."

I could hardly believe my ears. I did manage to keep my jaw from dropping. She was threatening to spank me before I even thought about doing something wrong. It made me sincerely wish that I had found something worth hiding from her. But I had survived as an MP, and knew a thing or two about officious authority. "Sure," I said, "our goal is the same, to make sure that whoever killed Aunt M is identified and brought to trial."

She narrowed her eyes at me, but decided to accept my acquiescence at face value.

She nodded. "And what is the story on Arlene Dorman?"

"What story?"

"How is she related to the Yates family?"

I thought it over. It seemed innocuous enough. "She's Ann's cousin, second cousin to be more precise. Ann's grandfather disinherited his sister, Arlene's grandmother, when she married for love into the wrong class."

"Arlene won't make that mistake, right?"

This was as good a place as any to make my principled stand. "If you want to know who she sleeps with, you'll have to ask her."

Lindstrom raised her eyebrows and grinned at me. "Aren't you one of those who believe that everyone should know everything about everyone's sex life?" She sat with her chin in her hand, looking steadily into my face. She showed very little of her thoughts or feelings in her blue eyes or surprisingly full lips. Good cop. Smart ass besides. Would probably make a good poker player.

I decided to bite. "Being out is a personal decision, but overall, it is the only real safety we have. As long as they can frighten us, keep us running and hiding and quivering in our closets, we can't be a force for change."

"Who is they, Darcy?"

"What?"

"Who is the they that have us running and hiding and quivering?"

I looked at her. I supposed she thought I was naive. First I meekly tell her I'll spill everything I know, then I have a complex of

64

some kind. I wasn't the seasoned veteran of the streets she was.

"Homophobes and those who aid them by deliberately maintaining their ignorance."

"I can't really say I've ever met a homophob, let alone been chased by one."

"Bull, Lindstrom. The department is full of them. They're everywhere. You might as well tell me you've never met a Republican."

She paused. Oh, damn. It could not be. She couldn't be a Republican.

"The department is full of ordinary people. Some have never met a gay person. Some see only the freaks at the pride parade. Several are nearly as far out as you. None of them has ever said a derogatory word to me."

"You have never heard a queer joke told by a cop?" I grinned. I knew I had her.

"Not directed at me."

I clapped my hand to my forehead. I could not believe this. This was worse than Republican. "So it's okay to denigrate fags so long as the butt of the joke isn't a Norwegian cop in a midwestern city?"

"No. Jokes like that aren't okay, either. But I've never felt like anyone told one to hurt me or to take my political power away from me. I just don't get my jollies by making the people around me uncomfortable. I am who I am. I've never denied it."

"Are you out to your family?"

"Of course."

"Wasn't telling them an important step to you?"

She paused, gathering her thoughts. "Talking to my parents about my life is hardly a political act. It is just about loving them. And them loving me. I don't love the assistant chief. He doesn't talk to me about his private life. I don't talk to him about mine."

"Does he have a picture of his wife and kids on his desk?"

"No."

"Does he bring his wife to social events for the department?"

"What does that have to do with whether or not I tell him that I'm gay?"

"He's flaunting his heterosexuality."

"Darcy, you are so full of it. I don't have time for this. Remember, withholding evidence won't do you any good."

"What are you afraid I'll find, Lindstrom? Something to shoot a hole in your theory?"

"Trying to compete with the police department is stupid. Don't be stupid."

She left without drinking the coffee I had brewed. I wanted to call her back, to start again, to tell her off for presuming on my hospitality to threaten me and call me stupid. To kiss her and take her to my bed. Instead, Harvey and I shared the chicken salad from the deli. I comforted myself with the thought that I had matured beyond the stage where wearing a gun visibly was necessary for my self esteem.

Tuesday morning Colleen announced that Arlene Dorman was on the phone. I didn't have a clue. Why would Arlene be calling me? I thought about telling Colleen to take a message, but my curiosity won out.

"Darcy here."

"Hello, Meg. Do you remember me? From Gateway."

"Yes, sure, Arlene. How are you?"

"Very upset. Something is going on here. Did you read this morning's paper?"

In fact, I had. I had read it pretty thoroughly in order to avoid the massive pile-up of manila folders on my desk. Walter had decided that we had to get rid of some old case files. I was supposed to pick out those that might have enduring significance and toss the rest. I hadn't seen anything in the morning *Post* that made me think of Gateway Nursing Home.

"Yes, why?" I responded.

"Did you see the article about Rudy? Rudy Carr? He was an aide here. His body was fished out of the Mississippi yesterday. He was murdered."

"Murdered? When?"

"I don't know. But he'd been missing since Saturday. He was supposed to work three to eleven, but he didn't show up or call."

All my alarm bells rang. That Aunt M and Rudy were linked in time and place and now homicidal death was too much to accept without questions. It turned out that Arlene agreed.

"Have the cops been there yet?" I asked.

"Yes, some fool named Schmidt. I tried to tell him that it was connected to Aunt M's death. But all he would say is, 'Yes, ma'am.' I could tell he wasn't paying any attention. The only questions he asked were about drugs."

"How long will you be there?"

"Until three. Are you coming?"

"Yes, I'll be there before three." We rang off, and I checked my watch. I fished the *Post* out of my wastebasket and flipped through it. It was a small article in the "Police/Court" box. The two-paragraph piece said only that Rudy Carr, twenty-five, had been pulled from the river by a fisherman. Police reported that the victim had been shot. I shivered. Couldn't help it. I'd seen Rudy Carr alive less than a week ago.

It was noon now. I decided to grab a bite to eat before enduring another visit to Gateway. I knew the sights, smells, and sounds at the nursing home would do nothing for my appetite. I walked down the street and got a burger from Hardee's. I could sort files and eat at my desk. Maybe make a call to Ann.

But when I returned, Colleen announced that I had a new client waiting in my office.

When Walter started Miller Security, he offered a full menu of services—whatever would make a buck he said. He soon realized he could make a living without doing divorce cases, that staple of many investigation services. Spying on his neighbors' personal lives made him feel like a slug he said. Two decades later the public perception that crime was increasing at supersonic rates made security a hot service to provide. Walter's many friends on the south side—union men, independent contractors, small industrial firms—provided him with plenty of business. The variety of our cases decreased. Some days I felt we were just a union hiring hall sending Walter's retired friends off to be nighttime security guards for lumberyards and warehouses. But Walter rarely turns down a small case from the neighborhood. He's against growing too big for your britches, a trait I find admirable. Frankly I think it's the human interest angle he relishes. Despite his aversion to messy divorce cases, he loves learning the quirky details of people's lives.

So I wasn't completely surprised when Colleen told me that a Mrs. Vogel was waiting for me. Colleen gave me a look that implied Mrs. Vogel was not a captain of industry or one of Walter's Korean War buddies.

She was sitting in the client's chair. She was tiny, even with a thick maroon shawl-collared sweater padding her heavy winter coat. She wore a head scarf tied under her chin and peered at me through thick glasses.

"Hi, I'm Meg Darcy, Mrs. Vogel. How can I help you?"

"You're Walter's daughter?" she asked sharply. Her voice had the tremble of old age.

"I'm his niece."

"This isn't a nice business for a young woman," she said, taking advantage of age's prerogative to insult the young.

I shrugged and crossed behind my desk and sat down. "You know, Mrs. Vogel, I spend most of my day right behind this desk." It was too often true and my least favorite part of the job. I can be nosy from a desk, but I can't stretch my muscles.

"Well, I wouldn't want a girl of mine doing it."

"How can I help you?"

"I was hoping Walter would handle it. He used to be my paper boy, you know."

"Walter isn't available right now." I was rapidly seeing why. "I'll do this first interview, but the whole agency will work on the case if we take it."

"But you've got to take it." A different tremble captured her voice. Her mouth collapsed inward, a prelude to tears.

I snatched a tissue from the box on my desk and hurried to her side to deliver shoulder pats. Her shoulders heaved under her coat.

"I'm sure we will." I kept patting till her sobs subsided. A powdery scent of lavender wafted by.

"My little Liebchen is gone."

I don't claim even a smattering of German, but I thought I recognized "sweetheart."

"Tell me all about it." I returned to my desk and took up my pen.

"He's been mine for eight years. That woman killed him. You have to help me prove it." She leaned forward and punched the air with a tiny fist holding wadded tissue.

"Would you spell the missing person's name?"

"Liebchen!" Any idiot would know.

"Spell it for me, Mrs. Vogel."

"It's not a person." She put a spin of contempt on the last word. "It's my dog, my poodle." Urgency spilled out of her. She began to shred the tissue.

"Hmm. Sure." I scribbled on my legal pad. "How do you spell his name, Mrs. Vogel?" Sometimes that works.

She glared at me. I was still a fool. But at last she complied. "And that woman killed him. My darling dog. I want you to prove it."

She was past her crying point and sobered by indignation.

"Mrs. Vogel, let me ask you some background questions." I took her through the preliminaries.

She was a widow living by herself, four blocks away. Liebchen was all the company she needed. The dog was her fourth poodle, yes, a small one. Not the smallest, that's a teacup. The miniature size. Definitely a lap dog. Not yippie at all. An insult to the sweetest little dog. Tears welled up.

"When did Liebchen disappear?"

"Monday. Yesterday. I called the police. They said they'd look, but I know they were laughing at me."

I bet. Though maybe that was unfair. I imagine lots of cops would rather be pulling kittens from trees and finding lost puppies than fending off drugs and guns.

"It's so cold out. I'm afraid he'll freeze. I can't search for him. The walks are too slippery. I'm eighty-two. I can't fall."

I didn't want to show how much I agreed with her. Even if Liebchen had survived city traffic, the weather had been terrible for a pampered older dog to endure. Maybe it was best to hope he'd stumbled into the kindness of strangers and was now sleeping at the foot of someone else's bed. But I wasn't sure I could console Mrs. Vogel with that.

I was tapping my pen on the pad, trying to think of how I'd approach the problem when Mrs. Vogel spoke again in her shrill voice. "I think Velma killed him. I know it's a terrible thing to say, but I really do. She hated Liebchen."

"Who is Velma?"

"The helper." She was impatient with my ignorance.

"The helper?"

"Yes, yes. The helper. The agency sends her." She bit the necks off the words. Just how dull was I?

I leaned back in my chair a moment and spun the pen with my fingers. Don't be afraid of silence, Betty says. I twirled the pen some more. "The woman who comes to cook and clean for you."

A brisk nod. "The helper."

"Velma the helper," I wrote. I nodded at Mrs. Vogel. "What's her last name?"

She frowned and shook her head. I could tell from her inward look she was searching for it. She warded off any comment from me with a gesture of her fist. "Riley. She's Irish."

I recognized the tone. Outsiders of all origins see that section of the south side as a white wall without cracks. But insiders are Italians, Germans, Irish with old tribal loyalties and antagonisms. Some still use labels as though they had real and permanent meanings. I wrote "Riley" after "Velma."

"Do you have her address?"

"Why she comes to my house every day of the week—between nine and eleven."

I sensed she was losing faith in my detecting powers. I didn't know common sense things. I tried to regain status. "Not on weekends, though."

"No, not then. You can talk to her right at my house."

I preferred not to, but I wasn't going to explain why. Instead I asked for and got a detailed description of Liebchen, all the way down to his inevitable red collar.

"I.D. tag?"

"Why would he need one? He's a house dog." A sniff.

I didn't argue. I asked for pictures. There are two kinds of people in the world, those who take pictures of their pets and those who don't. Mrs. Vogel was a don't. I'd have to rely on my purple prose for the posters.

I outlined our strategy—some door-to-door in the neighborhood, a call to the Humane Society, an ad in the paper, and posters.

When I wound it up, she was reluctant to go. Clients often are. If they could just stay and say one more magic thing. Finally she said, "You will tell this to Walter?"

"I promise."

She nodded. She struggled out of the chair and hung onto it to get her balance. "I'll pay you when my social security check comes in."

"Fine," I said.

I saw her to the outer office. She asked me to call a cab for her. Colleen called. Mrs. Vogel and I hovered near the front door till the cab came. I helped her into it, promising I'd be in touch with her soon.

When I returned, shivering, Colleen asked, "Big case?"

"The lost pet drill."

She reached for her memo pad.

"I'll write an ad. Let's put it in the *Post* and the *Suburban Journal* and the *American*," referring to St. Louis's African-American weekly. "Dogs don't know about racial tensions," I said. I paused to think.

"The police? The pound?"

"Yeah. And the city's sanitary crew. Just in case they've scraped a poodle off the streets lately."

She grimaced.

"Oh—can you do some fancy graphics on the computer for posters? We'll run it off at Kinko's."

"Sure. We've got a dog graphic, too. Maybe even a poodle," she said.

"Perfect." I handed her the notes I'd taken while Mrs. Vogel talked with me.

"I know Mrs. Vogel. A little. Can she afford this?"

"No. But we can."

She gave me a surprised look.

"Well, suppose it was Harvey Milk." I glanced at my watch. It was time for me to leave for the nursing home. Rudy Carr was on my mind not a missing dog, that's for sure. I went back to my office, took ten minutes to eat and clear off my desk, and on my way out told Colleen I'd see her tomorrow. I had something to go on now, my own angle, and I knew then and there I was not just a liaison.

At Gateway Arlene took me into her small cubicle of an office—assistant administrators don't rate windows. She didn't give me time to ask a question.

"Something is going on here. It can't be a coincidence that two people from this nursing home have been murdered within a week. The police won't listen, of course. They're sure Rudy was involved in some drug scheme and got killed over that."

"Why do they think it was drugs?"

"Schmidt said they found a pocketful of prescription medication on him. Which they assume came from here."

"Might he have stolen some drugs?"

"Of course, he might have, but that's not the point. Don't you see? He knew Aunt M. He almost always worked the wing she lived on. Someone killed him because he knew something."

I was skeptical. "What did he know?"

"I don't know. You need to find that out. It seems strange to me that the only people who profit from that poor woman's death aren't being investigated at all."

"You mean you think Ann's family killed Aunt M?"

"I'm not saying they did. I'm just saying that there was enough money there to be tempting to people who are so fond of it."

"Which of them wanted Aunt M's money that badly?"

"Ann and Greg are both great suspects if you ask me. The whole family worships money. Oh, they act like they don't. They stoop to care about causes, but when it comes down to actually doing the right thing one of them is as tight fisted as the next. And Ann's parents are no better."

"But what does Rudy's death have to do with this?"

"He must have seen something or known something about it. And they killed him to keep him quiet."

There was a knock on the door. Arlene sat back and said, "Come in."

A woman with carefully styled blond hair and designer glasses stuck her head in the door. "Arlene, Dr. Rolfing wants you. He's in his office." Arlene looked at me and asked me to wait. She left and thirty seconds later I did too. I left Arlene a note telling her I'd be back in touch with her and thanking her for calling.

I wanted to know more about Rudy's death than I was likely to find out from Arlene. I walked down the hallway. In Aunt M's favorite lounge, I found a tight knot of aides and nurses talking. They stopped when I came into the room. I noticed the pretty young African-American nurse that had been thoughtful the day we searched for Aunt M. She had made sure all the searchers got lunch and had obviously been upset about Aunt M's disappearance. I asked her if I could talk to her. She nodded and followed me out of the room.

She led the way down the hall to an empty patient room. I sat on a chair, and she perched on the end of the bed. She looked too petite for the heavy lifting of nursing. She wore white uniform pants and a light blue tunic. Her hair was short and well-cut.

"I'm Meg Darcy. Remember me from last Thursday?"

She nodded. "Yes, you're Ann Yates' friend, right?"

"Yes. Ann has hired me to look into Aunt M's death. I'd like to ask you a few questions." She nodded. "Let's start with your name."

"I'm Rachel Batson."

"You knew Aunt M well?"

"I knew Mary Margaret pretty well. I work the East wing most of the time."

"How long have you been at Gateway?"

"Eleven years." Not so young as she looked.

"Did you know Rudy Carr?"

"What does that have to do with Mary Margaret's death? I thought she was killed by that serial killer."

"She probably was, but since Rudy worked here and he was murdered, too, I need to find out if their murders are linked somehow. Perhaps he saw something."

She nodded again. "Yes, I knew Rudy. We worked together sometimes."

"Do you know if he was selling drugs?"

"No, if I'd known a thing like that, I would have told Arlene or Dr. Rolfing." There was indignation in her voice.

"How hard would it have been for Rudy to get prescription medication from here at the nursing home?"

"It would be possible, I suppose. All the meds are kept in a small room behind the main nurses' station."

"Is it locked?"

"It's supposed to be. Generally it's locked at night. But the lotion and rubbing alcohol and other stuff is kept in there too. So there's quite a bit of traffic in and out during the day." Rachel paused and was clearly deciding whether or not to add some other information or observation. I waited. Two-thirds of good interviewing technique is knowing how to use silence. Most people yearn to fill it. She began again. "They put a new lock on cabinets with prescription meds last month. We've been having some shortages. But the shortages didn't stop."

"Shortages?"

"Yes, more medicine is gone per week than should be according to the prescriptions for the residents."

"What kind of medicine has been missing?"

"Anti-depressants, sleeping pills, mostly what the little old ladies call their 'nerve pills.'"

"How much has been missing?"

"Not that much, really. Just a handful a week."

"So this is not a big drug operation."

"No, not at all."

"Who do you think has been taking the meds?"

"If I'd known that, I'd have told, wouldn't I?" Her tone was reasonable rather than petulant, but her smile looked strained.

"Had anyone accused Rudy?"

"No. Rudy was one of our better aides."

"Where did Rudy live?"

"I don't know. He didn't mention it. He had a girlfriend, though. Her name is Nikki. She used to come pick him up sometimes."

"Do you know of any reason someone might kill Rudy?"

"No, I don't. He was an okay guy. More cheerful than most."

"Thanks, Rachel. I appreciate your willingness to help. If you hear anything else, or remember something, will you call me?" I handed her a card and gave her my best serious PI smile. She went back to work somewhat reluctantly. I leaned back on the chair and tried to frame an interview with Rolfing in my mind. He already saw me as a pain in the butt. He hadn't liked it a bit when I encouraged Ann and the family to publicize Aunt M's disappearance.

My thoughts were interrupted by Rachel's return. She stood in front of me toying with her watch band. She leaned against the foot of the bed and began, "You know some things go on here that shouldn't."

"What kind of things?" I asked.

"Patients not being well-taken care of. They cut corners on staffing. Patients should be walked and talked to everyday. It helps them hang on to those skills and combats depression. But with only three aides on a wing, we can walk only a few each shift. Some patients go weeks without being walked."

"Has anyone died or been seriously injured from short staffing?"

"I'm sure Mrs. Grable could have made it if they'd given her more aggressive care. We could do more with prevention instead of just responding to crises."

"When did Mrs. Grable die?"

"In August."

"Was there any investigation?"

"No." She paused, obviously weighing the plunge. "This place was a lot better before Dr. Rolfing took over." She looked at me meaningfully, as if I were the caped crusader of nursing homes. This was troubling news, but frankly I didn't see what it had to do with Aunt M or Rudy's death. Or what I could do about it. I whipped out my serious PI smile again and thanked Rachel for helping me investigate. She seemed satisfied with that for the time being, and we parted friends.

My next goal was to find Nikki, Rudy's girlfriend. I thought about asking Arlene if she knew the woman's last name, but I was afraid of getting caught in another Yates-bashing session. I cruised the hallways until I saw an aide. He was tall with white-blond hair. He jerked sheets out of a large canvas laundry bag on wheels.

"Hi. I'm here to help with the investigation of Rudy Carr's death. Did you know Mr. Carr?"

The aide looked me over with some skepticism. I squinted my eyes and tried to give him my most cop-like scowl.

"Yeah, I knew Rudy."

"Did you ever see him outside of work?"

"Nah, we didn't hang. Just at work."

"Do you know who might have seen Rudy outside work?"

"Breezer did. Him and Rudy was pretty tight."

"Is Breezer here today?"

"Un-huh. He's down on the West wing."

"Thanks for your help." The aide nodded and went back to tugging on his mound of sheets.

I found him in the break room, munching chips. Breezer, as it happened, was Richard Breeze, a short, thin African-American who was pretty surly when I started my rap about investigating Rudy's death. He clearly didn't want to talk to a cop and was pretty unimpressed with my PI license as well. Monosyllables and grunts were the best I could get from him until I asked the third drug-related question.

"Listen. Cops don't know shit. So what if he had a few pills in his pocket? That ain't nothing. Nobody killed Rudy over a few damn pills. They wasn't worth shit. He just got a few for himself and shared with a couple friends. He wasn't no damn drug dealer." Breezer pushed back the molded plastic chair he was sitting on and started out of the room.

"Wait. Why then? Why did someone want to kill him?"

"I don't know, lady. But no damn cop is going to bust his ass over Rudy, I know that."

"Listen, just a minute. Do you think it might have anything to do with Mary Margaret Brooks's disappearance?"

"I don't know. I just don't know. He worked that night. We both did. We was the ones that went out looking for her. Tramped all over the damn neighborhood. But I can't see why anybody'd kill him about that."

"Just one more question, Breezer. Do you know Nikki?"

"Sure."

"What's her last name?"

"Dial. Nikki Dial. She stays on Kingshighway." He gave me the address.

After Breezer left, I tried again to visualize a conversation between Rolfing and me that was remotely productive. Finally I decided that the best defense was being offensive. Rolfing could easily unroll yards of silky platitudes. Maybe if I irritated him sufficiently, he'd lose his temper enough to unravel some truth.

His secretary was formidable. Her blond hair was a helmet. She assured me that Dr. Rolfing was busy this morning. I propped my left hip on the edge of her desk, crossed my arms, and offered to stay until he was free. She disappeared into his office, and presently he came out offering his hand and acting glad to see me. When we were settled in his office, somewhat less cubicle-like than Arlene's I noticed, I assured him I was here to make trouble.

"Dr. Rolfing, how long have you had prescription medicines being stolen?"

I saw him tense, but his voice was still controlled. "We had some small shortages earlier in the year, but we instituted stricter procedures with all medications and that problem has been resolved."

"According to your staff, the new locks didn't stop the thief, and there are still shortages, as you call them."

"I hardly see how this relates to the job you were hired to do, which was find Ms. Brooks. The police have completed that job now. Does the Yates family know you are trying to malign this institution?"

"The goal isn't to malign the institution, Dr. Rolfing; it is to find Ms. Brooks's killer."

Rolfing stared at me for several seconds without responding. Finally he said, "In case you haven't read the newspapers, she was murdered by a serial killer who unfortunately found her while she was away from our property."

"That would be convenient, wouldn't it? And just how was it that Ms. Brooks was 'away from the property' as you put it? Could it be that there isn't enough staff on duty to keep Alzheimer's patients safe and inside?"

"Ms. Darcy, I'm afraid I'm going to have to ask you to allow my staff to complete their duties without harassment. Ms. Dorman or myself will be glad to answer your questions within reason, but you will no longer be allowed to roam the halls of Gateway."

'Keep them off guard,' my old basketball coach said. I changed tactics. "Dr. Rolfing, if I'm convinced Gateway Rest Home had nothing to do with Ms. Brooks's death, I will recommend that the Yates family not sue you for negligence. I'm not a lawyer, but, as you probably know, agencies like ours have experience evaluating evidence for suits. You have more to lose than to gain by covering up." I stood up to enhance the drama. "What doesn't relate to Mary Margaret's death doesn't interest me. Think about it, Dr. Rolfing."

I gave him my most intense warning stare—one I'd used as an MP—and marched out before he could start a placating speech. I wanted some time for worry to undermine his arrogance.

It was time for me to talk with Nikki Dial.

Chapter Seven

The first time I went to the address on Kingshighway, Nikki wasn't home. I had tried to call, but there was no phone listing for either Nikki Dial or Rudy Carr in the phone book. Nor did information have a listing. So I grabbed another burger for dinner and called my office for messages. Colleen had left a note on the answering machine that said that Ann Yates had called twice. Patrick had called inviting me to dinner. Betty wanted to know if I could come help her trim the Christmas tree this weekend, and Maureen Hightower had returned my call. I decided to put off calling Ann. I felt sure she had heard about Rudy's death and maybe about Rolfing's displeasure with me. Instead, I dialed Maureen Hightower. The information I wanted from her I had to have from her in person. She couldn't see me that evening, but would meet me at Blueberry Hill tomorrow night at eight.

I hung up the pay phone and hurried back to the warmth of the Plymouth. It was completely dark at five-thirty. If Nikki worked days somewhere, she might be home by now. It took me three trips around her block to find a decent parking place, but finally I snagged one. I locked up the Plymouth and trudged back up the two flights of stairs to Nikki Dial's door. She answered the door this time and looked out at me with swollen eyes. Her dark blond hair was cut short. Her tired face and slumped posture suggested Rudy's death was not this woman's first tragedy. I introduced myself and explained that I was hired to investigate Aunt M's death and wanted to test any links with Rudy's murder. She let me into a tiny kitchen that smelled of garlic and onions and old grease. She lit a cigarette and offered me a soda or a beer. There didn't seem to be a chair to offer. We leaned against the counter, and she sighed as she pulled back the tab on a diet cola.

"I've just gotten back from the funeral home with Rudy's mom. She's such a hypocrite. She kicked him out when he was fourteen and hasn't helped him, not one single time since then. But now, she's acting like she's the big grieving mother. I thought she'd never stop crying while that man tried to explain things to us."

I nodded sympathetically. "This must have been a very difficult day for you."

"You can say that again, honey. I don't know how the hell we're going to pay for all this anyway. She says she doesn't have any money. I sure as hell don't."

"Didn't Rudy have any life insurance through Gateway?"

"Hell, no. Those tightwads didn't pay for any extras. Thank god I went back to work last month."

"What did the police tell you about Rudy's murder?"

Nikki's thin lips disappeared completely as she tried not to cry again. She let out a shaky breath. "They said he was found by some guy fishing on the river bank. God, I hope he didn't hook him. I didn't think to ask that." She put her hands over her face, and her shoulders started to shake. I put my hand lightly on her shoulder. I couldn't think of anything to erase the visual picture of a fish hook in her boyfriend's dead body. We stood silently for a minute or so.

"They said they don't know yet how long he'd been dead. I told them somebody killed him after work 'cause he never came home that night. Rudy never did that." She was breathing shallowly and talking faster as if she were afraid I'd interrupt her. "He always came home. That night he didn't call or nothing. I know he was dead that night. I tried to tell them. I called the police about three in the morning to make a missing person's report. They said they couldn't take a report like that on a grown man. 'Call us if he ain't back by Monday' they said. Like he was one of those guys who just took off without telling me. I tried to tell them he wasn't like that. Monday was too goddamn late. I went, though. Yesterday morning, first thing. You could tell that guy still didn't want to write nothing down. He kept asking me what we fought about. Like Rudy left me. I knew Rudy didn't leave me."

Her anger tumbled out, but I didn't try to defend those cops. She wouldn't care about their good reasons for not looking for Rudy sooner.

"Nikki, did anything unusual happen on Friday before Rudy left for work?"

Nikki rubbed her forehead. The nail on her forefinger was cracked. "He got a call. I thought he was a little nervous or mad about it, but he didn't talk about it."

"I tried to look your number up. Do you have a phone?"

"No, but the guy downstairs lets us use his."

"Did Rudy say who the call was from?"

"No. He wouldn't say anything about it. Just that he'd be a little late Friday night."

"Nikki, I'm sorry to have to ask this, but I'm sure the police have already told you about the drugs in Rudy's pocket."

"Yeah." She looked down at the cracked linoleum and rubbed

her forehead again. "He got pills sometimes. Not much. Just so he could relax. Sometimes he'd give some to friends. He'd never have many."

"Is there any possibility that he was deeper into drugs than you knew?"

"I wouldn't know then, would I?" She glared at me. I could almost hear her thinking, You're no better than the cops who wouldn't look for my boyfriend until his body was pulled from the muddy Mississippi.

"I know this must be painful, but it's important to rule out other reasons Rudy might have been killed before we jump to conclusions. If he wasn't killed over drugs, I'll do my best to see that the cops don't just brush this aside." She looked into my eyes for the first time.

"Look, it wasn't drugs. Sure, Rudy took some pills. He got them from the nursing home. That was wrong. But I swear to you, he wasn't on cocaine, he didn't deal. This wasn't some kind of drug ring."

"Do you have any other ideas?"

"Rudy had been talking about a big break last week. I thought he had a line on a better job. It had something to do with more money. He promised me he'd buy us a car."

Not to belabor a point, but that sounded a lot like drugs to me. Or that he was being paid to keep quiet about something. I paused. Before I could articulate the next question, she went on.

"I was afraid then that it had to do with drugs, but I asked him and he swore it wasn't. It was something he wasn't proud of, though. I knew because he wouldn't talk about it. He was such a talker. Eventually he always told me everything."

"Did Rudy ever mention Mary Margaret Brooks?"

She paused to think. "Not until she disappeared. He worked over that night to look for her. He called me from Gateway to say he'd be late."

"Was he afraid he'd be blamed for her disappearance?"

"No, but he was real upset when they found her dead."

"Did Rudy have anyone he was fighting with, anyone who hated him?"

"He didn't really fight with people. He was pretty easy going. His sister's boyfriend was mad that Rudy wouldn't loan him money, but I don't think Lonnie'd kill him."

I hated leaving her there alone with her grief in that cold and bare apartment. I asked if I could call someone to be with her. She said a girlfriend would come over later. I handed her my card with my phone number and asked her to call me if she thought of anything that might help. She put the card into her pocket, but she looked at me bleakly, her expectations low. She wasn't counting on any breaks from life.

Rudy had been expecting a big break, but instead he'd been shot and tossed into the river like a losing lottery ticket.

Nikki had given me plenty to think about as I drove home, but before I reached Arsenal I was shivering. I wished I'd laundered my thermal underwear. I ignored Harvey's greeting and popped a bowl of chicken soup into the microwave. Then I petted him and brought him up to date on the case. The microwave chirped and I ate half the big bowl before I peeled off my coat. I finished my first course and decided dry socks would improve matters. Harvey followed me into the bedroom—giving birth to dust bunnies as he went. He needs a full-time groomer.

I was just pulling on the second sock when the phone rang. I let the machine pick it up, but Arlene Dorman's voice produced enough guilt to send me racing back into the living room. I snatched up the phone before she'd finished her message. I blurted out an apology for leaving her office so abruptly that morning. She sounded cross about it but willing to forgive me if I appreciated her magnanimity. I tried to meet her expectations. My mom has an effortless charm, but mine requires heavy lifting.

She wanted to meet me for a drink. I looked at the clock. It was too early in the evening to beg off by using the excuse it was too late. After five minutes of circular negotiations I agreed to meet her at Mike's, an Irish tavern on Oakland.

I was glad for the dry socks as I headed back into the cold. All the Plymouth's metal surfaces were cold again, and I knew the heater wouldn't help till I was half-way there. Visions of a good book, Harvey on my lap, maybe some popcorn increased my churlishness about being out in this weather, and the ten-minute trip seemed long.

Mike's is a family tavern I was familiar with from being a guest at wedding and retirement celebrations over the years. It boasts good, if greasy, fried chicken and is one of the last places you can still get St. Louis's famous brain sandwiches. It's the kind of place where you can take your kids, but the regulars will still give strangers an unwelcoming stare. They did when I walked in. I gave the male bartender a nod and just kept walking. Stale beer and stale smoke and stale grease smells hung in the air.

Arlene was in the next to the last booth and was still in nurse's whites.

"There you are," she said as though I were hours late. A small glass with ice and pale liquid sat before her. She was turning it slowly with clean, stubby fingers. No rings, no polish.

"You're just off work?"

"Worked late. All this stuff about Aunt M and Rudy has us in an uproar. Rolfing has us double-checking everything, but the horse is gone. Whaddaya drinking?" She took a swallow of her own drink. "Seven and Seven," she explained.

I surmised it was not her first of the evening. "Hmm. What's their draft beer? No. I'd like a hot toddy. I haven't been warm in hours."

"I'll get it," she said and slid out of the booth to place the order with a fiftyish blond woman wearing an Ann Richards beehive. I'd seen the woman work the bar before. I unzipped my short coat but left it on.

"Want something to eat?" Arlene asked when she returned.

I did, but I didn't want to lengthen my stay. "Not yet."

"You really set Gateway abuzz with your questions."

I invited her to expand on the topic and she did. But nothing was surprising. Gateway wasn't one happy family, but it was a small shop. Rudy had been both young and cheerful, a rare and endearing combination. That he had been killed was as titillating as Aunt M's death at the hands of a serial killer even though the press coverage was less. Even stoic employees worried a bit about their proximity to danger, and everyone gossiped. Eventually every shift would know a PI had talked to Batson and Rolfing. She didn't mention Breezer. I wondered if this signaled a failure in her own intelligence gathering or was a meaningless oversight in her reporting.

The blond woman appeared with my toddy. "We've had more calls for these in the last two days than we've had all winter." Her voice was all smoke and whisky, and friendlier than her blue eyes. Those might have been chipped from the ice on the curb outside.

The aroma of the toddy was itself intoxicating. The first sip was as disappointing as whisky's taste always is for me, but its warmth spread quickly. I didn't care if it were false warmth. I wiggled my toes inside my boots.

"Thelma, Meg. Meg, Thelma. I'll have another." Arlene pointed to her glass.

"Hi, Meg." The introduction had melted a layer of ice. "You taking a cab?" she asked Arlene.

Arlene wasn't offended. "If I have to. Or Meg will give me a lift."

I smiled and nodded but heard the cage door snick. I tugged off my coat.

"So what did you find out?" Arlene asked after Thelma left. Arlene's eyes were her best feature, a dark brown and hooded.

"Not much. But I wanted to ask you. What do you think of

Rolfing? What kind of boss is he?"

"He's bossy. A real M. C. P."

I didn't get it.

"Oink. Male chauvinist pig."

I hadn't heard that one in a while. "Is he dishonest?"

"How do you mean?"

"Any way that would give him motive to kill Aunt M."

She finished her drink and slurped her cubes. "I told you who has a motive."

I sighed. It was irrational, but I resented Arlene's suspicion of Ann Yates while harboring my own. But I was seeing Arlene through Ann's eyes. I needed to look for myself.

I decided to switch topics. "How long have you worked at Gateway?"

"Since it opened."

"Ann said you recommended it as a good place for Aunt M to stay."

"It isn't Gateway's fault Aunt M got out," she snapped.

Thelma arrived with Arlene's drink, giving me a chance to reconsider my wording.

"Could someone from the outside have led Aunt M out without inside help?"

"Rudy's you mean?"

I nodded. She had a dark mole just to the left of her mouth.

She studied her glass. "I suppose. Ann and Greg often took Aunt M for walks down the hallways. For young people they came fairly frequently. I give them that."

"But you think they're greedy people."

She sipped her drink. "My grandmother died a poor woman because my great-uncle cut her off for marrying a poor man. My mother died of breast cancer. She was raised not to consult a doctor till you're on your last legs. We didn't have money for mammograms." She took the napkin from under her glass and sopped up the water ring. Her voice was oddly flat telling the most personal parts of her rage.

"But Deborah Yates sought you out."

A look I couldn't read passed over her face. "Sometimes she's almost convincing."

"About?"

"That we're all family. Despite all the years and what old John Brooks did."

"But Ann and Greg aren't? Convincing, I mean."

"They're snotty brats."

I figured she was a decade older than the brats and me. Was

that a factor? Or was it all about class and family grievances nursed too long?

Suddenly she grinned. It was a lopsided affair, tilted by the Seven and Seven. "But what do we care? We know how to live without wealth, don't we, Meg?" She raised her glass and winked.

This dance step nearly lost me. Was she coming out? Coming on?

"They say living well is the best revenge," I said. I raised my toddy and we clinked glasses.

"Are you living single, Meg?"

"Well, I..."

"Don't do it. Find a gal." She reached over and patted my arm. "It's the best way."

Unlike some similar pats under similar circumstances, hers ended briskly.

It was my turn to inquire about Arlene's marital status, but I was afraid it would signal too much interest. "What do you think about Ann's fiance?"

"Philip Seaton? Now there's an asshole defined."

We drank to that. The toddy was creeping further into my tissues, and a liking for poor Arlene spread with it.

"Are you out to the family?"

"I've never said, one way or the other."

"They seem fairly broad minded."

"Yeah sure, if you've got a million or two to leave 'em." She tapped the dark wood of our table with a short forefinger. "Look, I always knew I'd have to support myself. Nursing is a good profession if you're queer. But I also know, as far as Gateway goes, if there was trouble, Rolfing wouldn't stick up for me. He's too calculating."

"Is he a good administrator?"

"He's a mix. Like us all."

"Even the Yates?" I couldn't resist.

"Even them." Her head was drooping forward.

"Are you ready for that ride home?"

"Thelma will call a cab."

"I don't mind." And now I didn't.

We haggled. The compromise was that I waited till her cab came and saw her into it. She gave me a clumsy hug before crawling in.

Later when Harvey greeted me, I scooped him up and gave him an unwelcome squeeze. "I wonder if she has a good cat like you, Harve."

Chapter Eight

Deborah Yates had agreed to meet me at her home at eight-thirty on Wednesday morning. It was December ninth, exactly one week after Aunt M's disappearance. Dr. Yates opened the front door and led me through to a small breakfast nook at the back of the house. The wallpaper was creamy with yellow ribbons tied around small bunches of violets. She brought coffee and muffins to the table on an enameled tray, and we drank from tall glass mugs. I sat with a view into the kitchen. There were Braun appliances scattered on the cabinets, and the stove and refrigerator gleamed expensively.

After we had fussed with coffee and started our muffins, Deborah thanked me for coming to the memorial service and being a friend to Ann during this ordeal.

"You don't know how much it means to her to have you around. You are a calming influence on her. She relies on your competence."

"Some of what seems like competence is probably just having seen more violence than Ann has. It doesn't shock me quite as much," I managed to say.

"I'm sure that is true. Ann hasn't seen violence in any real way. None of us have experienced this kind of violence." Deborah looked out of the colonial window at her back garden. "But I've seen the violence that disease does to the body. Nature has its own violence."

"I asked to talk to you today because I need to settle my own mind about your sister's death. As you know, it's being treated by the police as one of the cemetery murders. But I'm not so sure about that. We know that Aunt M wasn't homeless, and the killer may have known that, too. Rudy Carr was murdered on the same day everyone heard the news about Aunt M. The murder of two people that closely connected rings warning bells for me."

"You aren't satisfied that Mary Margaret was murdered by the same person as the homeless women?"

"It looks like it on the surface, but it doesn't feel quite right to me. The cemetery murderer seemed to be making a statement by placing very poor women in wealthy surroundings. Aunt M's placement in Memorial Park just doesn't fit that pattern at all."

"Unless the murderer just hates old women, and cemeteries are just a convenience. After all, Bellefountaine and Calvary have the advantage of being handy isolated places to leave the bodies."

I nodded to encourage her.

"And he might have thought Mary Margaret homeless. She had that filthy coat on. And she certainly could have been babbling to herself. She must have been at her most confused to be wandering around completely off the grounds of Gateway." Deborah Yates turned her head and bit her lip. I wanted to reach out to her in sympathy, but something in her demeanor stopped me. Soon she continued, "But I think it is good for you to be asking questions. In a way, it is like research. We sometimes choose our own blinders. Maybe you'll keep the police from missing things because you aren't so wedded to their view of it."

"Can you tell me anything about Aunt M's life that might have led someone to be very angry at her or wish her dead?"

"No. I'm not saying her life was blameless, but I can't think of anyone who would have a motive for murder."

"Do you know how much money she left?"

"Mary Margaret was Dad's favorite, and she was unmarried, so he left the largest part of his estate to her. He said that I had Sam to take care of me, and my brother Thomas, Greg's father, was doing well with his distributing business. Mary Margaret invested wisely and lived fairly simply."

"Do you have some idea of how much her estate will be worth?"

"I'm not sure; we're scheduled to meet with her attorney about the will tomorrow morning."

I thought about pushing her again but decided that Ann would give me the information after the will was read tomorrow.

"What was her response to being in the nursing home?"

Deborah's eyes darted away from mine.

"She loathed it. She was always both a very private person and very much a gypsy. Being in an institution was the antithesis of her life." There was a long pause as we both chewed on that information. Then Deborah began again. "Twice when she was quite lucid she asked me to help her commit suicide. I lacked the nerve to do it. Now I wish I had helped her. So much better for her to die with some dignity than this horror." She paused for a deep breath and expelled it. She sent a weak smile to signal her willingness to continue.

I wondered if she meant what she said about regretting her refusal to help her sister commit suicide. Sometimes grief prods people to embrace guilt no matter which choices they've made. Suicide may have looked preferable to homicide in embittered hindsight. But I wasn't there to discuss ethics.

"Do you feel that Aunt M was treated well at Gateway?"

"Gateway is an institution for the care of those unable to care for themselves. It cannot be like home. Sometimes I felt more care could have, should have been taken. But mostly the employees are competent and occasionally even thoughtful."

"One employee told me that there often weren't enough staff on duty. She thinks patients are neglected."

Deborah twisted her mug in her hands. "Arlene assures me that Aunt M got the best care, and that is what I saw with my own eyes. Aides sometimes exaggerate their medical knowledge."

"Did you see any signs of a wide pattern of neglect at Gateway?"

Deborah's face hardened. "If I'd seen any signs of neglect at Gateway, Mary Margaret wouldn't have spent another night there."

The interview seemed to be at an end, so I thanked her for her time and the coffee. She recovered her graciousness, but not her warmth on our walk back to the front of the house.

As I walked to my Plymouth, a sleek, dark-blue Lexus pulled in beside me on the double drive. Philip Seaton was at the wheel.

I waited to exchange polite greetings. I saw a scowl forming on his face. I've spent years working to prevent knots forming in my stomach from his kind of disapproval. "Hello," I said blandly.

"What are you doing here?"

This was a new degree of rudeness. I didn't say anything. I just looked at him levelly, letting his words hang.

It took two beats before he shifted his eyes and his tone. "Is Dr. Yates home?" he asked more civilly.

"Yes," I said. "Nice seeing you again."

When I returned to the office, I borrowed Colleen for an hour. I asked her to drive while I tacked posters describing Mrs. Vogel's lost dog onto telephone poles. I couldn't help thinking of Aunt M and the signs Greg and I had posted. This time from the beginning I expected the effort to be futile. I shared my pessimism with Colleen after I'd climbed over my last mound of frozen slush and back into the Plymouth.

She nodded grimly. "I told Joey, my boyfriend, about Mrs. Vogel and Liebchen. If you don't find him, we'll get her another dog."

"That's a very generous thought."

"Mrs. Vogel's a really lonely woman."

I couldn't argue with that. In some ways she was lucky. Her mind was sharp enough; she had a home. But lonely. I stared out the window, wishing a poodle would appear.

I left Colleen back at the office and drove to Mrs. Vogel's address. I parked about a lawn and a half down the street. It was ten-forty-five.

All the houses on this block were modest one-story bungalows, sixty or seventy years old, and winter had robbed them of most of their dignity. The snow was patchy and soiled. At first glance the houses were neat, but without the distraction of leafy trees and flowers I could see sagging gutters and flaking trim. My guess was that several Mrs. Vogels lived on this street and that the middle-aged kids, their hands full of teenagers, didn't drop by most weekends. Or even, given Mrs. Vogel's age, were themselves not agile enough to do repairs that required ladders.

I kept the heater on and waited. Before I had time to really enjoy a fantasy in which I won the lottery and was seducing Lindstrom, a tall, substantial woman, bundled against the cold, emerged from Mrs. Vogel's house and walked briskly down the walk.

I sprang from the car and called out, "Mrs. Riley!"

She stopped and watched me approach. She wore a stocking cap and a scarf to match. Her mittens didn't match the set. Her down car coat looked cheap but warm. She was in her sixties and looking hale. At the moment she also wore a prudently wary look.

"Hi, I'm Meg Darcy. My uncle owns Miller Security. Mrs. Vogel has asked us to help find her dog."

She grimaced. "Oh, yes."

I handed her my card. "I'd like to ask what you know about it. Could we sit in my car?"

"I'm on my way to my next client. I have to catch a bus." Her cheeks were rosy, and her tone pleasanter than I'd expected.

"Could I drive you there? Or could we make an appointment for later?"

She peered at the card. "You're Walter Miller's daughter?" Obviously Mrs. Vogel had discussed her appointment with me.

"His niece."

She laughed. "Gert didn't get it quite right, did she? But don't make a mistake. She's still as sharp as a tack. Except when she gets an idea lodged in her head. Then try to change it." Her mittened hands sketched a gesture. Her own eyes looked keen behind rosy-lensed glasses. "My youngest brother went to school with Walter.

Ask him if he remembers Ken McInerny." She continued talking over my assurance that I would. "There was a long string of us kids. We were Irish. When that meant something. Nowadays you get two or three in a family same as—you aren't Protestant, are you? Isn't Darcy Irish?"

"It can be. In this case it's French. But my mother is mostly Irish."

"French." Mrs. Riley made it sound exotic.

"Mrs. Riley, I don't want to make you late. Can I drive you to your next appointment?"

We'd exchanged enough chit-chat, or I had listened well enough to gain her confidence. "Yes, you take me."

Once we were in the Plymouth she gave me surprisingly clear directions to her destination. When I said as much, she smiled. "I used to teach, you know. Elementary school till I married." She sighed. "Over forty years ago." She brushed her mittens together as though wiping away those years. "But you're wanting to know about the little dog."

"Yes. When did you last see Liebchen?"

"Monday, like Gert said."

"What happened?"

Mrs. Riley gave a muted hoot. "There's no denying I didn't like the little nipper." She gave me a sage glance. "Really a nipper, you know. He'd lunge at your heels. Just playful she says. Playful my foot." She pulled in a fresh batch of air. "But I'd never do harm to one of God's little creatures. So Monday I went out the back to take out the garbage. There's a fence around back where the dog can run free to do its duties. I can't remember if I shut the fence gate tight when I pulled the cans to the alley. They come through the back way, you know." She pointed ahead. "There's your left, at the next light."

"How did Liebchen get out of the house?"

"Gert has a little doggie door cut in the back door."

A silence fell. Mrs. Riley cleared her throat. "I've told her over and over that I'm sorry to my toes, but she won't get over it. When it's all said and done, it's only a dog, isn't it? I wished it no harm, but I can't bring it back. How much is it costing her, this looking for the dog?"

"She'll have to settle the fee with Walter," I lied. "But nothing till we find the dog."

"That's a funny way to run your business." She chuckled. "But I dare say you know best. Here we are." She pulled back her mitten to check her watch. "Early, too. They'll like that. A man and wife here. They don't get about as good as Gert. No pets, though."

I pulled up to the curb. "Thanks for your information. I know you're keeping an eye out for the dog."

She shrugged. "Glad to help. Tell Walter that Kenny's old sis said hello." She climbed out and waved a cheery goodbye.

I sighed at my case load of two loved ones each wandering beyond their prescribed limits. No doubt Liebchen would be taken for a homeless dog.

When I walked back into the office, Walter's broad back was the first thing I saw. He and Colleen were bent over looking under her desk.

"What's up?" I asked.

"I've solved the case of the missing pet poodle," Walter said.

Just then an irritating yap sounded from under the desk. Walter hooted as the dog ran out and across the floor. I looked down at a mass of dirty gray curls sniffing at my pants leg.

"Where'd you find it?"

"Around back at Meyerson's place. Sniffing around the dumpster. Came right up to me when I called it. Friendly little thing."

I reached down to scratch the dog's ears and picked it up. His button nose was smudged with dumpster remnants, but his bright eyes danced. I tried to get a look at his teeth.

"I don't know, Walter. This looks like a puppy to me. Mrs. Vogel's dog is eight years old."

"Nah. That's him. He just looks young because he's so small and feisty. Call Mrs. Vogel and tell her we're coming over."

"Shouldn't we give it a bath first?" Colleen asked.

Walter snorted.

"I guess we could. Think dish soap will be okay?" I asked.

"We'll use hand soap. Just a quick lather and he'll be as good as new." Colleen went back to run a sink full of warm water and I patted Walter's shoulder.

"Good detective work, Walter. I hope this is the right one," I held the squirming fur ball and followed Colleen back to our small kitchen. We have a single porcelain sink with a grooved drainboard. At an auction Walter had picked up a refrigerator that no one else had bid on because of its hideous avocado color. A white metal cart held the coffee-maker. The only new appliance, a small microwave, sat on a short, stout, three-drawer dresser that had once held my socks, underwear and tee-shirts from my infancy until I joined the Army. My mom had donated it to the office when she converted my bedroom to a sewing room. The linoleum was gray with black flecks, but Colleen had painted the walls a cheerful yellow the summer before. Colleen had laid a couple of dish towels out on the small kitchen table when I brought in the dog.

She tested the water and nodded. I tried to ease him in, but he wasn't having any of it.

"Hold him still," Colleen said.

"How? He's got more legs than I've got hands." Just then the suddenly muscular mutt leapt out of my grip and up on the drainboard where it stood shivering, eyes wide.

Colleen grabbed him. "I'll hold, you lather."

I pushed up my already wet sleeves and pumped a glob of liquid soap in my palm. I lathered his neck and back and tried as delicately as I could to daub his dirty face. Colleen lifted up his front legs and I rubbed his tummy and hind legs. We splashed some water on him to rinse, but the water was so filthy we drained the sink and held him under the faucet.

"He needs another go," Colleen said.

"Nah, he's clean enough. Besides I'm not sure this is the right poodle."

"He still needs to be clean." She put in the stopper and ran clean water in the sink. I got another gob of soap and started with his face this time. By now the dog was resigned to death by bathing and stood quietly quaking. We again soaped him thoroughly, and when we rinsed him, it was clear that his curls were gray, although a lighter shade than when we'd started. I was positive Mrs. Vogel had said white. Colleen dried him off with a dish towel and sat him down on the linoleum. He shook himself, dashed to the other side of the refrigerator, and squatted to make his puddle.

Colleen looked at me. "I thought male dogs lifted their legs."

"Not when they are pups. He's probably only six months old. We're looking for an eight-year-old-dog."

She grinned. "Dog piddle isn't in my job description."

By the time I had the floor cleaned up, Walter and the pup were engaged in a game of tug of war with an old tie.

"You ought to take the dog to Mrs. Vogel," I said. "She'll be really happy you found it."

"You did all the work. I just happened to see him. You should take him over."

"Walter, she really wanted you. Her old paper boy and all."

"I'd love to, but I've got an appointment in ten minutes. You go ahead. Tell her it's on the house. "

I didn't want to take this dog to Mrs. Vogel. I was sure it was the wrong one. Well, I wouldn't call and get her hopes up, I'd just show up. Then she'd know right away if it were Liebchen or not. I picked up the dog and headed out for my car. Colleen winked at me as I passed through the outer office. I think she meant to encourage me.

The scene in Mrs. Vogel's stuffy living room was even worse than I'd imagined. She burst into tears immediately when she saw the dog.

"That's not my Liebchen," she wailed.

I put the dog down to try to comfort her, and as I fumbled around looking for a tissue, the dog made a spot on her wall-to-wall carpet. Mrs. Vogel wailed louder. I stopped looking for tissues and started looking for paper towels. When I had blotted all I could, she instructed me to look under the bathroom sink for the spot remover. I fiddled with the carpet for fifteen minutes before Mrs. Vogel sniffed and said that Velma would do a better job tomorrow.

"Liebchen never, ever wets on the rug. He always goes outside."

I scooped up Not Liebchen and promised Mrs. Vogel that we would continue our search.

On the way back to the office the dog stood up on his hind legs in my lap and looked out the window. Small nose smears appeared on the glass.

We came back in and the dog greeted Walter with the joy of the safely returned arctic explorer.

"Are you going to take him to the Humane Society or do you want me to?" I asked Walter.

"He isn't Mrs. Vogel's dog?"

"No, Liebchen is an older dog, and white."

"Oh," Walter looked down at the pup, now with his teeth in Walter's trousers, pulling and growling in another game of tug-of-war. "Well," he said and paused. "I don't think we should take him to the Humane Society just yet. He probably lives around here somewhere." He reached down and patted the dog. "Colleen will just print up some more posters. And put another ad in the *Post*. His family will probably call in the next day or two. In the meantime, let's call him Mike."

I sighed, foreseeing many puddles between now and then. Colleen volunteered to go buy Puppy Chow.

"A small box," I stressed.

I put down some old newspapers in the bathroom and fished out the paper towels I'd used to sop up his earlier mistake. I put the paper towels on the paper and called Mike in. He ignored me, busy tailing the great detective into the kitchen. I followed them and scooped the dog up and took him back to the bathroom and showed him his smell on the papers. I hoped that would be the beginning of the end of the puddles, but I wasn't optimistic.

Chapter Nine

After lunch I turned my thoughts to the meeting I had scheduled with Maureen Hightower for later that night. I didn't want to admit how anxious I was—or face up to what it might mean if it had been Ann and not Maureen in the red sports sedan. Thinking of Ann led me to Arlene Dorman. Last night I had been cold and cranky and not thinking very clearly. I'd seen only poor Arlene. I'd felt some sympathy for her. But I hadn't taken advantage of her knowledge about Gateway. I picked up the phone and called her. I asked if I could meet her as soon as she got off work. I remembered a coffee shop in one of the strip malls where Greg and I had left posters. She remembered a small bar. I conceded but resolved to get there first, which meant I had to leave the paper work I'd just begun.

Mike was lying by Colleen's desk but hopped up to usher me to the door. "I'm surprised Walter didn't take him along to the warehouse."

"He said it was too cold to leave him in the car," Colleen said. She sounded cheerful about it, and the gray pup was scampering about. He had no complaints.

I got tangled in some early shift traffic and didn't make it to Revino's till three-fifteen. It was a small restaurant-bar a few blocks from Gateway and set in a small strip mall of flat-roofed, blond brick buildings. Dingy snow piles crowded the parking spaces. Revino's kept company with a barber, a pizza parlor, a wallpaper store, an insurance agency, and a pet shop.

Only the bar side of Revino's showed life signs. It was the kind of bar where strangers are the rule, not the exception. It was dark, hiding the chrome and vinyl that aimed for a cocktail lounge sophistication. At the end of the bar, the TV was on a sports channel, but the sound was low. The bartender looked too young for his trade. Two men, Walter's age, bulky in their suits, sat at the bar. My entrance stopped their conversation. They didn't bother hiding their stares. Toward the back I saw a man and a woman in a booth. Their heads were bent toward each other. I saw no sign of Arlene.

I picked the first booth in the line and slid in to face the door.

From the shadows a tall, slender woman in a short leather skirt and dark hose emerged. "What can I get you, hon?" I looked up. She was younger than I'd guessed. She looked and sounded unexcited about her work.

"I'd like a Coke. Biggest glass you've got." I wanted something hotter, but bar coffee drives you to drink. I didn't want to repeat last night's alcoholic camaraderie.

About five minutes later Arlene appeared, still wearing her uniform under a trench coat that looked pricey but worn. Like me, she elected to keep her coat on. Maybe Revino's was warmer with a crowd, but now it was too drafty for comfort. I pitied our server in her short skirt.

She came to collect Arlene's order. Arlene closed her eyes for a second's concentration. "A double martini. Up. Extra olives."

The server gave her a better smile than my Coke had elicited.

"Whew! What a day. Sorry I'm late," Arlene said. I thought she looked terrific for a woman who'd gone through a busy day with a hangover. "What's up?"

"I wanted to talk about the night of Aunt M's death. I know you've talked to Detective Schmidt and maybe others, but I'm just curious about a few details."

Arlene nodded and opened her coat and settled in. "Fire away."

"What's the evening routine at Gateway? Visiting hours? Bedtime?"

"Visiting hours are over at eight. There are exceptions, of course. On Tuesdays, Mrs. Peterson's daughter gets there at eight and stays till ten. The daughter's a nurse who works at Jewish Hospital. Her shift doesn't end till seven." She smiled at herself. "You don't want all that, do you? Usually we're shooing a few out till eight-thirty. The night Aunt M disappeared there weren't many visitors, and they were all gone by eight-thirty."

Our server was back with our drinks. She'd brought a saucer with four extra olives. She stood waiting. I had money ready. Revino's looked like a pay as you go place. I included a good tip and said, "We'll signal when we're ready." She smiled. I was shaping up into a better customer than she'd expected.

"What are you having?" Arlene asked.

"Rum and Coke."

"Takes all kinds." She took a big sip of her martini. "This would help you thaw out." She took a smaller sip, then dropped the extra olives into the glass. "We'll let those marinate. Now where were we?" She folded her small hands before her like a good pupil preparing to recite.

"So does it get quiet after the visitors leave?"

She grinned. "In my fantasies. After we shoo out visitors, we get real busy. And noisy."

I looked my question.

"Putting patients to bed. We say bedtime's at nine, but it's ten before everyone gets to their rooms, let alone bed. We're all scurrying around, rounding up the walkers, taking care of the ones in chairs, handing out meds."

"Is there a schedule? Would Rudy be responsible for certain duties or certain patients?"

She took a minute to sort her thoughts. "In theory, yes. But we have to be more flexible. Some of the patients pretty much stay put, but others, like Aunt M, are apt to wander off. Inside Gateway, I mean. Sometimes it takes a while to track them. And some don't like to go to bed." She used the fancy toothpick holding the original olive to fish out a new one.

I took a swallow of Coke and shivered.

"Too much rum?"

"No, no, it's fine. Just cold." I braved another sip. "Last Wednesday did anything unusual happen?"

"No, not a thing I can think of. I wasn't there, you know. Not my shift. But we've gone over it and over it with the staff that was. That tall blond cop asked us all a million questions about that night. Nothing special came up."

"Detective Lindstrom."

"That's it. Impressive. She went over everything twice. Rolfing looked like he wanted to puke. Pardon the language." She grinned and took another sip of her double martini.

I sipped more Coke. Of course Lindstrom had checked it out.

Arlene continued. "Like I told Lila, that was before Rudy was killed." She chewed another olive. "Then Detective Schmidt came. He wasn't so thorough. All he wanted to talk about was drugs."

"Rudy worked the night Aunt M was killed?"

"Yeah. And the card club—the four ladies who play in the lounge he used to take Aunt M to—say he walked Aunt M down that evening and used a wheelchair to take her back to her room."

Before I could stop her, Arlene snapped her fingers in the direction of our server. "This one's on me," she said. I could see her as an administrator then, not 'Poor Arlene'. She had a commanding presence in her repertoire.

When our server appeared, Arlene said, "She'll have another—"

"The same, the same," I overrode her and flashed them a smile. The server looked inquiringly at Arlene.

"I'm fine." Our server smiled half-heartedly and retreated.

"So when did things settle down that night?"

"Really quiet? Around ten-twenty, ten-thirty according to the head nurse that shift."

"When did they discover Aunt M was missing?"

"About eleven-o-five. The new shift does a bedcheck, makes sure they're all in bed, have had their meds."

"Richard Breeze said he and Rudy spent the night searching for Aunt M."

The server brought my Coke, and Arlene paid. She tipped handsomely and got a generous smile in return.

Then she looked at me. "So you've talked to Breezer."

"Yesterday. Were he and Rudy scheduled for a double shift that night?"

"No, they were asked to stay to help search. Did Breezer tell you about their little pills scam?"

I played dumb. "What?"

"Well, Rolfing caught him. Breezer. He finally admitted they'd been lifting a few on a fairly regular basis."

I couldn't tell what she thought or whose side she was on.

"Will Rolfing report this to Schmidt?"

"Oh, sure. He figures it explains everything." She ate another olive.

"Aunt M's room was at the opposite end of the hallway from that lounge, right?"

"Right."

"Is there an exit door there?"

"Oh sure. At the end of every patient wing."

"Can someone from outside come in those doors?"

"No, they're locked from the outside, panic hardware on the inside, strictly fire escapes."

"What's outside the one by Aunt M's room?"

"Nothing." Her face changed, grew more interested. "A little stretch of sidewalk to the staff parking lot and dumpsters. We bring supplies through the doors farther down."

"Is there a security gate back there? To the parking lot?"

She gave a scoffing laugh. "You're kidding. We had to hammer just to get Rolfing to put lights back there. But it's a pretty safe neighborhood." She stopped as though hitting brakes. "Not so safe for Aunt M and Rudy, I guess."

"Did any of the staff see someone else besides Rudy with Aunt M that night?"

She shook her head. "No. And no one else worked with her. We've asked everyone working that shift."

"Did anyone else besides the ladies in the lounge see Rudy

wheeling her to her room?"

"No, the patients in those rooms couldn't tell if they did notice." She whirled her forefinger toward her ear in the familiar sign for lunacy.

"What keeps a patient who can walk from using that exit?"

Arlene studied her hands for a moment. Then she took a deep breath and looked at me. "The fire alarm system includes a contact buzzer that sets off an alarm when the doors are opened."

"And it didn't go off that night?"

She leaned forward. "Breezer 'fessed up something else! He and Rudy and some other smokers have been fiddling with the contact alarm on that door for months. They untack it from the door and tape the contacts together so they can slip outside for a smoke."

We both considered this fact in appreciative silence.

"It was rigged that way the night Aunt M got out?"

"Well, Breezer claims they rigged and unrigged it each time because they didn't want to take the chance of a patient getting out and the alarm not going off." She speared another olive but didn't eat it. "Breezer swears that's true, but Rolfing doesn't believe him. I don't either." She popped the olive into her mouth and spoke around it. "Not human nature. I think they took their chances. At least during each shift." She chewed the olive. "Is your drink strong enough? I didn't see them put the rum in. Some bars cheat."

"It's fine. Just the way I like it." I twirled my glass. "If Breezer is telling the truth, the alarm should have gone off. If he's lying, maybe Aunt M did go wandering off by herself into the fog and no one's the wiser."

"Yeah. Rolfing's torn. He wants to believe that Aunt M left on her own, but he just can't swallow it. Besides, Breezer would lie to Rolfing just to yank his chain. They despise each other."

"If the alarm were set, Aunt M didn't leave on her own."

Arlene's face sobered. "That's right. And she was a pretty nice old lady. Despite, you know." She repeated the lunacy sign.

"Not so old."

"No, but that disease ages you fast."

"When did Breezer explain about the door?"

"Today. Rolfing finally took some advice and offered some money for information connected to Aunt M's death."

"Breezer took it?"

She chuckled. "Oh no. A pal told. A guy who was in on the door rigging but not the pills."

"Some pal."

She shrugged. "Do you know that Lindstrom? I think she's musical, maybe sings in our choir."

Thanks to Alix Dobkin I understood her point. "Hard to tell these days."

She laughed. "Ain't it?" The *ain't* was jocular. The martini was hitting home I figured.

"Did Breezer say how Rudy acted the night Aunt M disappeared?"

"Un-uh. You won't get that from Breezer. Unless it's true that Rudy acted the same as usual." She paused. "Maybe he did."

"Did they search together?"

"Part of the time."

"Could Breezer have let Aunt M out?"

"If Rolfing has to involve Gateway at all, he'd like to pin it on Breezer. But I don't think so. Breezer worked almost all the three to eleven shift with Judy Sarkin. She's an RN. She had her suspicions about Breezer and the pills, so she was keeping an eye on him." She took a tiny sip of her drink. "You know, I like Breezer. He talks that race crap all the time, but he's got his own code. He's not a tattle-tell."

I was impressed that Arlene admired Breezer's reticence. Administrators usually find tattle-tells useful. "What about Rudy?"

"Well, he was popular with patients and most of the staff."

"But what did you think of him?"

"It's what he thought of me. We butted heads once, and he called me a 'bulldyke.' In front of some aides, too. He figured I wouldn't confront him on it. He guessed wrong. He held a grudge."

I considered it. "How did Rolfing take Rudy's accusation?"

"Like the loudmouthed bullshit it was." She sounded angry. "I mean, what does he know about my sex life? Rudy was just mouthing. Rolfing didn't care. If it rocked a boat, caused bad PR…" She shrugged. "But otherwise it would be easier to replace Rudy than me."

"It was gutsy of you to call Rudy's bluff."

She looked sheepish, not accustomed to direct praise. "I figured Rolfing's a practical guy. Like I said, most medical people don't have time to sweat the small stuff. They've seen life and death."

"When did Rudy come back to work—I mean after he finished the double shift the night Aunt M got out?"

She thought. "I went over that with Lila. Just to get it straight." She tapped her toothpick against the saucer's edge. "He would have reported back that afternoon at three."

"Did he?"

"Oh yeah. And helped with some of the searching that evening."

I remembered then that I'd seen him in the cafeteria drinking some of the hot chocolate Nurse Rachel Batson had provided. Hot chocolate and coffee and sandwiches.

"How did he seem then?" I wanted her opinion.

"Well, you can guess how people talked after his death. Remembering his last hours. Remembering their last contacts with him." She speared her last olive. "He acted worried about Aunt M. Like he would. One of the reasons he was popular was that he seemed to like the old ladies."

"Did he search at all with any of the Yates family?"

That took her by surprise. Her brown eyes blinked. "I don't remember. Maybe. But I don't know."

"Think you could find out?"

"Breezer would know. But Breezer's gone."

"How about Rachel Batson?"

"Why Rachel?"

"Well, she was in charge of giving snacks to the searchers. She might have noticed who he came in with or went out with."

She nodded. "Good idea. I'll ask her." She glanced at her watch. "What about the night he was killed? Did he work then?"

"The three to eleven shift."

I thought. Aunt M had disappeared the previous Wednesday, exactly a week ago. Rudy had helped search till Thursday dawn and had resumed Thursday night. Aunt M's body had been found by the cemetery workers on Thursday, but the police hadn't made the necessary connections and notified the Yates family till Friday.

"When did Rudy learn about Aunt M's death?"

She gave me a look. "Well, the police came to Gateway about noon on Friday. I imagine he learned when he reported for his evening shift."

"Did anyone notice if he acted upset?"

"We were all upset. Of course, Rolfing made it worse by running around and telling everyone to stay calm and not to talk to the press." She grinned. "In the long run maybe he did us a favor. He was so annoying he distracted us."

"And Rudy checked out at his usual time?"

She nodded.

"There you are!" a cheery voice announced. I looked up. A plump woman with long lashes over warm brown eyes was beaming down at us.

"Meg, Lila. Lila, Meg," Arlene said. She looked up at the standing woman. "Sit down, hon."

"Let me get a drink. How about you two?"

"I'll have another, since you're driving." Arlene looked at me. "Want to join us for dinner?"

"I'm fine," I told Lila, clapping a palm over my Coke. Lila went to the bar. To Arlene I said, "Thanks. But I have to get back to the office."

"They do a good lasagna on the other side."

"I'm sure they do. But really I need to go."

Lila slid into the booth by Arlene, and they clasped hands and smiled at one another. Lila wasn't a classic beauty, but she had the sort of pleasant face you'd like to see every day. Her sandy hair had silver and gold strands and was clasped into a loose bun. Her lipstick had faded. She opened her long coat. She was wearing a soft, red wool dress. Across the table and over Arlene's gin I smelled a lush perfume.

"Has my sweetie been talking your ear off?"

I shook my head, still taking her in.

"She does rattle on." Lila patted the hand she held.

In spite of my mother's best efforts I've never learned manners. A big reason I became a PI is so that I could be nosy. "How long have you two been together?"

They beamed, glad to be asked. "Twelve years," Lila said.

"Is that all? Feels like a hundred," Arlene said and winked.

"Feels like twelve delicious years," Lila said, leaning into her partner. Betty has the same kind of magic. Says the corniest things and makes them sound just right.

Poor Arlene indeed!

Since I was to meet Maureen Hightower later, I went back to Miller Security after leaving Revino's to do some of the weeding out of files that Walter had assigned me. I was tired of the pyramid of manila folders on my desk and steeled myself to be ruthless.

The neighborhood with its small, mostly family-owned businesses tended to be deserted on evenings and weekends. Cars speeding by on Gravois and the noise from the Quick Pick across the street provided a reminder that I wasn't truly alone.

I had started with the intention of not stopping until I saw the R.J. carved into my desktop, but about six-thirty that intention was starting to weaken. I did have a large pile of folders that were destined for the dumpster, but I also had a moderate pile of 'maybes' that I needed to look at again before refiling or tossing. Indecision had crept into the process, slowing me down considerably. I was getting a kick out of reading some of the cases Walter had handled before I came to work with him. Most fascinating were his jotted notes about individuals he had come across during investigations. One file contained a marginal note with the terse comment 'delusions of adequacy.'

There was the case in which a wife had hired him to find her husband. When Walter was finally done with the investigation, he had found the husband and three more wives, none of them divorced. Walter continued to make notes in the file from time to time, commenting on the legal tangle that ensued, both criminal and civil. In the end, the man was sentenced to probation and Walter got paid only half his bill.

At six-forty-five there was a knock at the outer office door. I looked through the front blinds and saw Philip Seaton on the step. I opened the door. "Hello, Philip. What can I do for you?" I stepped back to invite him in and pointed him toward my office while I relocked the door. He spent the walk taking off his gloves, carefully folding them into the pocket of his leather jacket and unwinding a cashmere navy scarf. He settled into a chair without an invitation.

"I'm glad I caught you. I didn't know if you would be here this late."

"We're not open really. I stayed to get some work done." We both looked at the mound of folders on my desk with more scattered on the floor. Philip just managed not to purse his lips.

"I've come to talk to you about what you're doing to Ann and her family," he said as he crossed his legs. The crease in his pants was seven a.m. sharp.

"What I'm doing to them?"

"Yes, all this charging around questioning people is keeping Ann and her family stirred up. They could get on with healing if you stopped agitating them."

"Ann specifically hired me and is paying me to do the work I'm doing."

"No, she hired you to be a liaison with the police, not to look for reasons that Aunt M's friends and family might have killed her. We have nothing to do with her death, as you well know. The cemetery murderer will be caught by the police, and your efforts can only make this ordeal more painful for the family. The Yates did everything possible to keep Aunt M safe."

As I listened to Philip's speech, it occurred to me that this was more of a defense of Deborah Yates than of Ann. Perhaps my interview with Ann's mother had upset Dr. Yates more than I'd realized. "Have you talked to Ann about this?"

"Yes, if it's any of your business, I have."

"Well, if Ann has changed her mind about our agreement, I'll be glad to discuss terminating our contract. In the meantime, Mr. Seaton, I have some work to do." I stood to show him to the door, but he didn't budge.

"You know you're not doing the family any favors by alienating Dr. Rolfing and casting suspicion about. I assure you Ann will be ready to stop this by the end of your contract on Friday." Then he went. I didn't see him to the door, and he seemed to find it on his own.

He had just strengthened my intention of seeing this case to its conclusion. Even if it meant irritating Lindstrom again. I had to find out who killed Aunt M, Rudy Carr, and the others. Seaton had just landed himself on the list of suspects. Didn't he plan to marry one of the heirs?

I stood outside in the cold in front of Blueberry Hill, University City's trendy rock and roll bar/restaurant.

University City is in St. Louis County, just west of the city. U. City, as it's called, is an integrated middle-class neighborhood of primarily Jewish and African-American professionals. Its Loop area was rediscovered a few years ago and rapidly became a magnet for the young with a few dollars in their pockets. One of the wonderful features of the neighborhood is that, on Delmar, sections of the sidewalks are embedded with brass stars and plaques giving short biographies of St. Louis's own such as Maya Angelou, Chuck Berry, Kate Chopin, and Scott Joplin.

Blueberry Hill, right in the heart of the Loop, has the largest collection of jukeboxes currently in use in the St. Louis area and the walls are full of Elvis memorabilia and other rock and roll oddments.

I was outside because I wanted to see Maureen Hightower drive up. And at eight-o-five my heart soared as I saw a cherry red Mazda RX 7 pull neatly into a meter on Delmar. I hadn't realized what a load I'd been carrying, fearing Ann secretly had a connection to another of the victims in this case until I saw that car. I waved at Maureen. I noticed right away a resemblance to Ann; Maureen was also slender with auburn hair, and she wore a suede jacket and white silk scarf that looked expensive. But up close no one could mistake them. Maureen was a decade or so older. We ducked into the warmth of the bar. I introduced myself and explained briefly that I was helping with the investigation of the cemetery murders.

"Is Leanne all right?" she asked. "I've been worried sick about her with all this killing going on."

I said that I'd never actually met Leanne, but that someone had told me a relative of Leanne's took Lubbie to the Currency Exchange last month.

"Yes, that was me. I met Lubbie when she and Leanne were both at Malcolm Bliss, and I see her from time to time when I'm out looking for Leanne. That was why I was looking for Leanne that day, to take her to cash her check and make sure her rent got paid. I couldn't find Leanne, but Lubbie caught me and asked me to take her over to cash her check."

"Doesn't Leanne have a payee for her S.S.I. check?"

"No, the damn social security administration decided when she turned twenty-one she could handle her own money. She's been homeless at least once a year since that time. But do you think anyone in that damn bureaucracy would listen? They don't lose any sleep over Leanne or go searching through the shelters and soup kitchens just trying to make sure she's alive and taking her medicine." Tears welled up for a moment, but she fought them down. "Schizophrenia is hell. And no one, not the hospitals or social security or law enforcement will force her to live at home where she would be safe and comfortable and we'd have at least a fighting chance of keeping her on the medication that allows her to function normally."

I made sympathetic noises and hoped like hell Marty at Malcolm Bliss wouldn't call Maureen next week and ask her how Leanne was recovering from her stitching up. I felt like a virus for adding to this woman's misery. She asked about where the killer was picking up victims, and I shared with her what little information I had. I left her with my card and a promise to call her if I found Leanne in the course of my investigation.

Chapter Ten

The next morning, Thursday, I pulled into my spot on Miller Security's asphalt parking area behind our squat red brick building. Colleen's old red Escort was in its place; Walter's black Oldsmobile was not. Leanne and Maureen had been on my mind all night and I hadn't slept well. Nothing about this investigation was going right. My misery factor was pretty high and St. Louis's early December gloom wasn't helping. As I walked along the street up to Gravois, I did a double take. A girl, about nine, was leading a small white poodle along on a rope.

I smiled and waved at the girl. I crossed the street to her. She waited but looked wary. Her light brown bangs extended below her knit cap. She had on thick new jeans and a down jacket.

"Hi," I said. "I was just noticing your dog."

Her brown eyes looked up at me solemnly; she nodded.

"He looks like a great dog. Have you had him a long time?"

The girl shrugged, then shook her head. She looked toward home, torn between the two inviolable rules of not being rude to an adult and never talking to strangers. I kneeled down and attempted to pat the dog, which growled and bared yellow teeth.

"The reason I asked was because a friend of mine recently lost her dog and this looks like hers." The girl looked stricken. Why had I chosen a profession in which I routinely made people miserable?

"Could we talk to your mom together about it?"

She brightened, a reprieve. "My mom's at work."

"What about your babysitter?"

"My dad's at home."

We walked silently to a medium-sized frame house where the dog led the way up the walk. He had made himself very much at home. The little girl opened the door and called out to her father.

A short, muscular man in Levis and a red flannel shirt came out of the kitchen drying his hands.

"What is it, Jenny?" When he saw me, he stopped.

"Hi, my name is Meg Darcy. I work at Miller Security, up on Gravois."

He nodded his head and stuck out a hand. "Ted Zelker." His face was an older and coarser version of Jenny's, including the sprinkle of tan freckles across his nose and cheeks. His face wanted to ease into a smile, but I was a stranger who'd followed his little girl home.

"A couple of days ago a Mrs. Vogel came to us because she had lost her poodle. You may have seen the posters in the neighborhood."

His wariness melted to sheepishness. "Yeah, I saw one yesterday. I told Jenny we'd have to call that number this afternoon. She was just so attached to the thing." He trailed off.

"This dog seems to match Mrs. Vogel's description of her dog. I'm pretty sure this is Liebchen, but if it isn't, I'll bring him right back, okay?" I looked down at Jenny. Her lips were pressed together tightly. "Do you and your dad want to go to Mrs. Vogel's house with me?"

Jenny looked up at her dad.

"Let me get my shoes on. Then we'll go," he said. He disappeared down the hall and Jenny kneeled down to hug the little dog. The poodle licked her face and danced up on his hind legs.

It was a long, silent, three blocks to Mrs. Vogel's house.

Velma answered the door, and I saw the answer to my question in her face. She grimaced to see her old nemesis, but her voice was cheery as she called out.

"Gert, come see. It's your little dog come home."

Jenny sagged into her father, and he put a hand on her shoulder. As soon as the poodle saw Mrs. Vogel, he dashed forward, and to our amazement, jumped into her arms and licked her face. I'd never heard such a joyous whimper before.

Mrs. Vogel's tears this time were easier to take. She fussed over Liebchen a bit, but soon remembered her manners.

"Oh, I can't thank you enough," she said to Jenny. "I've been so lonely since my little Liebchen was lost."

Jenny sniffed and stiffened her spine.

"I took good care of him. He slept right on my bed at night."

"I can tell you are a very sweet little girl."

There were a couple more strained exchanges, then I figured Jenny had had enough. We said our goodbyes. On the way home Zelker told her she had done the right thing and had been very brave. Then he offered me his hand for a shake, but Jenny didn't want to meet my eyes. Only when he nudged her shoulder did she say a polite goodbye.

"Don't worry," her father said. "We'll go to the Humane Society this weekend. We've been thinking it's time for a pet. We'll get her a puppy."

The whole episode had taken under a half hour, and I was

uncertain how I felt about it. Mrs. Vogel deserved her dog back, and Jenny had been promised a replacement pooch. Yet, I was left with Jenny's face struggling to be grown-up about her disappointment. She was far less petulant than Mrs. Vogel had been when she'd come to report Liebchen's disappearance. I did some struggling of my own—against the stereotype of the old and selfish and self-absorbed. Was Mrs. Vogel's love for her little Liebchen any more ridiculous than my attachment to Harvey? Millions were spent every year to promote the idea that Jenny's fresh-faced childhood was somehow more important than Mrs. Vogel's wrinkled old age. Had there really been cultures where the old were truly venerated, or was that one of history's lies?

Mrs. Vogel, however lonely, was probably safe in her snug little house, even if she felt terrified by headlines about violent crime. Yet the line between her and the homeless women who'd been killed seemed thin to me. Society didn't make the welfare of old women a top priority. Nor that of small children, either, I argued with myself. But why should there be a forced choice?

Perhaps I should go to the pound and find a puppy for Jenny. No. Stupid meddling. I just wanted to see her face light up, at least lose its sober look of renunciation when Mrs. Vogel claimed Liebchen. Well, at least Liebchen looked happy. He'd been in luck to have Jenny pick him up.

Now, all I had to do was find Leanne for Maureen Hightower and Aunt M's murderer.

I dealt with my mixed feelings by going for lunch. I drove through a Steak n' Shake and grabbed two single burgers with mustard, pickle, and lettuce and headed back to the office. I'd eat at my desk while I finished the Vogel file with a summary of my morning's activities. When I walked in, Colleen told me Ann was in my office. I gave her a quizzical look and she shrugged: Don't ask me, I just work here. She buried her nose in her current filing project.

I left my sack of hamburgers on the nearest file cabinet. Inside my office Ann Yates was sitting in my client's chair—a secondhand scarred oak. Ann twisted around as I came in, and the look on her face stopped the usual greetings.

"What's happened?" I asked urgently.

She was wearing her suede jacket and white silk scarf and clutched thin leather gloves in one hand. Her hazel eyes showing consternation, she said, "Meg, I've just come back from Aunt M's attorney."

I nodded encouragingly and perched on the edge of the desk.

"We met in his office for a preliminary reading of the will so that we'd know what to expect before it was probated." She spoke slowly enough, but there was a vibrato of tension under the surface. "My parents were there, and Greg and Arlene."

I made a guess. "Did something surprise you?"

She gave a tight smile. "You could say that. Bill Curtis was there. He was Linda's nephew. You remember Linda—Aunt M's lover?"

She meant as one of the cast, not personally. I nodded.

"Well, after the smaller bequests are subtracted, Bill gets one third of Aunt M's estate."

I suppressed a grin. Ann's tone was one of total indignation. There was an assumption that this was such an outrage that anyone else, certainly including me, would be indignant,too.

Still, she was a client and a friend. "And?"

"And nothing. That's enough. It's totally out of left field, totally unexpected. We were all shocked." I could tell 'shocked' wasn't the word she really wanted, but maybe my calm was tamping her down a bit.

"Was Linda's nephew shocked as well?"

That stumped her for more than a half-minute. Strangely enough she hadn't considered it, though it seemed to me an obvious thing for her to notice. "I guess not. Evidently he had had fairly frequent contact with Aunt M."

"You hadn't ever met Bill Curtis before?" I wondered if she'd pick up my incredulity.

"Only twice. He sometimes fed Aunt M's cat when she was traveling. He didn't even go to Aunt M's memorial service."

"Who gets the other two-thirds—after deductions?"

"Greg and I do. Just as we expected—" she paused and amended "—had been led to expect by Aunt M and Linda." She leaned forward a bit. "But the main issue is Bill Curtis. How did he get into Aunt M's will?" She shook her head in exaggerated bewilderment. "Where did that come from?"

We both knew I couldn't answer. I shifted gears. "If I may ask, exactly how much does that leave you and Greg to play with?"

Always before she'd been carefully vague about the exact number of zeros. I didn't know if she'd wanted to avoid underlining the gap between our incomes and lifestyles or if she just had a rich person's conservatism about money matters. Certainly I'd been reared myself not to ask about income, age, or weight. But as a PI, I had learned to overcome my upbringing.

She paused, then gave a small sigh, and said, "We'll each get about two million." She was a little less indignant.

Well, it was all in the point of view, like lottery winners who find out someone else will share in the prize. She and Greg had gone from inheriting three million apiece, to two mil. I guess it would be disappointing. Still, it was hard to sympathize with someone who'd just become two million richer.

She was smart enough to know that. "We're wondering if this is legitimate."

"Isn't the lawyer the one to tell you that? And the probate court?"

She shrugged that off. "Up to a point. But that's after the fact. Who is this guy? Why does he have a right to one-third of her estate? Did he unduly influence Aunt M?"

I admitted those were interesting questions, but I had another thought. "Maybe she just didn't want to disappoint you and Greg ahead of time. I hate to put it this way, but maybe she thought you'd be sweeter to her if you didn't know she planned to leave some money to someone else."

She shrugged again. "Maybe. But that still leaves unanswered my questions about Bill Curtis and how he wormed his way into her will."

A silence fell. She examined her gloves again, then looked up at me with all her charm and elegance winning me over. She added candor. "You think we're greedy, don't you?"

I tried maintaining direct eye contact, then sidled off with a little laugh. Caught! "Let's say that my sense of the injustice of it is a little less strong."

She gave her own little laugh. "If you think I'm upset, you should have seen Greg. He was so furious he didn't even explode."

I understood that. "Just turned icy?"

She cocked her head engagingly. "He flared up at first, then sort of pushed it down. He sat there glowering and looking as though he were chewing burnt muffins. He didn't even pretend to be polite to Mr. Curtis. You don't know Greg well enough to see how mad that means he was."

Not pretending to be polite to someone whose guts you hate has something to recommend it, but I didn't offer that thought to Ann.

"I'm sorry this has further complicated Aunt M's death for you," I said in my best therapist's voice. My mom does this stuff really well, but it's not a gene I inherited.

"You're busy, and you think I'm wasting your time." She held up a hand to forestall any attempt on my part at polite pretending. "I do have a reason to come here with this complaint. I want you to investigate Bill Curtis, find out who he really is, what he does, and, if possible, how he came to get so close to Aunt M." She slapped her gloves lightly against my desk.

I sensed she wasn't finished. She wasn't. She drew a deep breath and continued, "And to see if it's at all conceivable that he killed her."

I let that lie there a moment. "Isn't that far fetched?"

Her smile held its touch of rue. "It's a bad world, isn't it? People are killed for ten dollars—or two. I don't know this man or what two million would mean to him."

She was convincing in ways she didn't intend. If losing an extra million meant that much to her and Greg, folks who were already well-cushioned, one might suppose it would mean more to Bill Curtis. Though maybe not. If he didn't have wealth of his own, he might not have lived thinking about it so much. Not knowing him, I couldn't speculate.

About him. But I did speculate about Ann and Greg. Ann wasn't a stranger to me, but I didn't know her in the same way I knew friends of longer standing. I was sure Patrick wouldn't kill someone for a million, though he might joke about it. Did I know that about Ann? I knew even less about Greg.

I tried not to let that show. I walked around my desk and sat down. I leaned back in my chair, put my feet on a half-opened drawer, and tried to project my relaxed, folksy side. "I'm worried about taking more of your money in return for very little help, Ann. Isn't there something about pouring good money after bad?"

"You can't argue that this isn't a job that Miller Security wouldn't take normally. You do deep background checks."

She had me there. "All right. But let's set some limits." I went on to propose some on time and expenses. She agreed readily enough, no doubt remembering how easy it had been to keep stringing me along on the original investigation.

I walked her through a few background questions and found out that Aunt M had made her will before entering the nursing home and hence before Linda had died.

"Perhaps Aunt M put Bill Curtis in her will to please Linda?"

Ann shrugged, clearly not mollified. "Perhaps."

I did have one other question that to me seemed obvious.

"How did Arlene take this development?"

Ann looked genuinely baffled. "Arlene? She didn't expect anything more." Case dismissed.

Again I kept my thoughts to myself. It's hard to know what people expect as their due. Who'd have dreamed that pretty, poised, financially secure Ann Yates would have counted on an extra million? The giddy relief I'd felt by learning that Ann hadn't taken Lubbie to the Currency Exchange was melting faster than light snow.

I spent Thursday afternoon struggling to get comfortable on a bench in the hallway of the criminal court building waiting to give testimony on a case Miller Security had carried far too long. The Sheldon case had dragged out since early May despite the fact that Sheldon's brother-in-law couldn't afford a decent attorney. I had to bring the file with me to brush up on dates and times. It had been Walter's case originally, but I had been on stake-out the night the suspect had carried twenty-three boxes out the back door of Sheldon's Car Stereo Store just before midnight. So I was stuck testifying.

As I waited in the hallway to testify, the most obvious thing to me was that Lindstrom wasn't in sight. I missed not having her waltz in with her notepad, eyeing me with a mixture of scorn and latent desire. It made me realize what an added dimension she gave to my work. When at last, after hours day-dreaming of Sarah Lindstrom and how I could break the ice long enough to seduce her, it was my turn to sing. Then the defense attorney just looked over his wire rims and declined to cross-exam. I sighed with gratitude and shot the suspect a withering look when he panted at me. Another day, another dollar. But I still didn't know how I'd seduce Lindstrom.

With my first cup of coffee Friday morning, I called Rudy's girlfriend Nikki Dial again. I was able to reach her at her neighbor's phone and she agreed that I could drop by right away.

The metal steps leading up to her apartment were wet, but clear of snow and ice. This time she invited me into the living room and I sat on the short couch. She went to get us coffee. The first thing I noticed was the complete lack of printed matter—no books, magazines, not even a newspaper cluttered the room. Her living room was about the size of my own, but longer and narrower. The furniture, like mine, was largely secondhand, although the big television looked new. On the table at my elbow was a picture of Nikki holding a blond baby. Her hair had been longer then, and her face not so care worn. She smiled when she saw me looking at it as she returned with our coffee.

"That's Jason. He's my nephew." She held her hand up to her waist. "He's this tall now."

"He's certainly a handsome boy."

"Yes. He's my sister's boy. He's six next month. I keep him sometimes when she works."

I put the picture frame down and sipped my coffee. It was good and hot.

"Have you found out anything about Rudy's death?" she asked.

"Nothing concrete yet, but I do have a couple more questions for you." She nodded as I continued, "Rudy worked a double the night Mary Margaret Brooks disappeared, right?"

"Yes. He called me at eleven-thirty and told me that one of the patients had wandered off and he had to work overtime to look for her. He told me to go ahead and go to bed. I was working days, so I had to get up in the morning."

"And he went back to work for his regular shift on Friday afternoon?"

"That's right."

"Can you tell me any more about the call he got on Friday?"

She scrunched up her eyebrows. "Donny pounded on the pipes. That's how he lets us know we've got a call. Rudy was just getting out of the shower, so I was going to go down and get it. But he said he would and pulled on his jeans."

"What did he say about the call when he came back up?"

"Nothing really, just that he'd be late from work. I told him not to work another double. Since I got another job, he shouldn't have to work doubles so much. He said he wouldn't." A lost look came over her face, but she didn't cry.

"When he got home Friday morning what was he like?"

"Tired, a little grouchy. I figured it was because he'd worked those sixteen hours, and eight more to go with hardly a break."

"What did he say about Aunt M's disappearance?"

"Just that they hadn't found her and that the family was still looking."

"Have the police released Rudy's body, yet?"

"No. They said maybe next week. His mom wants to have an open casket. I can't believe it."

I bit my lip and hoped the funeral director would be able to convince Rudy's mother otherwise. Rudy had been in the Mississippi from when he was killed—my guess was late Friday night or very early Saturday—until Monday afternoon. He couldn't be a pretty sight.

"Tell me about Richard Breeze. He was a friend of Rudy's?"

"Yeah. They met at Gateway. Breezer's an okay guy."

"He was involved in taking drugs from the nursing home, too."

"I don't know. They didn't really talk about that. Rudy knew I didn't approve, so they didn't talk about it in front of me."

"Has Breezer contacted you since Rudy's death?"

She looked away, then down at her coffee cup. "Why do you ask?"

I tried to sound reassuring. "Because if Rudy's murder was connected to Gateway in any way—about the drugs or about Mary

Margaret's disappearance, Breezer probably knows something that will help."

"You know they found out about Rudy and Breezer?"

"Yes."

"Breezer had to leave St. Louis." She shrugged. A fact of life.

"Where to?"

"I don't know. I didn't ask. He wouldn't have told me. He just wanted me to know why he wouldn't be at Rudy's funeral. He didn't want me to think he didn't care." A tear escaped, but she wiped it away and looked up at me. "I don't know where he is, but if he had known anything about Rudy's death, he would have told me. He was angry because there was such a big fuss made about that old lady's death and nobody gives a shit about Rudy. Except you. I told him that you were working on it."

"Did he say he'd be in touch again?"

"Not really. He just told me to take care of myself. And that he'd drink a beer for Rudy on opening day." She looked away again. "They liked to watch the Cards game on TV." She looked back at me. "Rudy was a good man. He wasn't perfect, but he was kind, and he never hurt anyone."

"Do you know if Breezer has family or other friends in St. Louis?"

"I don't know about family. He broke up with his wife about a year ago."

"What's her name?"

"Sheila. Sheila Breeze. I never saw her after she left Breezer."

I scribbled the name in my notebook. "Any idea where she lives or works?"

Nikki shook her head negatively. I thanked her for the coffee and told her I'd keep trying to figure out who killed Rudy. She walked me to the door and actually hugged me good-bye. I didn't hurry her. She was hurt and lonely. And I couldn't go to some humane society and simply replace Rudy for her.

Chapter Eleven

After I left Nikki, I climbed into the cold Plymouth and headed downtown. It was still cold and cloudy, a bleak, depressing day for bleak, depressing errands. I turned up my coat collar and decided I'd ask Betty for a scarf this Christmas.

Like most cities, St. Louis has seen a tug of war over its downtown area. Suburbs and their elaborate malls have sucked some of the life from once thriving downtown businesses—small stores to shop in, restaurants to dine in were dwindling. Nowadays the middle-classes, white and black, make forays into the city like surgical strikes during the Gulf War, landing in predetermined safety zones—the riverside Laclede area for tourists, St. Louis Centre for shoppers, the looming corporate fortresses, and, of course, Busch Stadium. Around the edges, still nibbling like rats, are the dirt and fear and desperation that drive away the timid and test the mettle of survivors.

I found Bill Curtis's pawnshop on an otherwise abandoned block that once had featured a dry cleaner's, a shoe repair shop, a Chinese takeout. Even pawnshops can't exist on thin air, and I wondered how Curtis was surviving, and if he would have to move soon to a neighborhood which might attract more customers. Perhaps if Mary Margaret Brooks's will held up through probate, he wouldn't have to. He could retire with two million bucks.

I hadn't got much about Bill Curtis from Ann except this address. The shop entrance was small, a door on one side, a small display window like a jeweler's on the other. Both hid behind stout bars. In the display window were a handful of watches, two camcorders, an electric guitar.

When I opened the shop door, a bell tinkled. The traditional three balls to indicate a pawn shop had been painted in red on the door. Inside the shop Curtis had the symbol displayed in brass hanging from the wall over the cash register. Probably it had been displayed outside once, but no longer, not in this neighborhood.

I took a minute to let my eyes adjust to the fainter light inside the store. Like many shops it was both longer and wider than you'd guess from outside, but it still seemed narrow because of the large glass display cases on each side and an abundance of junk—globes, a harp, and other free-standing merchandise in the middle.

A young white woman came forward from behind the counter on my right. She was small and plain with her mouse-colored hair parted in the middle and drawn back tightly from her face and behind her small, neat ears, each of which bore a tiny gold hoop. Her hair flowed smoothly and cleanly down her neck and back. She looked like a prim hippie. She wore no makeup and had on a drab green shirtwaist dress in a soft material; over that she wore a thick wool cardigan in dingy gray. No wonder. The shop was cold.

"May I help you?" The voice of a prim librarian.

"Yes. I'd like to speak with Mr. Curtis, if he's here."

She looked at me a long moment as though my statement were a trick question. I stood and looked back in my most forthright manner. I had the fantasy that she wasn't a hippie at all, but a member of a fundamentalist sect who was about to reprimand me for wearing pants.

"Come this way," she said before I could develop that thought or my defense.

She led me toward the back of the store and through a green velvet curtain that looked exactly like one I'd seen in a B movie, and I followed her through a small, shelved storeroom stuffed with dusty junk—once someone's prized possessions I supposed. Then we were in a wider, lighter room. The right half of the room was lit by overhead fluorescents. That side held gun cabinets with rifles and shotguns crammed into them.

The other side of the room looked like a combination of workroom and study. A collection of books in built-in-shelving looked eclectic just from the variety of sizes and covers—some new with bright paper jackets and some old, faded cloth bindings. There was a large and comfortable-looking easy chair in maroon velvet that looked used but not shabby. By its side was a table holding a tea tray with a proper porcelain pot, thin cups, sugar, and cream. Close to me a long table with folding legs, the sort found in school cafeterias, was spread with model cars and the small tools necessary for repairing and painting them. Despite the amount of paraphernalia, the table looked neat rather than cluttered. A work space, not a dust catcher. Two free-standing lamps provided the softer light on this side of the room, though a good desk lamp was clamped onto the work table.

Sitting at the table was my man, or so I presumed from the way in which the young woman drew to a halt. She immediately confirmed this hunch by saying, "Bill, here's someone to see you."

Her tone sounded hostile, just an edge to it. That she hadn't called him out to see me or asked me some basic questions before inviting me into this inner sanctum seemed hostile, too.

But he looked up cheerfully enough, and a tentative smile spread his thin lips into a welcome look. He was not exactly what I'd expected, even though I had tried to keep an open mind. He was small—perhaps a couple of inches shorter than I with just the tee-niest pot belly pushing against the handsome vest he wore over a clean, white shirt. The vest was a lovely subdued burnt orange with brown designs. It was muted yet rich, inviting touch. He wore a dark brown tie with the merest suggestion of small gold stripes running across it.

His head was slightly larger than his small body warranted. His hair was auburn with reddish gold highlights; it curled and waved outrageously and was wispy at the edges and thinning at the top. He had luxuriant, old-fashioned sideburns, white at the bottom. He was otherwise clean shaven with pink cheeks, a small-ish nose, that wide, thin mouth, and a good cleft in his manly chin. He reminded me of somebody. I realized then that I'd seen him at the memorial service. Maybe Ann hadn't recognized him or maybe even seen him because she was sitting in front and had been so absorbed in grief. He had sat among all the elderly women mourn-ers in front of Lindstrom, Neely and me. He must have slipped out of the service among the women before the family noticed. And I thought I hadn't seen anything worth note at the memorial! I had seen him as part of that group.

He rose off the stool he sat on behind the work table and came round to my side. He cocked his head to one side and looked up, a gesture that was once perhaps engaging and now looked merely practiced.

"How can I help you?" As he spoke, the young woman who had ushered me into the room returned to the front of the store—or so I presumed.

I pulled my card out of my pocket—the one that correctly iden-tifies me as an agent of Miller Security.

I gave him a second to look at it. He took the time, then looked up again. This time he lifted his considerable eyebrows. "Are you selling security equipment?"

"We do. But that's not why I'm here. I'm here because Ann Yates has hired me to investigate the murder of her aunt."

"Mary Margaret Brooks," he said enthusiastically, the boy who got the right answer. "There can't be that many murdered aunts about," he added.

"That's right," I said.

"Well, then, why not have a seat right over here?" and he touched my elbow lightly and steered me toward the easy chair.

I sank into it and was pleased to find that its looks did not deceive. He perched on his work stool, pulling his feet up to the bottom rung and hunching forward in a friendly fashion.

"So, you're looking into the circumstances surrounding our Miss Brooks's death. A terrible business this—the murdering of harmless old ladies—though maybe not so terrible in her case."

He spoke rather rapidly and with some slight lisping impediment, barely noticeable and not unpleasant.

I played along. "Why not in her case?"

"She was once a bright and articulate woman. To see her shrink to a witless, petulant child was heart-breaking for everyone who'd known her, don't you think?" He didn't use grandiose gestures, but he threw some body language into every speech.

I wasn't sure if he expected an answer, but I said, "I'm sure it was. Do you think someone loved her enough to attempt to ease her out of it?"

"A mercy killing?" He lifted his curling eyebrows theatrically.

"Perhaps seen as such."

"By family?"

"By anyone who cared for her," I said.

"A doctor? A nurse? An aide?" He was enjoying himself. Anything that gave him lines to speak.

"Possibly. What do you think?"

"Oh, possibly, yes, possibly." He waved toward the bookcase. "And there are philosophers who wouldn't condemn such a deed." He made a dramatic halting gesture. "But wait—would you like some tea before we continue this discussion?"

"No thanks, I've just had coffee," I lied to forestall his insistence. He shrugged elaborately to indicate his acceptance of this feeble excuse, and I pressed on. "So, if someone who knew her killed her, your premise is that it was done to relieve her suffering?"

"Or to relieve their suffering at her suffering. And I say *their* advisedly. It might be a cabal who joined together to help her." He dramatically emphasized 'kay-BALL.'

I was beginning to think I had wandered into a movie. Before I could compose my next question, he leapt ahead. "But that isn't my premise at all. It's just one of many possibilities. Possibilities you—and the police—have the advantage of actually investigating, while I can only speculate."

"What other possibilities have you speculated about?" I wasn't sure if it were a question or a cue.

He cocked his head from the other angle this time. "Clearly"— and he put a dash of remonstrance into the word—"not everyone is equally at a loss because of Mary Margaret's death."

"Meaning?"

"Deborah Yates was perhaps the most genuinely and purely grieved. She lost a beloved sister, though I think even she might have felt some relief. No matter what one does with an Alzheimer's patient, one always feels one isn't doing enough. So perhaps a soupçon of grief and a ladle of relief." Here was a man who enjoyed drama, who enjoyed gossip, who enjoyed his own titillating wickedness.

He held up a forefinger. "And wait!" I waited. "Not to mention that your client and Greg Brooks and Bill Curtis find ourselves enriched by Mary Margaret's passing." His eyes—were they blue or green or gray?—showed his amusement. "Proportionately I am more enriched than the other two. Do you suppose that makes me a greater suspect?" The last question was full of mock innocence.

"Not necessarily. I've heard the rich enjoy getting richer." I was a little irritated to be defending him.

"Ahhh. You assume the other two are rich."

"Don't you?"

"Richer than I, yes. For a certainty." He held up that warning finger again. "But suppose my assumption is wrong? Suppose one isn't so rich? Or both? I don't know their bank accounts. Do you?"

He knew the answer to that question I reckoned. But I tried to look as if he didn't. Instead I looked around the little room, just a brief, surveying glance. "Perhaps your holdings extend beyond this shop."

"Perhaps," he said delightedly, as though he had successfully induced me to join a game. "Or I have the Hope Diamond on pawn. Who knows? Appearances deceive."

"Things are not what they seem," I said, thinking that he was scattering disinformation through the reliable technique of snowing meaningless chatter. He was colorful if you hadn't caught his act before.

I tried another question since he was obviously intent on seeming to be open. "How did you come to be a friend of Mary Margaret's?"

"Attached enough to be a recipient of two million, you mean?" He smiled as though he'd caught me out. I nodded, and he continued, "She and my aunt Linda were lesbian lovers." He watched me carefully. "Perhaps you understand." He let that dangle before me.

I didn't take the bait. It didn't matter to me if he identified me as lesbian.

I shrugged to signify my letting his remark pass. He continued, "When they lived together, they traveled a great deal. Like many lesbians, they loved animals and had a houseful of pets. I often looked after their animals while they were gone."

He paused and looked at me with a bright smile. "I also traveled with them a few places—to Florida, to California—places they could take their animals. I'd stay at the motel or whatever while they did day trips."

"To look after the pets," I said.

"Yes, though I was useful in several ways. Mary Margaret and I enjoyed discussing books and plays. We came to play chess together. She was better than most women." He sent a wider smile. "Oh, I know that's not politically correct, but it's true." He shrugged a 'lovable old me' shrug.

"You think that's why she left you the money?"

"Because I looked after her pets and played chess with her?"

I risked it. "And danced attendance on her?"

He laughed. "Oh, but I didn't. I turned them down many a time, many a time. I wasn't a very affectionate nephew really. I think Mary Margaret was fonder of me than Linda was."

"Do you have a theory as to why she left you the money?"

"Several. But if I tell you, won't that reduce the number of hours you can bill Ann for?"

I laughed, then crossed one leg over the other and settled back, saying, "But you don't know me. I may be richer than I seem. Humor me and give me your best guesses."

He laughed again, not so genuinely. "At least you pay attention. That one doesn't anymore." And he nodded toward the front. "And that was the key, maybe. I didn't dance attendance, but I did pay attention while Mary Margaret was still young enough and alert enough to notice. I never asked for favors. We both liked rather macabre stories. We liked cutthroat chess. I didn't care what they did in bed—not much by the time I traveled with them, I suspect."

"What happened to the animals?"

He cocked his head again and beamed at me from his stool. "An astute question. You know, I don't think Ann or Deborah or Greg asked. I took the little dog who had to be put down soon after Linda's death, and I have the two cats upstairs."

"You live over the shop?"

He nodded, not volunteering more for once.

"Will you continue to live here?"

"For a few months. Then it's back to Florida I suspect. I don't like St. Louis anymore."

"Who do you think killed her?"

"A serial killer who's been stalking homeless women, killing them, and transporting their bodies to cemeteries." He said it mockingly.

"You really believe that?" I leaned forward a bit, looking into his shining eyes.

"It's a possibility." Still beaming, still mocking.

"Did you know Rudy Carr?"

"Who?" The single word shot out before he could wrap a pose around it.

"A young man who worked at Gateway Rest Home. He was one of the attendants who looked after Mary Margaret."

"The blond with acne?"

"Yes. He was murdered."

For the first time there was a long pause as though his quick mind were racing up several paths, testing each for the hidden ambushes. "I think I know the lad you mean."

"Do you think his murder might be linked to Aunt M's?"

"Why ask me? Surely you have the advantage here?" Evidently he'd found the safe path, the one that doubled back to me. I heard the bell in front tinkle.

"I just want your opinion."

"I think he was a doper."

"And?"

"Oh, that suggests many things, doesn't it?" He was relaxed again.

The young woman came through the storeroom. "There's a customer here you need to see," she said. Her tone was superficially matter-of-fact, but underneath she still seemed angry with him.

He hopped from the stool. "So sorry to break off this lovely chat, such a pleasure to meet you, send my greetings to Ann." He was talking and moving as the woman followed after him.

I could scarcely believe they'd just left me there to find my way out. I hopped up myself and made a quick survey of the room trying to notice anything I'd missed before. There was a desk tucked into a far corner covered with the usual desk debris: bills, invoices, his checkbook. I glanced through the checkbook. He hadn't deposited his two million yet. On the top inside cover under the plastic he'd written his social security number and some phone numbers on a card. I jotted them down. The center drawer of the desk was a jumble of pens and pencils, rubber bands and paper clips. But no dramatic documents. The big double-drawer on the right was locked.

Quickly I moved into the storeroom. Another look there wasn't enlightening. I moved through the velvet curtains. Bill Curtis and his assistant were behind the glass counter. On the other side was a middle-aged Asian man in a brown bomber jacket and brown slacks. A gleaming pistol lay between them. I heard the customer talking about self-defense, and Curtis fluently responding.

As I opened the door, I glanced back. The woman was looking at me stonily, her pursed lips the only emotional indicator. Somehow I suspected she didn't like me.

Outside the shadows were gathering, and the temperature had dropped ten degrees. I pulled on gloves and made a dash for the Plymouth. I was sure Ann Yates hadn't talked to Bill Curtis at the will reading. If she had, she'd have been more infuriated than she already was.

Chapter Twelve

Back at the office I walked into the most amazing scene I'd ever witnessed on the Miller Security premises. Colleen was leaning against the front of her desk, and Walter was standing by the outside door. Colleen shot me a helpless look as soon as I crossed the threshold.

"Oh lord, Walter, what have you done?" I blurted.

In the center of the reception area stood a sheepish Mike. His curly head was drooping, and he was shifting his tiny feet. His eyes had that woebegone look of a dog who's being scolded for pooping on the carpet. He was wearing a bright red and black plaid poodle coat.

I looked at the dog and I looked at Colleen. She turned her head, compressing her lips to stifle sound.

"It's a good color, don't you think?" Walter asked. His beefy face was nearly as red as the coat. I walked over to him but couldn't smell a whiff of Wild Turkey. He rolled Mike's blue ball toward the dog.

Walter seemed not to have been drinking, but I thought I needed a snort. Instead I said, "It all depends on how he accessorizes."

Walter wasn't listening. He was lowering his bulk to the floor. "Come here, Mikie. Come to Daddy."

Usually the pup raced to Walter, obeying his least command. This time the dog collapsed on the floor and belly-crawled over. "That's right," Walter said. With effort he bent over from his squat to scoop the pup up for a kiss.

Colleen met my eyes briefly, then turned away.

"I figured if I can keep him warm, I can take him with me when I make some of my calls. That way Colleen won't be bothered entertaining him." Walter was now sitting on the floor, and Mike was standing in his lap, licking Walter's chin.

"Good plan. Have you got any response to the newspaper ads?"

Colleen rolled her eyes.

Walter cleared his throat, but he still sounded gruff. "I told Colleen to cancel 'em. Mike's got a good home now."

"Un-huh. And a great wardrobe, too." I gave Walter a pat on

the head as I walked by. "Colleen, will you give me a hand?"

When we reached my office, I closed the door, and she collapsed against it. We both needed tissues to wipe the tears.

"If we'd bought that coat, we'd be dead meat," I said.

"Dog food," she said, and we were off again.

But she was sniffing and patting her eyes dry when she added, "Under all that bluster, he's a sweetie."

I thought she meant Walter.

That pretty much ended the working day. Colleen pulled on her coat, and Walter carried Mike back to say good-night. The pup was getting used to his new outfit and looking less like a canine candidate for death by shame. Of course, Walter was taking Mike home with him every night, and I suspected he'd convinced a barkeep or two that the little poodle was some special kind of support dog.

I dialed the Clark Street police station number and asked to be put through to Lindstrom. I wanted to find out her take on Rudy Carr's murder.

"Lindstrom here."

"Got anything on the cemetery murders, yet?" My tone was derisive.

"Yes, I think I have."

This set me back quite a bit. "Suppose I buy you dinner and you tell me all about it?"

"I'm nowhere near celebrating yet. I just questioned the suspect for the first time this morning. But I think he's it."

"Someone I know?"

"I think not. Listen, I need to get back to work. What do you need?"

"To talk to you about the case. Even if you can't celebrate, you need to eat. When do you get off?" I could hear the hesitation in her silence. When would she get over thinking I was such a threat to her?

"I've got to go look at something in your neighborhood. I'll stop by your apartment on my way home. We can talk a few minutes."

I beat it home in record time and had both living room and kitchen straightened up in less than thirty minutes. Lindstrom hadn't told me what she had to look at, so I didn't know how soon she'd arrive. After I stashed the dirty dishes in the oven, I went to my bedroom and opened my closet door. Nothing, absolutely nothing to wear. There was a knock at the door. I wished I'd taken a moment to brush my teeth. I opened the door with my best smile.

"Hi, sweetie. What's up?" he asked.

"Oh, Patrick. You scared me. Come help me pick out something to wear."

"What's the occasion, Meg?"

"Lindstrom's on her way over; I need to look sexy, but totally non-threatening."

"That's a tall order, and I suppose we don't have time to shop." I pulled him into my bedroom.

"Can I assume the Ice Queen is warming up?" he asked.

"Nope, not a bit."

Patrick waded into my closet and emerged a few seconds later with my green corduroy pants and a green and tan plaid shirt.

"Do you have a turtleneck? Off white or green?"

"Off-white." I turned to my dresser drawer and found it on the first grab.

"This should do it. She's tailored, right?" he said.

"Very."

"Well, you don't have any of the elements for a decent fifty's femme, so we'll have to make do with this. You wouldn't act the part anyway. So we might as well have truth in packaging." I started untying my tennis shoes, and Patrick turned to get my boots from the floor of my closet.

I had just finished brushing my teeth when we heard the knock on the door. Before I could stop him, Patrick answered it. I followed him to the door, hoping to get rid of him quickly and quietly. A lost hope with Patrick. "Hello, Detective Lindstrom. How are you this evening?"

I cut in, "This is my friend, Patrick Healy."

Patrick obligingly stuck out his hand for his manly handshake. Lindstrom didn't have much choice. She shook his hand. Patrick turned and smiled at me. "I'll be right back."

He disappeared out the door, leaving it open, and I couldn't guess what he was planning. I led Lindstrom into the living room and offered beer, soda, or coffee. She chose soda. I walked back out the door. I met Patrick in the outer hallway with a tray full of food. "Here's dinner. This is Hungarian Stew. Don't let it boil, it has sour cream. The sauce goes over the noodles, and here's some stuff for a salad. Do you have a bottle of red wine?"

"No. I wasn't planning on fixing her dinner," I sputtered.

"She'll be more likely to agree if you keep her talking till she's good and hungry. Then she won't have to be seen out with you. It's safer. I wish I had a red." He transferred the tray from his hands to mine and kissed me on the cheek.

It was a measure of Patrick's love of match-making that he was willing to help with Lindstrom. I knew he thought she was exactly the wrong woman for me. I sometimes suspected as much as well. I returned to my favorite cop with a can of soda and a glass of ice. Accepting both, she continued to peruse the titles of my books. She stopped and looked at a small, framed painting. "You like daisies?"

"They're my favorite. I bought that print in Texas years ago." I didn't mention San Padre Island where I had first noticed her on the beach long ago. "So tell me about your suspect, Lindstrom. Has he confessed yet?"

"No, no," she said as she sat. "He's a loner, meets the profile to a tee."

"Unemployed, maladjusted white male with a grudge against women?"

"Not unemployed, but self-employed. He's been heard preaching about a final solution for homelessness and the mentally handicapped. Thinks the human race is on the down-hill slope as a result of genetics."

"Killing off homeless woman one at a time seems a rather ineffective approach. Is he a neo-nazi?"

"We're looking into that, but it doesn't look like it. It's not a racial thing. He thinks all the world needs to improve its gene pool. Not just one group."

"These women were too old to bear children."

"Yes, but he sees them as vermin, sponging off the public purse."

"The public purse?"

"He talks that way. In a rant."

"Why not old men?"

"Women who can't reproduce no longer have value. But a man might." She shrugged. "The value of a penis." It was the most political statement I'd ever heard her make.

"This guy sounds like the vermin."

She nodded.

"What's his name?"

Lindstrom smiled and shook her head. "I can't give you that yet. When we arrest him, the papers will pick it up." At least she didn't look me in the eye this time when she told me to get my information from the newspaper.

"You know Mary Margaret Brooks may not be a part of the series of killings at all."

"Forget it, Darcy. You don't have a case here. Believe me. It's the same guy."

"How do you know it's not someone with a motive to kill one of the women who's just killing the others to cover up?"

Lindstrom frowned at me. "Guys like this love the killing. It's not really about motive. They just make up some ornate psycho-babble to fit their love for killing people."

"Why did he kill Rudy Carr?"

"Who is Rudy Carr?"

"An aide at Gateway Rest Home who was fished out of the river on Monday."

"Gateway…the nursing home where the Brooks woman stayed?"

"Yes, in addition, he often worked with her and was on duty the night she disappeared. His girlfriend says he was very upset when they found her dead."

Lindstrom stared at me for several seconds, then gave a slight shake of her head. "I don't know. Maybe it is related. I'll look into it."

"Are you holding your suspect?" I asked.

"No, but we're keeping an eye on him. We don't have enough to hold him yet. Why did you go private instead of becoming a cop?" Nice footwork, but I noticed the switch.

"I guess I was doing the work before I made a real career choice. I loved it, so I just kept doing it."

"How were you doing it before you made a choice?"

"My uncle owns the firm. I was serving summonses and doing background checks for him while I was in college. By the time I got out of the Army, he had more work than he could do, so he hired me as a temporary solution. I've been there ever since."

"You know, being a cop has its advantages. You have a struc-ture to work in that allows you to do more real crime work."

I looked at Lindstrom's light blue eyes and wondered why she was trying to sell me on her choices. "I've got more freedom where I am. I'm not accountable to whoever graduated from the academy the year before me. I don't have to worry about how the citizenry thinks I'm doing my job." I wanted to say 'I don't have to huddle in the back of my closet, always afraid I'm going to lose my job.'

Maybe 'citizenry' triggered a thought. She offered a smile. "You can tell the Brooks family that we're close to making an arrest, and there won't be any more deaths."

"Good. It must be a great feeling to stop this horror. I'm going to put dinner on. Do you want another soda?" She looked up at me and just shook her head.

I decided to take that as an agreement she would have dinner with me and went to put Patrick's meal on. We talked about college and the Army and the police academy while I fixed dinner. I was setting it on the table and apologizing for the lack of wine when her beeper went off. She was on my phone for two minutes and out the door a minute later.

I knocked at Patrick's door. He opened it quickly.

"Are you hungry?" I asked.

"Where's Lindstrom?"

"I'm jilted again." I expanded on this as we made the short trip back to my kitchen where Harvey Milk was calmly sampling the stew. We salvaged a good portion, and as we ate, made a thorough dissection of the Ice Queen's behavior. Patrick, ever the romantic, argued that her seeming willingness to be seduced into staying for a meal was, "highly promising." I pooh-poohed the notion just to keep my cool intact, but inwardly I hoped.

Much later I was deep into a dreamless sleep when I heard sharp knocks. As I staggered to my door in a faded tee with Harvey holes and striped boxer shorts under a gray sweat suit, I was trying to guess who was banging on my door at one o'clock.

For once I exercised caution worthy of a PI whose main line of work stresses security and put on the chain lock before opening the door to squint out into the dim hallway light.

"I saw your light on," she said.

I keep a living room lamp on for Harvey and me in case we make middle of the night treks to the bathroom or kitchen. I didn't explain. I just stepped back and unlocked the door and let her in. Part of me tingled, pleased by the flattery implied by her voluntary return. But I was groggy and grumpy, too. Why did she think she could barge in here in the middle of the night?

"Were you in bed?" she asked innocently.

She looked different, highly charged, a kid with a secret. She had a thick brown car coat on and leather gloves that she was pulling off and stuffing into its pockets.

I nodded and yawned, just barely covering my mouth in time.

"You look like a little kid in her jammies," she said.

I bristled. That wasn't how I wanted her to see me.

"Have you eaten?" I asked, proving I could sound just as protective.

"No." Her blue eyes were dark and intent.

With my shoes off she could more easily look down on me. I straightened to parade posture.

"You hungry?" I was fumbling through a possible menu: a dish of stew I could microwave, some Kraft cheese slices from plastic envelopes.

"Yes," she said in a choky voice and reached for me.

I wasn't ready. First off, in all my fantasies I reached for her, and our first kiss was slow and sensual, and I directed the tongue traffic.

Instead, our faces collided. I subconsciously recoiled from what I'd so long sought, then tried to meet her halfway. But she wasn't having that; she definitely planned to be in charge. She pulled me forward by the shoulders rather in the manner of my second-grade teacher who once shook me for climbing too high on the playground jungle gym set. Then she executed a break-and-enter kiss.

I resisted, framing my protests as fast as my mind could churn. Then I said to myself: Wait a minute. Go with the flow. You can turn this around.

I shut my eyes and tried to let the moment in. Her hands, now caressing my face, were still cold. Her tongue tasted of coffee and of her. I could still smell the cold night clinging to her coat, maybe in tiny, melting flecks of snow. The sense of lean, muscular strength under Lindstrom's winter layers came through as she pushed against me, pursuing my tongue as though it were a prime suspect.

I twisted my head away. "Lindstrom," I said, with perhaps less dignity than I'd hope for.

"Darcy," she said dryly. Mocking me? This was backwards.

She slid her hands down and under my t-shirt, yanked it up, and pulled me forward. I gave an involuntary yip as her fingers touched the small of my back.

"Too cold? Perhaps you can warm them," she said, definitely mocking now. Her hands were sliding down my hips, then back over my buttocks, and the technique was working. Her hands were warming, and so was I. Something like melted honey trickled toward my lower lips. I felt the flush on my face.

For a few minutes we danced clumsily, stuck in one spot but shifting to accommodate body parts. She resumed kissing me, using her tongue like a butterfly to undermine and distract me. I managed to undo her coat and press against the cable knit sweater and cords there, but she grumbled, "Don't interrupt me." I'd have lodged a full protest, but she was kneading my butt, tickling the backs of my thighs, feather touches that flirted and promised.

"Assume the position," she whispered in my ear, her voice husky with wanting.

I spread my legs, accepted her finger and rode it home to glory, thrusting and bucking to a climax that exploded like a starburst. I collapsed against her, sweaty and flushed, my gray sweats dangling down my thighs. My lungs hurt. My pride hurt. None of this was in my script.

"Darcy, say something."

"Again," an evil ventriloquist answered.

For the first time I heard her laughter as something light and free, erasing her caution. Gleeful, joyful—and, yes, irritatingly triumphant.

I didn't care. I wanted to ride again. I was hungry for the motion. I was angry, too. I wanted to be in charge. I pulled her head down into a kiss I initiated. If the first ride was a frenzied gallop, the second was a slow-motion canter. I'd ride up to the edge of the cliff, then backtrack. She caught on and followed me. The second time caught me unaware. Rocking along easily, I was suddenly just too full to contain the pleasure spilling over. I clenched tightly. "Hard and fast," I said. And she did and did and did while I galloped past finish lines until the last one was marked by sweet exhaustion.

When I could breathe enough, I asked, "You okay?"

"I'm strong," she said. But not bragging. She was stroking my head with her dry hand and bestowing little kisses on my crown. I let her.

When I could breathe even more, I said, "I want to do despicable things to you."

"Do you?" Vintage Lindstrom.

But she didn't resist when I grabbed her hand and pulled her into my bedroom. My old-fashioned full-sized bed looked pathetically small for us, and my covers typically tangled.

She had shucked her jacket and was starting to undo her cords when I said, "Let me." For the first time in the last hour she looked uncertain.

"Relax. I'll be gentle."

She smiled. "But can I trust you?"

I was already struggling with the clothes that came off so easily in my daydreams. Still, despite needing her assistance, I managed to cover her with kisses as I removed her clothing. I tickled a bare foot when I pulled off the last sock. She bore it stoically, but I think it was mind over matter. When she was entirely nude, she lay back, squarely in the middle of my bed and more beautiful than I'd dared to believe. She was milky white with blue veins and silky dark blond pubic hair and breasts like pears. I wanted to speak poetry.

"You're beautiful," I said. The words weren't enough.

She looked impatient. "What is that?" She reached for me, tugged me on top of her. "Weren't you going to do despicable things?"

I tried. I worked at it for more than an hour, using every body part and all my ingenuity. She seemed to cooperate. But we were stuck.

"Don't worry," she said. "Sometimes I can't."

I knew I wasn't supposed to argue or quiz her about her past sex life. I was supposed to be gracious and light and not pelt her with reassurances. I wasn't supposed to feel like a failure. Or to blame her for not responding to the wonderful skills that had brought hundreds—okay, maybe a half dozen—other women to technicolor climax.

I was lying with my head resting in her groin. She was lifting strands of my hair and letting it fall, lifting and releasing, in a sleepy rhythm. The smell and taste of her floated through my senses.

When we'd been silent for a time, she asked. "Are you okay?"

"I'm embarrassed."

"Don't be. It's—" Her voice was strained.

"I want you to make love to me again. Touching your body has made me—" I stopped. I was shameless. Greedy.

She laughed. Not quite the same peal of joy as before but definitely pleased.

We negotiated positions with murmurs and grunts. I stayed on top for a while, then she rolled me over. I was dizzy, queen of the universe. On top she pushed aside one leg, straddled the other, bore down hard with her thumb. While I slipped and slid beneath her, she rubbed against me, and suddenly, as my hips bucked under her, she moaned in release. But she didn't lose track of me till I stretched under her in a final spasm.

We lay in a long silence. Then, "Just scientific curiosity," she said. "How many times?"

"I lost count at thirty-six." I picked up her hand, kissed it. "Scientific curiosity!—Liar."

She gave an inquisitive grunt.

"What you're really after is bragging rights," I said. My voice had stayed light, but I spoke true fears. I'd just showed her my deep desire, my lust, my naked self. I'd been caught wanting her.

She laughed—I'd made a joke.

"What brought you back tonight?" I asked. Venturing out on thin ice.

"I wanted to get into your pants." Light. Teasing.

"Worked like a charm, didn't it?"

"Hmm." I didn't know 'hmm' could sound so smug.

I snuggled into her shoulder. "Were you working since you left?"

I felt the slight withdrawal. "Yes."

"The cemetery murderer?"

"Yes. Things are moving fast. We found some rope."

"Where? Who is it?"

"I can't, Darcy." She heaved a hound-dog sigh. "Don't ask."

I shifted upward, using my elbow as a prop. "You have just used me wantonly for two—no, three—hours. What do you mean,

'Don't ask'?"

Her jaw tightened, and she looked away. "Look. There's a lot cops don't even tell their wives."

I couldn't even list the ways that made it worse.

She risked a glance at me, then grinned. "Looks won't kill, Darcy. Get over it. You'll read it in the *Post*."

Oh, compounded errors. "You don't trust me." In more ways than one.

She regarded me steadily. "Don't oversimplify this."

"Meaning what?"

Harvey, perhaps feeling the storm of noise had subsided, chose that moment to jump onto the bed. He pranced over to Lindstrom, purring and arching his back. She turned to him gratefully, fussing over him and ignoring me.

"Who am I going to tell?"

"The Brooks family, Ann Yates, Patrick," she reeled off as if she'd clearly thought about it. She kept her eyes on Harvey.

"Not if you asked me not to."

She regarded me again. "You strike me as an independent woman who marches to her own drummer. Sometimes breaks other people's rules."

"You don't trust me."

"I don't know you." A rueful tone, but her jaw was set.

Maybe if I could have made a joke then—that she knew me better than my gynecologist—we'd have been out of the muddle. But I was pissed; at her for her lack of trust; at me because the shoe pinched. I can keep secrets, but I'm loyal to my own code. I wasn't ready to swear blind fealty to Lindstrom.

"Shit," I blurted.

"Ah, well—" She was rolling over, away from me, out of my bed. Methodically, without haste, yet all too quickly, she redressed herself.

She caught me in a shiver and threw my sweats to me. I sat there, the sheet tangled in my lap, clutching the sweats.

"I can let myself out, but don't you want to latch the chain after me?" It was a form of caring. But not enough.

I shrugged. "I'll get it later."

She did her own shrug. "Take care of yourself." She reached down to pet Harvey. "Don't stay angry, Darcy."

"Who's angry?" I couldn't say more without choking.

She gave her social chuckle. Then she was gone.

Harvey followed her out.

I got up and tugged on the sweats. I smelled of sex. My body felt drained and there was a raw throb in my pubic region. I ought to have been floating in bliss, but my stomach was queasy. Damn her anyway. She hadn't stuck to one line of my script. She'd held me in the palm of her hand, sometimes literally, and stayed aloof. She'd pulled rank as a cop. She'd out-butched me.

I sulked as long as I could, but before dawn my body betrayed me. Just as I was sinking under, Harvey rejoined me. His rough cat's tongue licked my sweaty cheek. Cynics say cats like the salt, but I figured he knew.

I slept late that morning, another bleak, cloudy day that invited a Saturday sleep-in, until I stretched. My body screamed reminders, not all unpleasant; then I recalled the not-so-grand finale. Lindstrom's refusal to trust me loomed as scalding rejection.

I dashed to the shower to scrub away the ripe body smell that betrayed my willingness to trust her. Well, I'd shown her mine, but she hadn't reciprocated. I replayed it all in slow motion and wallowed in my self-pity with generous dollops of anger whipped on top. Still, when I finished toweling down, my body hummed. Despite tender places, I felt the satisfied thrum of a woman who'd been well made love to.

While I dressed, I tried to focus on the content of our earlier conversation—the part about the profile of the murderer. Had a copy cat killer murdered Aunt M? Lindstrom's claim that forensic evidence linked them all wouldn't convince me until I saw it. She was honest, but not infallible.

I hadn't even started coffee when Patrick knocked. He announced he had another Saturday off and invited me over to his place. I always hate to be reminded of what a slob I am. His apartment nearly sparkles, and he doesn't allow the noun *clutter* to cross anyone's mind.

His two princely boys, Quentin Crisp and Oscar Wilde, pranced over to inspect me and rub against my legs. I gave them some serious attention. I was relieved to have the two Siamese to fuss over. Lindstrom was on my mind, and I didn't want Patrick reading it.

Patrick had a small breakfast table sitting in his bay window. He'd covered it with linen and a delicious brunch; bagels, lox, cream cheese, marmalade, orange juice, hazelnut coffee. He looked great, too, in stylish slacks and a new crew neck sweater.

"Patrick, this is too good to waste on me. You need a steady boyfriend."

He gave an exaggerated sigh. "Too right. Sit down, sit down."

"But next week could we have those eggs with salsa and refried beans?"

I was helping myself as I put in that order, and he flicked a linen napkin at me.

During brunch we talked about movies and the new books coming into the bookstore where he worked, plus tidbits of gay gossip. Patrick gathers it, but I relish it. It may have been the love of gossip that got me into business as a PI.

After breakfast we split Saturday's *Post*. Patrick is the perfect host; he gave me the front section and the *Everyday* section which includes the comics.

The top headline was that the Task Force had arrested William Nelville Bishop on suspicion of the cemetery murders—this was Lindstrom's suspect. I skimmed ahead quickly, then read portions of the article aloud. William Nelville Bishop was fifty-six, the owner of a used bookstore. I knew him slightly and so did Patrick.

Bishop had operated his bookstore in downtown St. Louis for years and his uncle had run it for years before that; so anyone seriously interested in used books would know him and his store. Bishop was a bibliomaniac who wanted to own books, stacks and stacks of them. He didn't read them and he did not want to care for them, he just wanted to accumulate them—and to talk about them in a superficial way, implying that he knew their contents well.

For years he had managed to hang onto his store, though as downtown neighborhoods changed, he had to be losing business. He had moved several times to seedier locations, jamming thousands of books into underheated buildings whose aisles were teetering stacks of books. His shelving systems quickly broke down under the strain of ever-increasing inventory in ever decreasing space, so finding a particular book was a discouraging challenge and he didn't always volunteer to help.

A tall hulk of a man who in winter was thickened by layers of sweaters and bulky overcoat to fend off the cold, he often wore a dirty plaid scarf. His thick black hair looked unwashed, and he wore a stubble before it became fashionable. He liked to stay by his space heater, holding forth to any customer he could buttonhole to hear his right wing theories of sociology and governance. But these were only the exteriors. I thought him a loud and arrogant bully, a discount Rush Limbaugh, though the veneer of good humor was even thinner.

The old-fashioned term "blowhard" always came to my mind. He had a gift for slimey innuendo. He was one of those men who make me squeamish, as though rape is never far from his mind. Running into him was a little like running into a spider web in the dark; I never felt clean of the clinging strands. He looked and sounded like the sort who would molest little girls and murder sweet old ladies. No wonder he was an attractive suspect. The paper quoted unnamed sources that accused him of haranguing listeners about final solutions against the homeless.

No surprise that Lindstrom had been so charged last night—no, early this morning. She'd arrested Bishop. She'd come to celebrate. But I was a prop, her personal champagne, not a partner to share the good news with.

Partner. Now there's a tricky word. Did I want a partner? A spouse, a mate, a more than a sometime thing? Or had Lindstrom given me exactly what I wanted from her and in just measure?

Patrick interrupted this train of ironic thought by whistling. "Wow—sounds like the Ice Queen has the killer."

"He is the kind of guy whose teachers will remember him as a little weird."

"Always tearing the wings off flies and torturing cats." Patrick picked up a bagel scrap and jellied it. "I always thought he was a creep."

"Me, too. But I'm not sure that means he's a serial killer."

"Why ever not? Or is it just your ACLU leanings?"

"Partly that. It's easy to railroad a guy this obnoxious. But being guilty of creepiness isn't quite the same as serial murder. Somehow he doesn't fit at all with Aunt M."

"Tell that to Lindstrom."

"I'll try, Patrick; I'll try." Maybe there was something in my tone. A silence fell. I looked up to see in his eyes the same considering regard Lindstrom's had held during our tug of war over trust. "What?" I managed. A tactical mistake.

"You're holding out on Uncle Patrick. All morning there's been something. You're twitchy."

"Twitchy?" If I'd settled on one note I'd have been better, but I tried for both innocence and indignation. Straddles never work. Except, of course, during great sex.

"Yes. Charged. Nearly giddy. But with a touch of not-so-pleased. What's going on, Meg?"

Of course, I'd wanted to tell him right away. But privacy considerations had restrained me. That and the shame of confessing I wasn't such a hot lover, albeit a selfish one. Plus, I hated to prove Lindstrom right by spilling pillow talk. But she hadn't been cautious about that. What she'd worried about was my revealing secrets about the case. And the truth is Patrick is my great confidante in matters of the heart and hormones. Maybe because we're of different genders we find it easy to be non-judgmental. Or, if that was how it was at the beginning, the now is that we love each other enough to go easy. He's always on my side.

Or, to put it more bluntly, I had more loyalty to Patrick who was still regarding me steadily, questioningly. "The whole truth, Meg."

I confessed. In five minutes I told him all that inquiring minds want to know in a PI's succinct report.

His blue eyes widened. "The Ice Queen melted?"

"No, Patrick, that's the point. She didn't. I did. I was in complete *China Syndrome* melt-down. The very fillings in my teeth were molten liquid. She took me, used me—" I'd jumped up from the chair and was marching to my drummer.

"Don't pace, Meg. It makes Quentin nervous."

I threw myself down on his sofa. "But when it was her turn, I couldn't—she couldn't—"

"Oh, girlfriend, I've had so many boyfriends like that!"

"So, what did you do?"

"Well, first of all, a man would never think his partner's sexual failure was his fault."

I took too long to realize he was joking. He made a face at me and continued. "Meg, there could be a dozen reasons why she didn't come under your ministrations. Maybe she was just too tired by then and even her excitement about arresting Bishop and making love to you—not in that order, of course—weren't enough to keep her pumped up." He shook his head. "You aren't giving yourself enough credit. Just touching you set her off."

"I wanted to be more in charge, Patrick."

He gave me a look. "Surprise. But you were. You decided to hand yourself over to Lindstrom, to enjoy being in her power." He smacked his lips leeringly. "Haven't we all loved those delicious little moments of just letting go?"

"No, I meant in charge of her."

He shrugged. "Who's in charge? Now that's an interesting question, isn't it?—Master or love slave? I'd bet she would have found it hard not to follow your lead last night. Know what I mean?"

I was blushing so I did. "Yes, but—"

"Un-huh. No buts. You don't know what was going on in her head. And that's where it all happens, isn't it?"

"Not quite."

He smiled appreciatively. "Well, some of us think with our dicks."

I stuck out my tongue—but not as sexual gesture.

"Besides, haven't you ever been stuck—wanting to come, not quite able to get there? Seems to me I remember an MP story involving some drinking and—"

"Don't rehash old news."

He reached down to stroke Oscar Wilde's beige face. "One other thing, Meg. Ask your body. Do you want Lindstrom to make love to you again?"

"Oh, shut up, " I snapped. Only partially addressing Patrick.

Chapter Thirteen

Patrick and I whiled away the Saturday browsing at Left Bank Books and Paul's and The Big Sleep and Our World Too, a bus man's holiday for him and a distraction for me. I alternately wanted to throttle and cuddle Lindstrom. Patrick was patient with my sporadic eruptions of complaint about the previous night's encounter with her even though repetition usually bores him. Saturday night we took in a movie at the Tivoli, a newly refurbished miniplex of gilt, glitter, and gay-friendly films.

Later, I was surprised at how quickly I bounded up the stairs that night to check my answering machine—and how disappointed I was to find only a call from Betty.

Sunday hardly dawned. A gray film between mist and sleet enveloped the day like shrink wrap. Patrick had traded shifts, so he was working at the bookstore. I paced around my apartment till I had Harvey twitching his tail in agitation. I vowed I wouldn't sit pining by the phone like a moony teenager, so I paced some more.

At noon I checked my cupboards, hoping a miracle had rendered them less bare. I bundled up and decided the treacherous walk to the St. Louis Bread Co. would be a hair less dangerous than driving the Plymouth. I was currently reading Rosellen Brown's *Civil Wars*, which fit into my parka pocket easily. I slipped twice on the way over but witnessed a fender bender on Grand that justified my decision to walk.

I had soup, a sandwich, and a giant cinnamon roll with three cups of decaf hazelnut at the Bread Co. The place was warm and homey and several faces were familiar from the neighborhood. What could be better than a place where the smell of freshly baked breads and newly brewed coffee filled the air and Rosellen Brown's words fed the mind? Except Lindstrom's face kept creeping onto the page, blotting out Brown's nuances.

On the way back to my apartment I fell twice, skinning my palms and jarring my self-esteem. Ironically the temperature was climbing, but that left a wash of water over ice.

I limped back up stairs, sure I wouldn't have any phone messages and irked to be right.

"Okay, Harvey, desperate times call for desperate measures," I said, waking him from his snooze. I decided that cleaning the two bottom drawers of my file cabinet was the likeliest counter-irritant to dislodge Lindstrom from my mind. Obviously, she owed me a call. She'd had her slam-bam, and I was still waiting for the, "Thank you, ma'am."

The files didn't work their usual soporific magic. Somehow my gears never engaged with my task, and I kept 'coming to' with a start to realize I'd skimmed five files without once making mental contact. Yet, I'd managed to re-write my major sex scene with Lindstrom twelve ways, ranging from nearer to my heart's desire (she lay panting at my feet, groaning in gratitude for my artful skill as a lover) to a pyrotechnic confrontation in which I lambasted her as a cold, self-centered, self-absorbed bitch.

I think it was 'bitch' that snapped me back to reality. I hate the word. It didn't fit Sarah Lindstrom. Cold, self-centered, self-absorbed would do.

That settled, I started working over my notes on Aunt M's disappearance and murder. Something didn't sit right with me about her murder, but Lindstrom seemed cocksure—a word I enjoyed applying—about all the murders being committed by the same serial killer.

By bedtime I was stiff from my two tumbles which overrode my body's aching reminders of my recent robust sexual athleticism. My sulking about Lindstrom's silence was freezing into an attitude, too. I'd thought her manners were better than love 'em and leave 'em, but maybe I'd been mistaken in this as in other things about her. Oh, I could concede that arresting Bishop might tie her up. Still, she'd made time for that celebratory fuck, hadn't she?

The temperature outside kept climbing right along with my blood pressure. I went to bed thinking it might be sweet revenge to prove Lindstrom wrong about at least one of the murders.

The next day back in the office, I pushed into high gear. If Aunt M's murder really wasn't related to the others, then I needed to figure out who else had motive, means, and opportunity. Ann had given me Greg's office number, and I called to make an appointment. It took me two tries to convince his secretary that I should talk to him in spite of the fact that she had never heard my name and that I refused to tell her what I wished to speak to Mr. Brooks about. Once he was on the phone, he was his usual charming self. Of course he'd see me, why didn't I plan to have lunch with him? I passed on that and made an appointment to see him in his office at one-thirty.

In the meantime, I consulted the phone book, but could find no listing for Sheila Breeze. I called information, but had no luck there either. My friend in the Department of Motor Vehicles wasn't in that morning, so I stared at the R.J. carved into my desk. Sheila Breeze, where are you? And where is your husband, the small time pill-popping buddy of the dearly departed Rudy? Probably Breezer didn't tell his ex-wife where he was going anyway. Nikki said they had been split for a year. Probably didn't pay his child support either. That little cynicism gave me an idea, and I dialed the Department of Family Services. Bingo! Sheila Breeze was in fact an AFDC recipient and her address was on Natural Bridge. All obligingly given to me, because I was employed by the city health department, sexually transmitted diseases division. I decided I had time to whip by Sheila's house before I met with Greg.

An erect black woman at least seventy years old with wispy white hair answered the door. She kept the screen door firmly latched. Sheila wasn't home. She was at work. The woman wouldn't tell me which beauty shop. She didn't want me bothering her over there. She just got the job this week. No, she didn't know or care where Richard Breeze might be. She didn't know that he'd left his job and St. Louis. She didn't know where he might go or if he had family anywhere. She didn't know if he'd ever lived anywhere besides St. Louis. I ran out of questions before she ran out of negatives, so she reminded me as I turned to leave that there was no point in coming back. Sheila didn't know or care where Richard was either.

Downtown St. Louis was at its bustling best. The Arch gleamed even in the faint winter sunshine. Traffic was busy but not completely clogged at this time of day. Christmas decorations and lights festooned many of the buildings. Greg's office was in one of the medium-sized glass and steel towers. A quick look at the building directory showed mostly brokerage firms, insurance offices and a scattering of other services, including two psychotherapists. Would the proximity of help keep brokers from jumping out those reflective windows if the market crashed again?

The firm Greg worked for was one of those named for partners. There were six names in the firm title, and none was Brooks. The elevator rose silently and smoothly to the ninth floor. The doors opened with a whisper, and I stepped onto a thick maroon carpet. There was a short hall to the left and a long hall to the right. Directly facing the elevator doors was a heavy oak door with only the partners' names on the black and brass plate.

I pushed it open and was immediately in the parlor of a fine old home. The carpet was a medium gray with a border of the maroon.

It was furnished in gleaming dark wood tables and upholstered chairs. I walked to the left side of the room where a large mauve and gray couch faced the center. On the coffee table in front of it was today's *Wall Street Journal*, neatly folded. As if by magic a door opened to the right of the couch. A fortyish brunette in a gray wool skirt and blazer smiled at me.

"Whom were you wishing to see?"

"Mr. Greg Brooks, please."

"Ah, Ms. Darcy. Mr. Brooks will be free presently. Shall I bring you coffee while you wait?"

I declined the coffee and sat on the couch. I briefly entertained the idea of propping my feet on the polished coffee table. At precisely one-thirty-five the receptionist invited me through the door.

The huge window behind his desk looked out at the skyscraper next door. Greg's desk was a light wood as were both client chairs and the three-drawer filing cabinet to his left. Above it hung a diploma from Harvard's School of Business. A credenza behind him held a top-of-the-line computer and its accouterments. A dozen exotic sea creatures, only two of which looked like fish, swam in a fifty-gallon aquarium to his right. Beside the fish tank was a wooden coat rack that held his umbrella, a black cashmere coat and a beautiful white silk scarf that looked like it cost as much as my winter coat. If surroundings were any measure, Greg was doing pretty well for a thirty-nine-year-old. He stood up and walked around his desk to shake my hand.

"Meg, I'm glad to see you. Ann says you've been so helpful to her."

"I haven't done much, really. But the case may be closed soon."

"Yes, I saw the article in Saturday's paper. What a relief to know they have the killer."

"Yes...I don't know much about Lindstrom's case against him, but she's good at what she does."

"Do you know who this guy is?"

"Just that he evidently believes that the weak should be culled from society."

Greg shook his head. "It's just so hard for me to imagine someone's killing helpless old women. He must be some kind of nut."

"Probably. I've been following up on something a little different, just in case this guy turns out not to be the one. I talked to Bill Curtis on Friday."

If I had been expecting Greg to spit, he disappointed me. His face and body language were completely calm. "Yes, his inclusion in the will came as a bit of a surprise to us. I had no idea that he was that close to Aunt M."

"He seems to have spent a fair amount of time with Aunt M and Linda. He said he generally cared for their pets when they traveled." Greg nodded absently and thumped his index finger against the edge of his desk twice.

"What I came to ask you about was the possibility that Aunt M may not have been a part of the cemetery murders. Her killer may have just used that device to make her death look like it was part of a series."

Greg shook his head. "I don't know, Meg; I guess anything's possible, but I think she was probably just very unlucky to be out wandering, looking like a homeless woman on the same night that Bishop was out looking for another victim."

"Did you know Rudy Carr?"

"No. Who is he?"

"Rudy was an attendant at Gateway. He often worked with Aunt M."

"Oh yes, I know the Rudy who used to help Aunt M. He was very good with her."

"He was murdered a week ago."

"Oh, I didn't hear that. How terrible for Gateway." He paused, then asked, "But how is that connected to Aunt M's death?"

"It may not be, but it's an odd coincidence that two people connected with the nursing home should be murdered in the same week. Maybe Rudy knew something about her disappearance." He nodded encouragingly as people do who want to hear more. But I had another question. "Greg, do you know any reason why Ann would need Aunt M's money right now?"

"Heavens, no, Meg. I can't believe you'd think it. You know Ann lives on her salary from the university. All socially responsible, she barely touches her investment income."

"And what about your financial situation?"

Greg laughed and shrugged. "At least that's a little more believable. I've always been fonder of filthy lucre than Ann has. But I get my pleasure from earning it, outwitting the big boys on Wall Street."

"Did you talk to Rudy after Aunt M's body was found?"

"No, why should I? Look, Meg, I know you're trying to turn every stone and do a good job for Ann, but really, is all this necessary? If you just keep her informed about the investigation of this man Bishop, I'm sure that will be what Ann wants."

I sighed because I, too, feared I was flogging a dead case. But Walter has always encouraged me to follow my instincts, and my instincts kept coming back to Rudy's death. It was connected to Aunt M somehow; I just needed to figure out how.

"Rudy's death interests me. Even if it's not related to Aunt M's death, I don't think the police are on the right track."

"How so?" He seemed genuinely interested.

"Rudy had a handful of pills in his pocket when he was pulled from the river, so naturally the only motive that the police are chasing is drugs. We've become so drug-obsessed in the last ten years. But his girlfriend is pretty certain the pills were just a small amount for his own use, that he wasn't dealing."

"But how could his death be related to Aunt M's?"

"Several possibilities—maybe he saw something when he was out looking for her. It's even possible that someone paid him to let Aunt M out."

I could see that hit a nerve. There was a silence while we both considered the idea of a conspiracy to kill Aunt M. First he looked at his fish tank in search of answers, then at me. "You know, that's a real possibility. It could explain how Aunt M got out. How will you find out what happened?"

"I just keep asking till I find someone who saw or heard something."

He wished me luck, and we both reasserted our horror at the senseless murders. I didn't want to ask him how he'd handled Aunt M's finances until I'd done background checks.

"I hope that William Bishop is it and that Lindstrom gets the goods on him soon. It would be a relief to know that Aunt M would be the last. Thanks for your time," I said.

I started to rise, then sat back. "You know, I'm curious. Your father was an extremely wealthy man. How did you feel when he left most of his money to homeless shelters?"

Of course it was a rude question, the sort people in his social circles may have thought but not said aloud. He stared at the aquarium and the colorful fish circling lazily. "My father had the medieval notion he could buy his way into heaven." He turned to give me a dazzling smile that didn't connect to his eyes. "I'm grateful to him. It gave me an opportunity to use my own wits."

"To be a self-made man?"

"To master my own fate," he said. The smile disappeared from his handsome face.

In for a penny, in for a pound. "You must be one of the most eligible bachelors in town."

He looked surprised, then sly. "Are you flirting with me?"

I clamped down on the swift ripostes. "Just making an observation."

"Well, I don't have time for as much social life as I'd like." His tone was nakedly defensive. But not more so than your average venture capitalist defending neglect of family.

"Who does?" I smiled, and my smile didn't include my eyes either.

As I left, we shook hands again and I plucked a caramel from the bowl on his desk. Any man that likes Werther's Originals can't be all bad even if he did worship the almighty dollar. I wondered if there were any PIs in the country operating out of offices as plush as this one. Magically, the brunette met me in the hallway outside Greg's door and made sure I didn't peek in at any of the partners on my way out.

At two-fifty I got back to the office. I hurriedly sat down and dialed the number for Gateway Rest Home. I wanted to catch Arlene before she went home. She was there. I thought Arlene was probably the type that would work for Gateway for twenty-five years and never once sneak out early, but she was turning out to be a woman of surprises.

"Hi, Arlene. This is Meg Darcy. How are you doing?"

"I'm fine." Her voice was warm.

"I've been following up some leads on Rudy's death and any possible connection to Aunt M's. I need some more information."

"Dr. Rolfing has given orders that you aren't to be allowed in the building. If you come around, we're to call the police immediately."

"Thanks for the warning, Arlene. Look, I was wondering if you'd be willing to help me with the investigation?"

"Sure, Meg. What can I do for you?"

"I'm looking into various people's financial situations, and it would help to have some social security numbers."

"Mary Margaret's?"

"Yes and Greg Brooks's; legally he handles her bills so it should be on a form at the nursing home. And Rolfing's."

"I'm not sure I can get Dr. Rolfing's, but I'll try."

"Thanks, Arlene. This will be a big help."

She signed off quickly, and I booted up the computer to begin searching data bases.

At three-thirty Colleen told me Arlene Dorman was on the phone. I figured Arlene had gotten cold feet to be calling back so soon.

"Hi, Arlene."

"I got them, Meg." She was breathless. "I just walked into his office and told the secretary he had a file I needed. He had some letters from an insurance company in his desk. His social security number was printed right on top." She read it to me.

"That's great, Arlene. You'd make a good detective. Did you get the others?"

"Those were easy." She laughed. "I didn't even have to lie to get those." She read me first Mary Margaret's, then Greg Brooks's.

"Thank you, Arlene. This is a big help."

"No problem, Meg. By the way, I asked Rachel Batson and she says Rudy didn't pair up with any of the Yates family during the Thursday night search for Aunt M."

"Thanks. Also, would you let me know if you hear that Rolfing has any contact with Mary Margaret's family or if you hear anything unusual going on with Rolfing?"

She promised cheerfully, and we signed off.

After I put the phone down I stared at it a moment. Still no call from Lindstrom. I dialed her home number and listened to her brusque 'leave a message' message. Damned if I would call her. I slammed down the phone. Friday night had been all about power, and Lindstrom had won. She'd had me begging her to touch me. Well, that was the end of that. I wasn't interested in being the Ice Queen's call girl, hanging out, waiting to be wanted for celebration or comfort. As I walked by Colleen's desk, I noticed our caller ID boxes. I blushed. Please, goddess, let Lindstrom not have caller ID.

Tuesday a weak, watery sunshine wasn't enough to jumpstart my day. I needed some of Colleen's decent coffee. When I reached the office, she was chipper and poured a mug of coffee for me before I could even get to the pot.

"Walter in?"

"He's staying home. Has the flu," she said. She was pulling a file from a drawer; I couldn't read her face.

Sometimes 'the flu' is Walter's cover for a night of drinking. On the other hand, a real flu was making the rounds.

I shrugged and picked up the *Post* that waited for Walter. I hadn't had time to read mine at home. I walked with it back to my office. The headlines under the fold announced that William Bishop was out on bail. The judge stated that although the police had been reasonable in charging Bishop, there wasn't enough evidence to hold him without bail. This was news indeed. Since his arrest the paper had run at least one story a day, delving into his background. The *Post* wasn't a tabloid, but this was one of the grisliest cases to come along. A series of brutal murders and an unsympathetic suspect were irresistible.

Today's story announced that James Burke Greber was now acting as Bishop's defense lawyer. Greber was one of the city's high-powered defense attorneys. Not as famous as F. Lee Bailey but the attorney well-to-do locals called when their sons did more than run a red light. Well, well. Who was paying Greber? If Bishop himself had the money to hire him, he certainly was a long way from needing a court-appointed lawyer, a fact I'd assumed all along. Bishop's book business might be down at the heels, but he was not starving.

Lindstrom had been asked to comment and had refused to give the paper any raw meat beyond a curt statement that the investigation was continuing and Bishop still held the Task Force's attention. Lindstrom was too smart to rail at due process, but she must have been grinding her teeth anyway because many people in the community don't keep up with the niceties of the Constitution and would blame the cops for 'letting him go.' I didn't envy Bishop either. Between the cops and the press his life would be miserable. I expected Bishop to sound off, but Greber muzzled him, holding him to a strict 'No comment.'

Well, well. I re-read the story and wondered what were the weak links in Lindstrom's case that persuaded the judge to allow the bail. He had set it high. That raised a question, too. Who'd footed that bill? Did Bishop have that much stashed away?

Colleen interrupted my musings by coming in with a list of Walter's appointments. Which did I want to cover and which should she cancel? It took a few minutes to work that out. I had some calls of my own to make after that was settled. The last was to Ann Yates.

I reached her at her UMSL office and set up a meeting. With that done I plunged into my day, one of those desk-bound days that moved slowly.

By four-thirty I was glad to escape into the cold and make the drive to the designated coffee shop. It was tacked onto a strip mall and had a bleak exterior. The inside matched. Calendars, bulletins and posters looked older than the walls they hung on. The front window glass was steamed over, and pungent aromas of fresh coffee, stale doughnuts, and greasy hamburgers set me salivating. I'd had a cellophane bag of peanuts for lunch.

Four of the six tables were taken with students. For a moment I felt a pang for my college days. I remembered the free-wheeling conversations that had been a vital part of each day usually in a grungy setting like this one. I took the table next to the window and realized that my left arm and leg were going to stay cold. Before I could consider a move to the last empty table, it was taken by a laughing group of four.

I had ordered coffee and drunk half of it before Ann arrived. The hamburgers were smelling better.

She looked strained. A frown creased her forehead, and her

shoulders sagged. "I'm sorry I'm late," she said, pulling off her suede gloves, loosening her silk scarf. "A student with a problem caught me on my way out."

I smiled. "Not a problem. I was glad for a chance to relax."

She smiled back but tightly. "Relax? That sounds good. Maybe we should have met at a bar."

"A rough day?" I said, inviting her to tell more.

But she dismissed it. "Yes, but you didn't want to talk about the ups and downs of teaching."

A burly young man with a grin that suggested he was only a puppy lumbered over to take her order. She ordered coffee, and I said more of the same. Something told me the hamburgers couldn't be as good as they smelled.

Ann turned back to me, a more rueful smile on her face. "I know I sound naive, but I find it hard to believe they've let Bishop out." I imagined people all over St. Louis were saying the same.

I looked at her. Our last meeting when Ann had complained about Bill Curtis's share in Aunt M's estate had been fairly tense. I wasn't comfortable with a disagreement. I wished we could return to meeting just for fun. But there was no help for it; this was business.

"I know it's a surprise, Ann," I began, trying to soften my message. "But as I read between the lines, I think the case against Bishop may not be airtight. I don't think the judge would have let him out if it were."

She wasn't soothed; her voice raised a notch. "You mean they may not be able to make the charge stick?"

She might be a lawyer, but she was human, too, and wanted an aunt avenged.

I nodded. "That could happen, of course."

"And?" She correctly read my face.

"And maybe Bishop isn't the one who did it."

The look that crossed her face then made me glad I wasn't one of her students. It was a nuanced blend of disapproval and disappointment. Somehow I felt it was directed at me and not the system.

But she couldn't make the argument that he must be guilty if the cops had arrested him. Even her humanity couldn't take her that far against her legal training. Instead, she switched arguments. "I thought you said Lindstrom was good."

"I think she is. But she might make a mistake. She's only human." I kept my personal thoughts about Lindstrom off my face. I reached out to touch her hand, but her face discouraged me, and I started twirling my coffee mug. "But even if she's done everything perfectly, a case has to be developed. What looks airtight may spring holes. In any case, you know the judge has to treat Bishop as innocent until he's proven guilty."

She was impatient with this speech, but she couldn't really counter it. "I know that. I just hope they'll keep a close eye on him."

"I think you can count on that." I sipped some coffee just to make a pause. "The reason I asked you here is that I've run past our contracted time. Do you want me to continue?"

She frowned. "I don't see the point. Even if the Task Force can't prove it's Bishop, I consider it settled."

I gave her one of my most steady, penetrating looks. As a lawyer she should have recognized it as the address to the jury. "I'm not so certain, Ann. Maybe Bishop killed the others. But I just can't quite shake off the feeling that Rudy Carr's death is connected to Aunt M's."

"Arlene says Detective Schmidt thinks Carr was killed because of some drug deal gone bad."

I nodded and kept the eye lock. "Maybe, but I'm not sure."

"What's changed?"

"I'm not sure I can say clearly. It's a hunch. If Rudy knew something about Aunt M's disappearance, he'd be dangerous."

"Blackmailing Dr. Rolfing?"

"Maybe. Say someone paid Rudy to let Aunt M out. Rudy could have done that."

"You've been talking to Arlene. She's paranoid." But her tone had some good humor in it.

I grinned to show I wasn't without humor myself. "Maybe so. Now that you mention it, Rolfing certainly didn't welcome my questions."

"In real life, who does? It's only Washington media that believes the public has a right to know. The rest of us want to keep our grubby little secrets to ourselves. Who wants to be embarrassed?"

"You're right, of course. Rolfing stands to lose money if Gateway Rest Home's reputation gets tarnished. It isn't always a question of criminality."

She nodded. "So what's the point of pressing on? You didn't find anything out about Bill Curtis, did you?"

I shook my head. "No—unless a malicious sense of humor counts. He's enjoying upsetting the apple cart."

"Well, my mother has calmed me down a bit. Aunt M wasn't really leaving me shut out in the cold, was she?" She gave another rueful grin.

"I can understand if you don't want to spend more money on this." I shrugged. "I just would like not to give up too soon."

She considered me carefully. Finally she said, "Now there's a new tune. I practically begged you—indeed, I did beg you—to take this on. Now am I going to have to pry you off it?"

"The thing is, I want to spend a bit more of your money."

"Oh?" But it wasn't frosty. More intrigued.

"I want to get some people's financial records checked. I would appreciate your not saying anything about this to anyone—Philip, Greg, your parents."

"Are you going to check mine?"

"Do you want me to be thorough?"

For the first time she paid attention to her coffee. She put some sugar in, stirred it slowly—all that while the meter was ticking. "Isn't there an irony here? You're thinking Bishop might not be guilty, and you're back to thinking I am?" She pulled a smile across her lips. I noticed her eyes were a little teary.

"Not at all. I'm trying to make sense of what happened."

"How much will this cost me?" I keep forgetting that the rich stay rich by paying careful attention to money.

I told her my best estimate. But I could tell she'd already decided to agree. With no further hesitation she signed an extension of our contract. She didn't even blink as I asked her to write down the name of her bank and her social security number.

She had news of her own. "The police called yesterday. They released Aunt M's body to us. We're having a private graveside service in Bellefountaine tomorrow. Will you come?"

I said yes to her invitation and she provided me with the details. Neither of us was in the mood for further small talk, and she was frank enough to say so. She said her goodbyes and headed for dinner with Philip and her parents. I called Colleen from the pay phone and asked her to come in early the next morning. I asked about messages. None. Damn Lindstrom. Then I ordered a hamburger.

Chapter Fourteen

Wednesday morning my alarm went off at seven-thirty, and I stretched and turned over. I could hear the wind blowing through the branches of the large tree on the east side of the building against my living room window. It was going to be a cold one, and I was going to spend yet another hour in a cemetery. I tried to organize my thoughts as I stood in the shower. What did I know about this case? What did I need to know? Money. If I had lots of it, I wouldn't be going to work that morning. If there were any motive for Aunt M's murder besides the random rage of the serial killer, then it was money. As Walter frequently says, "Cherchez la cash." Who needed money? That was a simple question. Perhaps even a question I could find the answer to.

When I got to work, Walter had already arrived and brewed a pot of coffee. He and Mike were in his office reviewing video tape made by a security camera. I got some coffee and went to my office.

I called Les Collins, a buddy of Walter's who specializes in financial investigations, for some advice on snooping via the computer. He had several suggestions, including Internet addresses for major banks and credit agencies.

A few minutes later Colleen stuck her head in the door.

"Hi. Sorry, I wasn't here sooner. Joey's truck wouldn't start this morning. I had to take him to work."

"No problem. I've just been doing some preliminary information gathering. Get a cup of coffee and leave the phone on the answering machine."

"Sure. I'll be right back."

I set to writing a telephone script with me starring as a loan officer from Mercantile Bank. When Colleen returned, she hooked up the modem and got connected to the Internet. I explained to her some avenues that Les Collins had suggested.

We picked over the possibilities, and she called a friend who was a computer hacker for additional advice on what was available on the Internet, and I compiled a list of credit agencies.

After a few phone calls in which people were obligingly free with information about who owed whom money, I looked over at Colleen. Her face was rapt as she stared at the Macintosh screen.

She grinned and mumbled to herself as she tapped out another prayer to the information demigod. I had guessed right when I had given her this job. I had chosen the telephone for myself because I assumed I was the better liar, but I was tickled that Colleen really enjoyed snooping and fibbing. She barely looked up from her keyboard when I left for Aunt M's burial.

I'd worn my best gray suit so that I could go directly to Bellefountaine. Ann had told me the family was meeting at eleven at the cemetery's office and would caravan up to the grave site. I slid the Plymouth into line at eleven-o-five just as three cars were pulling out to drive up into the cemetery. I couldn't see into the funeral limo, but Ann, Philip, and Greg were in Philip's Lexus. Bill Curtis was by himself in a black Bronco.

The procession stopped on top of a knoll not that far from where Rita Bellis had been found, a fact I intended to keep to myself. Ann's parents climbed from the limo, followed by Dr. Yates' friend Shirley, who'd helped search for Aunt M, Arlene Dorman, and the young priest who'd presided over the memorial service. A slender young undertaker slipped from the front passenger seat and ushered us onto a green astroturf carpet to the graveside where a small tent sheltered the coffin which waited our arrival.

Under the carpet and snow the terrain was frozen and lumpy. This time Sam Yates and friend Shirley supported Deborah Yates. Everyone wore dark, thick coats and looked somber. Curtis and Arlene had fallen behind, side by side, but they seemed to ignore one another. Arlene turned halfway and gave me a thumbs up sign and a broad smile. I returned the smile but felt a twinge of disloyalty that I was here almost in the bosom of a family that I had dedicated the rest of this day to investigating.

I noted that a low stone curb marked off a larger plot which held a towering Brooks obelisk, and I saw headstones marking the resting places of bygone Brooks. The individual headstones of John the grandfather and of Thomas, Greg's father, were of richly carved marble.

The cold had reined in the handsome young priest. After we'd awkwardly gathered alongside the coffin, he said two introductory sentences and then prayed with merciful brevity. A sharp wind was numbing my legs despite the lining in my best slacks. Unconsciously, we'd all drawn close, seeking warmth and shelter, like sheep in a pen, except for the priest who braved the elements alone. I leaned into Arlene. The wind ruffled the auburn wisps of Curtis's curly hair. The cold muffled the perfumes and colognes emanating from our small huddle. The hairs in my nostrils froze.

I always peek during prayers, usually just to check what's going on. This was a well-behaved group. The other heads were bowed. Perhaps they were tucking their chins into scarves. I stared at the bright spray on Mary Margaret's casket: 'Beloved Sister' said the bright gold ribbon.

When the prayer ended, we filed back to our cars. Ann waited for me. "Thanks for coming," she said and gave my arm a squeeze. For a moment we felt like friends again. I smiled and nodded, and she turned back to Philip.

I watched the family, dry-eyed but solemn, climb back into their cars. I got back into the Plymouth and shivered in its first blast of air. I headed back to Miller Security, eager to resume my investigation of this family. Despite my ambivalence, it was, I assured myself, my best possible tribute to Aunt M.

I picked up a Chicago-style pizza with everything from Talayna's on my way back to the office. Colleen juggled the pizza and the typing without getting sauce on the keyboard or cheese on her chin. I stopped and ate. I can't sound like a bank official with my mouth full of pizza.

At four-thirty we quit and exchanged information. I started with what I'd learned about Dr. Rolfing. "Rolfing's paying exorbitant interest rates on Gateway. The business was making a profit when he bought it in 1985 and has continued to do so for ..." I shuffled through my notes, "...um, about three years. Then he started losing money. It doesn't make much sense. The beds are always full, and he's applying for and receiving about the standard amount from Medicare quarterly. The only unusual things I could find were his bank loan for Gateway and his expenditures on pharmaceuticals."

"Drugs?" Colleen asked.

"Yes. It's an eighty-four bed facility, and he's spending forty thousand a month on medicines. No other nursing home in St. Louis with fewer than a hundred beds spends more than twenty or twenty-one thousand."

Colleen snorted. "Well, he's behind on his child support payments, but he managed to buy a twenty-five thousand dollar car last month." Colleen had learned to be cynical. We spend a fair amount of time tracking down dead-beat dads.

"I think he's losing it. Surely, if anyone audits him, they'll jerk his license." I said, trying to figure a way Rolfing might find it profitable to kill Aunt M.

"What did you find on Greg Brooks?" I asked her.

"Greg lives a bit beyond his visible means of support. The house of cards hasn't fallen yet, but it's bound to happen soon. All his credit cards are at the limit; he's refinanced his house and is still behind on the mortgage. If his investments for his clients are as bad as his own, he'll probably be unemployed soon. He buys almost exclusively high-risk stocks for himself. He's hit big a couple times, but overall, he's lost money every year but one." Colleen shook her head in wonder at human folly. "He also has incredibly high travel expenses and buys a ton of stuff at sporting goods stores."

"Yeah, he's into spelunking."

"So, is his checking account."

"Then two million would help Mr. Brooks quite a bit?"

"Not unless he gets smarter on the market. He'll be through that in four years. Probably less," she said.

I declared a seventh-inning stretch and brought us sodas from the avocado fridge.

"Anything on Bill Curtis?" I asked as I resettled into my chair.

"He's doing okay. He's really conservative with his money." She clearly approved. "Has three employees. Pays himself a straight salary. On paper the pawn shop doesn't make much profit, but he's got some investments, and he owns that building the shop is in."

"But two million dollars might be tempting," I said.

I shuffled through my notes. "Ann checks out okay. She has a trust fund, lives within her salary, reinvests her interest income. She'll be able to retire at forty-five if she likes." I didn't tell Colleen, but I'd felt a wave of relief when I discovered Ann didn't seem to have a financial motive to kill her aunt.

On the other hand, I also didn't tell her my disappointment that Philip Seaton didn't seem to have a motive either. His career path had reversed Ann's. After getting his law degree, he'd taught, then gone into corporate law.

"He's not a millionaire yet, but he's on his way. And clean as a whistle," I reported.

"So he isn't after Ann's money," Colleen said approvingly.

"Seemingly not," I said, not willing to relinquish all my suspicions of Philip.

I changed the subject.

"Thanks for all your work today. You really liked it, didn't you?"

Colleen grinned. "No secrets are safe anymore from computers. It's better than reading your sister's diary."

I spent the next hour typing up my notes on the case and trying to look at everything with fresh eyes. By the time I was finished I had decided to tackle Rolfing again, but that would wait until tomorrow. I heard Colleen leaving and a few minutes later Walter's heavy steps stopped in front of the door. I listened to him grunt as he bent over to put the plaid coat on Mike. Five minutes later I grabbed my own coat and headed home to Harvey.

When I got home, I turned on the evening news and rummaged in the refrigerator looking for something that appealed. I got only as far as the soured milk when something caught my ear, and I rushed back into the living room. Another cemetery murder. A woman, assumed to be homeless, Edna Marie Haley, had been found murdered in Oak Grove Memorial Cemetery on St. Charles Rock Road. A haggard-looking Lindstrom told the young TV reporter that she had no comment at this time; as soon as they'd gathered all the evidence, she would have a comment. She wouldn't answer the reporter's high-pitched query about William Bishop's premature release.

I sank on the couch and stared at the screen. I couldn't believe it. Even though I didn't think Mary Margaret fit in with the others, I thought the serial murders would end with Bishop's arrest. I couldn't fathom that he could kill again. Lindstrom had to have a tail on him. Had he evaded the tail to strangle another woman? If so, there was no doubt that Lindstrom's ass would be in a sling. The entire community would blame the police even though freeing him had been a judge's decision.

A wave of grief washed over me. I had never known Edna Marie Haley, but it was as if I'd been told someone I knew had been murdered. I felt guilty and sad and angry. I couldn't sit still. I grabbed my coat and headed out to Oak Grove Memorial Cemetery.

Of course, when I arrived, I couldn't get anywhere near the place. The rotating blue and red lights of police cars only accentuated the darkness of that unlit portion of St. Charles Rock Road. Oak Grove was the last of three cemeteries that sit side by side. Uniformed cops weren't letting people stop or park anywhere along the highway. I drove by twice, trying to see what was happening.

Finally, I pulled off onto Hanley Road, parked at a dry cleaners, and hiked back to the cemetery. I was grateful the morning's piercing wind had died down. I walked into the back of the cemetery and was able to watch the scene-of-the-crime officers combing a large headstone and surrounding area for evidence. I squatted and leaned my back against a medium gray stone that was engraved with the name Bernard Armbruster. I sent up a quiet thanks to Bernard for sharing his resting place with me. The scene before me was strange and busy, with everyone moving in short, jerky rhythms, in and out of the circle created by three flood lights. Many of the graves around me had artificial flowers or wreaths or evergreen grave blankets. A huge gray stone mausoleum sat farther in the distance, its dome lit by dusk to dawn lights.

A photographer dressed in jeans and a navy pea coat was taking pictures. Three uniformed cops were setting up yellow police-line tape around a grave site. I could see Lindstrom with Neely standing behind her. She was pointing off to the left, and Neely walked several feet in that direction and peered at the ground. He gestured to one of the uniformed officers and was handed a flashlight which played over the grass, then he walked around. Finally, he knelt and peered closely at the brown grass. He gestured again, and the flashlight officer walked over and laid down some yellow police line tape in a rectangle roughly four feet long and two feet wide. Lindstrom went to the man taking pictures and talked to him for several seconds, then she turned and walked, head down, to her car. Presently, Neely followed, and they drove slowly toward the exit. Just looking at her was like watching *An Affair to Remember* all alone on New Year's Eve.

By the time the picture-taker finished, I was thoroughly cold, and my anger was spent. I walked to the front of the cemetery to see if Lindstrom had left. I couldn't see her department-issue car anywhere, so I turned to walk back to mine. As I passed behind the main gate, I noticed a tall column between the entrance and exit. Around the bottom were engraved the words: Liberty, Justice, Humanity.

I got back into the Plymouth and headed over to the New Life Shelter. Maybe I could find someone who knew Edna Marie Haley.

There, I parked on the street right in front of the door and watched several small knots of men huddle. One group was surreptitiously sharing a quart-sized brown bag. To the left of that group stood one person alone. I couldn't determine the gender. There was a tangle of black hair, a muffler wound around the face, and an old black cloth coat. Sticking out the bottom of the coat were a pair of work pants and dirty tennis shoes. I got out of the car and walked over to the figure. When I got close enough to say hello, he or she turned and scuttled around the corner. I didn't want to approach the drinking men, so I walked to the other side of the large shelter and up to two hunched figures. We stood in silence for a beat, but neither ran from me. I cleared my throat and asked if they had heard about the cemetery murders. The taller one responded immediately.

"Yes, indeed. Yes. Yes, I did. That was horrible and after the fire, too. I told them not to. It was so bad and momma was so mad.

She liked to skin us alive. I told 'em. Yes. Yes. Yes. Yes."

I tried again. "Did you stay at this shelter Wednesday night?"

"No, ma'am. No, no. No, this place is new. Just been here today. No, no, it wasn't me. No, sir. That just wasn't it. You know that top is gone. Like a top in the night. You know how it is. Un-huh. Gone for good now. Yes, indeedy. That's right. Gone like a top." He stopped and nodded in agreement with himself. I looked at the shorter figure. She was staring intently at her brown work boots which were unlaced.

"Did you stay here Wednesday night?"

"No."

"Where did you stay?"

"The park."

"Why not here? It was cold."

"Not so bad. You can only stay here three nights in a row. Then you got to go somewhere else."

"Did you know Edna Marie Haley?"

The man broke in again. "That top is gone. Yes. Yes. Yes, gone a night. For good now. You didn't see it, but I did. I was there. I know how it is. Yes, indeedy."

I re-addressed the woman, "Did you know Edna, or Sophie or Lubbie or Rita?"

"No."

"Have you heard anything about the murders?"

"Don't go with strangers. They told us at the mission."

"That sounds like good advice. Does your friend need to be in the hospital?"

"No. He just got out Monday."

"Does he take his medicine?"

"How's he going to get medicine? He hasn't got a medical card. He's okay. I'll make sure he gets in tonight." I handed her a twenty and thanked her. She shook her head and crumpled the bill in her hand.

I hadn't learned anything about the killer, but my urgency about this case had doubled. Protecting the living suddenly loomed larger than avenging the dead.

It didn't occur to me until I was home that a twenty-dollar bill might well make her a target in the shelter. I pulled the covers over my head and listened to Harvey's purr until I fell asleep.

153

Chapter Fifteen

On Friday, Ben Able, NPR's local weather forecaster, said the temperatures would top out at fifty-one degrees, but that most of the day would be cloudy and chilly because of gusty winds. I believed him. I can never figure out why a December fifty-one feels too cold, but a March fifty-one encourages me to run about in my shirt sleeves.

I was up early and had time for two cups of coffee with the *Post*. It was clear from the paper's reporting that William Bishop wasn't a suspect for this latest crime and that made him less of a suspect for the others. I flicked on the TV. St. Louis's morning anchors are pretty steady folk, but ratings affect coverage. A reporter on one station managed to suggest that Bishop's release on bail had resulted in the fifth murder. Lindstrom had admitted to a reporter that a copy cat killer might have murdered Edna Marie Haley.

By the time I'd reached work my frustrations over the case were running high. But I put my mind to the paper work on my desk and looked forward to an afternoon appointment at a warehouse on south Broadway that was thinking of upgrading its security. I was restless enough to pace, but I stuck to my chair as though I'd been superglued—that old Army discipline learned while standing post.

I was two hours into good behavior when Colleen buzzed me and informed me that Detective Lindstrom was there to see me. An unexpected ripple surged up from the base of my spine. Attraction and repulsion at the same time. How I wanted to see her again— and again and again. But also I felt invaded in my lair. I hadn't invited her to my office—in fact, I hadn't invited her to my home a week ago. And she hadn't called. Shit. Colleen waited patiently for an answer. I imagined Lindstrom's cool stare at Colleen. The palm that clenched around my telephone was sweaty. "Okay, Colleen. Tell her I'll be out to get her in a minute." I took a deep breath. Then another. Ran my fingers through my hair. Pulled my shoulders back. None of it helped.

Lindstrom was constitutionally unable to look shabby, but she did look dispirited. She looked like a woman hip deep in corpses and political heat and thwarted by judicial and criminal intentions.

I'd been reading and watching the press chewings she'd been taking, and I imagined some high-powered politicos were leaning on her as well. A tendril of sympathy crossed my mind. She really was in a bad spot.

She gave me a low-wattage grin. "I'm the one with the problems, Darcy. Why is your hair standing on end?" Colleen giggled.

I reached up and patted down the damage my earlier finger-combing had done. "Come on back, Lindstrom."

She settled herself gracefully into one of my oak clients' chairs. I asked if she'd like coffee. She would. Cream, no sugar.

I grabbed my cup and walked back to the kitchen, located my least favorite mug, a white plastic one with MONSANTO in blocky red letters. I tipped half and half into both cups and picked up the coffee pot. My hand was shaking. How dare she? What did she want? To pump me for information, arrange another quickie? To check out how I reacted to her?

I took the coffee back to my office and slammed hers onto the desk.

She started without preamble. "The case against Bishop was unraveling before this last murder, Darcy. Bishop found a pal to provide an alibi for the first murder. You'll keep this confidential?"

"Sure," I sputtered before I realized that the question was insulting. I lost my concentration for just a moment as I looked steadily into her blue eyes, thought about tracing that chiseled jaw line with my finger, fantasized kisses above the collar of her dark brown turtleneck.

She quickly refocused my attention. "Do you still think the Mary Margaret Brooks case doesn't fit with these killings?"

I ran over my argument for her, stressing Rudy Carr's murder. I told her about the call to Rudy the day he was killed and that he'd expected to come into some money. I told her about Rolfing's financial woes and Gateway Rest Home's missing medicines. I ended with the fact that one member of the Brooks' clan was on shaky financial ground.

"You can't withhold evidence that obstructs an investigation," she reminded me. She knew I was hedging.

"I know," I said, trying to sound calmer than I was. I definitely have a law and order streak. Why else did I get a thrill from nabbing employees who stole goods from warehouses or embezzled funds? On the other hand, there was this strong rebellious streak that loved thumbing my nose at authority. Lots of cops have it, but I think maybe Lindstrom doesn't. Or is it buried, deeply, alongside her sense of humor and her sense of sexual ethics?

"I called Detective Schmidt from the Vinita Park police and

talked with him. He thinks Carr's death was drug-related," she said.

"I don't blame him. On the surface it looks good. Rudy probably made some small change in the drug trade. But I think maybe he was killed because he knew how Aunt M got out of Gateway Rest Home. Maybe he knew who wanted her out. Maybe he even helped."

She stirred her coffee. The brisk, minty scent I was starting to associate with her wafted over the hot cup.

I had a question of my own. "Why do you think it's possible this latest killing is a copy cat thing? Do you have some evidence?"

"Evidence is a tricky thing. We're back to the anything is possible stage." She attempted a smile. "Except it is not possible that Edna Marie Haley was killed by Bishop. Not only was he closely watched, he spent most of the evening in Neely's company."

I raised an eyebrow.

"Like a lot of small time crooks, he likes to talk. So when Neely dropped by, our William Neville spent the evening spinning yarns about himself and his exploits and his theories for world order. He doesn't like the homeless. He is contemptuous of old women. But he didn't spend Wednesday night murdering Edna Marie Haley."

"Small time crook?"

She shook her head like someone ducking an annoying fly. "Don't hold me to an ACLU standard here. We think he fences some hot goods—not steadily. Just opportunistically."

"Do you think he killed any of these women?"

She sighed. "I did think so at first." She ticked off points on her fingers. "He was heard threatening Lubbie when she loitered in front of his shop. In his back room at the bookshop he had rope of the kind used in the killings." She caught my look and answered. "Not a rare type but still a good link. We're still trying to match fibers in the lab. He has the right kind of vehicle."

"Which is?"

"A van like newspaper carriers use. Ideal for transporting bodies. I'm talking too much." She shrugged again, but the weariness didn't roll off her shoulders, even as she reached across my desk and clasped my forearm. I tried to ignore the tingle that started because it was obvious from her face that she just wanted to assure my attention. "And don't you dare feel sorry for his being falsely accused. Let me tell you, Darcy, this man is glorying in the thought that half of St. Louis is sure he's a serial killer. He thinks that makes him sexy and strong in their eyes. Trust me."

The distaste in her tone made it clear that she wasn't as detached from her job as I'd imagined her to be. 'Trust me' had a nice ring to it, but I doubted she knew what it meant. Obviously her years as a homicide cop had squeezed closed her trust mechanism. Trust was a one-way currency she used to get what she wanted from suspects and witnesses. She'd released my forearm and took another sip of Colleen's coffee.

"I know Bishop. Well, slightly. My friend Patrick and I like to cruise bookstores." I saw her brows lift. "For books. We both like books." Her brows didn't come down. "On Saturdays, just for something to do," I finished lamely.

Maybe she lacked social skills. She left me hanging on those remarks, then glanced at her watch. "I need to move along. Neely and I are going out to do more questioning of the homeless. The usual drills."

"Getting much cooperation?"

"It varies. Some of them are zonked on cheap wine or pills. There are some reports of aliens. Some cooperate by saying what they think we want to hear."

"Where are you asking questions?"

She shrugged. "Stay out of it, Darcy. Even without the serial killer, these aren't safe places."

"Well, the shelters, I thought—Larry Rice's place and the Cathedral," I said defensively, trying to deflect her attention from my ploy.

"Neely and I have got it covered," she said firmly. I did bite my tongue and stop "Edna Marie Haley wouldn't think so" from coming out. I don't think she had a clue how arrogant she was. In a funny way she was protecting me. A better person would have relaxed and been grateful. Perhaps a person who hadn't been taken for a roller coaster ride, then dumped at dawn's early light.

"What you do know about this guy is that he's taking lots of risks," I said striving to keep bitterness out of my voice. "Using victims he doesn't know, hauling the bodies off to cemeteries. And now—killing again after Bishop was let out. He should have stopped. Surely he knew Bishop was being watched?"

"It would seem obvious. And this killer is a control freak as well, so he'll be seeking out all the information he can. Maybe, at this point, he can't stop. If that's the case, he'll make more mistakes."

"Why do you say he's a control freak? Does that fit with all the risk-taking?"

"Sure. You can tell he needs to feel in control. The careful placement of the bodies, the choice of garroting. That's a control kill, not a passionate one."

"A control-obsessed, risk-taking misogynist?"

157

Lindstrom sighed. "I don't know. He doesn't rape them. So I'm not sure we're looking for an overt woman-hater. The victims aren't people to him, just symbols to manipulate. To me, he's not sending a gender-based message."

I thought she was naively apolitical, but I changed the subject. "We're both referring to the killer as 'he.' Any chance it is a woman?"

"Not very likely, really. When a woman does more than one victim, it is generally within the family. Poisons her husband and mother and old auntie with anti-freeze or something like that."

"I wish you luck, Lindstrom. The whole city hopes you get lucky."

"The old women need me to get lucky," she said. She stood up and looked down on me. She looked tired but not as dispirited as I'd thought on first seeing her. "And I will. This guy is going to slip up. Hard work is going to pay off."

I thought I was going to let her walk out then. But it boiled out of me almost against my will. "What in the hell is going on here?"

She looked up, her face completely blank for a second and then a narrowing of her eyes. "What, Darcy?"

"What was last Friday night about?"

She turned and glanced at the open office door. So I strode over and slammed it. Colleen isn't an eavesdropper, but this might get too loud for her to avoid hearing. I turned to face Lindstrom.

"Why don't you tell me why you are angry?" she asked, folding her arms across her chest and leaning back on the edge of my desk.

"Angry? I'm angry because you drop by for sex, ignore me for a week, then arrive uninvited and unannounced to pump me about murder without so much as a thank you, ma'am."

"Thank you for the great sex, Darcy. I enjoyed it." She couldn't keep the grin off her face.

Suddenly I wanted her out of there. I wasn't positive that I could keep the tremor out of my voice. Or keep from throttling her. "Is it being a cop, Lindstrom, or were you always an emotionally stunted asshole?"

"Why does enjoying sex make me emotionally stunted?" The surface was all you would expect from an Ice Queen.

"Forget it." I opened the door and waved her out. This was going nowhere.

She walked over to me and closed the door, then put both hands on my shoulders. "Darcy, you're pissed at me because I haven't called. I'm sorry. It's been the week from hell on these murders. But you didn't call me either. You've never tried to get to

158

know me as a person. And don't even try to pretend you haven't been coming on to me for a long time. So we both wanted it, and it happened. Don't set yourself up as the ravished maiden."

"Well, it won't 'happen' again, believe me."

She blinked and dropped her hands from my shoulders. "Okay, if that's the way you want it. Take care." She walked out of the office and shut the door very quietly behind her.

I slumped into my chair and played fifteen games of solitaire before my curiosity and urge to rub Lindstrom's nose in the dirt prodded me back to my case notes. I had lost my utter conviction that Lindstrom would find the killer. I needed to work harder on this case. Aunt M would have expected it of me.

Overnight it had gotten much colder and snowed about three inches. A mild warmup followed, creating a gray and drippy Saturday. The snow had been scraped from the street, but was piled against my curb. Later that day I was going to go back to some of the homeless shelters, and I thought I might as well take some of my castoffs. My foot landed in a charcoal pile of ice and snow as I tried to toss a garbage bag of clothing into the backseat. I looked down at the sludge of winter and sighed. Most of it shook off my foot, but some had gone into my shoe, and if I didn't go in and change right now, my right foot would be wet and freezing all day. So I trudged upstairs again and found a clean pair of socks and another pair of tennis shoes.

I was on my way to see Dr. Rolfing at Gateway. When Arlene had called back the day before, she had said he would be in this Saturday morning, probably until about noon. I hadn't had much time to think about Rolfing since Colleen and I had done our research. I had been focusing on Edna Marie Haley. But as I drove north on Grand, by the hospitals, I wondered if perhaps Rudy Carr had stumbled onto Rolfing's double orders of drugs. That would be another explanation for his death, although it would mean it was unrelated to Aunt M's. Perhaps Rudy had been Rolfing's retail outlet. Rudy had only a few drugs at a time, according to his girlfriend Nikki, but perhaps that was just the portion he kept for himself. That, too, might explain his expectation of having more money— although it didn't fit with his actual poverty.

I had asked Arlene not to tell Rolfing I was coming; I hoped she kept her word. Gateway had its old familiar smell. The blond wasn't on duty this morning, so I stepped up to Rolfing's door and tapped on it twice. He mumbled "Come in," so I did.

"Good morning, Dr. Rolfing, I've come to ask you a few more questions." I helped myself to the chair in front of his desk, as I could see from his facial expression that he didn't intend to invite me to sit.

"Ms. Darcy, I'm afraid you've come at a bad hour, I have some rather pressing business and won't be able to spare you the time this morning. Perhaps you could call on Monday..."

I interrupted his brush-off. "Dr. Rolfing, I don't intend to wait until Monday to ask why Gateway spends twice as much as other nursing home on drugs. I can ask you or I can ask my friend at the *Post*."

"I have nothing to hide, so your threat of exposure does not intimidate me."

"Then there is a straight-forward explanation of why you order so many drugs and how you turned a profitable business into a shambles?"

"Someone has misled you. The nursing home buys no more medications than those needed by the patients here. As for our profits, it has been a difficult period for all long-term health-care providers. The gap between what it costs to care for a patient and our reimbursement from Medicare and Medicaid grows each year. You'll find that two nursing homes in the city of St. Louis closed down last year due to these financial pressures."

"What do you know about Rudy Carr's death?"

"Exactly the same things you do—what I read in the newspaper and what the investigating police officer told us."

"So you had no relationship with him other than here at work, you never saw him outside Gateway?"

"Not even once, and I hardly spoke to him here. Marie supervises the aides. Now, if you don't mind, I'm going to have to ask you to go."

"I don't intend to leave this alone until I know why you buy so many drugs every month. If you're selling them, I'll make sure that is known."

"Ms. Darcy, this institution is carefully monitored by all the appropriate agencies. I assure you that if anything were wrong, you would not be the first to notice it. I will take action to protect myself against harassment or libel. Now will you leave, or shall I call security?"

"Did Rudy let Aunt M out of the nursing home the night she was killed?"

For an answer, Rolfing picked up his phone and asked that security be sent to his office immediately.

I leaned across his desk, resting my right hand on the leather blotter. "Look, Rolfing, all you have to do is answer one more question for me. Where were you the night Rudy Carr was murdered?"

The look he sent was hateful, but he answered. "I spent that evening emceeing a charity variety show to benefit muscular dystrophy. We held it at Cheshire Inn. It ran quite late. Afterwards a small group of us—doctors and wives—had a midnight supper and drinks. Does that satisfy you?"

Actually it disappointed me. I had been warming up to the notion of Rolfing as suspect. This alibi would be easy to check.

"Thank you, Dr. Rolfing." I removed my fist from his blotter. "You know you ought to check with a better security agency. Your boys are slow."

I let myself out before they arrived.

Chapter Sixteen

I left Gateway and realized I had to go back to my apartment before I did more foraging at the shelters. I did feel safer in my grubbies. And I thought if Patrick had worked the early shift at the bookstore, he might be up for going with me.

Harvey threw himself at me when I came in the door. I knew he wasn't hungry; he hadn't finished his breakfast yet. So maybe he was lonely. I sat down on the couch, and he landed in my lap. We had a bit of a chat about the case and matters closer to the cat heart. His opinion was that I should note carefully how each of the suspects smelled and report back to him. Harvey was certain that much killing would leave an olfactory residue. After our chat, he curled up on my lap for a nap. Gently I picked him up and put him on the couch and went to change my clothes.

Patrick hadn't answered his door when I came in earlier. I tried again as I left, but still no luck. I consulted my street guide and headed for the Salvation Army shelter. I stopped at a Quick Trip on the way and bought five packs of cigarettes.

The clouds were low, and snow was predicted for tonight and tomorrow. For the twentieth time, I replayed the scene in my office with Lindstrom. This time she confessed to being cold and controlling and asked me if I knew a good therapist. On the twenty-first time she threw me down on the desk and ravished me again. But this time when I touched her, she exploded time after time.

By the time I arrived at the shelter, the wind had picked up and ragged leaves and scraps of fast-food bags were swirling on the sidewalk. The shelter wasn't open yet, and no one was lurking outside waiting for the doors to open. So I flipped back in my notebook and found the address for the soup kitchen that Nina had given me. It was housed on the first floor of a crumbling brick two-story in the Hyde Park neighborhood in the shadow of Holy Trinity Church. It was just before serving time, and there was a line outside the door.

I parked the Plymouth around back in a spot set aside for volunteers and walked to the front of the old brown brick building. The smell seeping out of the structure wasn't all that appetizing. It was a mixture of cabbage and beef that was a day too old. I got in line behind a short black woman wrapped in an old army issue raincoat.

"What time do they open the doors?"

"When they get ready. Most days about four."

"What do you have to do to get a meal?"

"Just show up. They supposed to have you on a list, but they done gave that up. Too many mix ups."

I nodded and rubbed my arms with my hands. "What time does the Salvation Army shelter open up?"

"Seven, but you better be there before that, you want a bed tonight. Cold nights they fill up pretty fast. Where you stay last night?" I hadn't expected that question.

"I've been staying with a friend, but he got kicked out. Now I've got no place, really. I'm scared. They haven't caught that guy who's killing women and dumping them in the cemeteries."

"That's the least of your worries. You just don't talk to strange men, you'll be all right."

"Did you know any of those women?"

"Un-huh. They say he's just getting the ones that sells themselves. I won't ever do that. I'll get by till my check comes."

"You think he's somebody who works at the shelter?"

"No, that's just talk. You'll be all right."

Suddenly the line started to move, and the woman turned around to shuffle forward. I debated for a moment and then stepped forward, too, keeping my place in line. I turned to see that there were four people behind me in line. When I reached the door, the smell of cabbages was much stronger. We shuffled down a short, dark hallway and then into a large, open room. There were twelve long tables and metal folding chairs on both sides of each table to the right of where we stood. To the left of the line there were three tables spaced about four feet apart which constituted the serving line. At the first table was a woman pouring coffee and some vile-looking orange drink. I picked up a cup of coffee. At the next table we were offered trays and plastic spoons and forks. I nodded and smiled at the woman who offered mine, but she didn't look at me. At the third table we were handed a bowl of soup; its main ingredient was cabbage. At the final table they had either bologna or peanut butter sandwiches and some apples. I took peanut butter and looked around for an open table. I avoided the table that the woman ahead of me chose; I wanted to talk to someone new.

There was one seat left at a table that held both black and white men and women. I asked if the seat was saved. A white man who looked to be in his thirties with a scraggly goatee shook his head and gestured for me to sit down. The talk that swirled around me was mostly about the weather. Exactly how cold it had gotten last night compared to the night before and last year and the big freeze in '89. Then there were complaints about the soup, which wasn't as bad as I'd expected. Finally a white man two chairs to my left mentioned the cemetery murderer. He, too, thought the murderer was choosing victims who were willing to trade sex for money. But a young black woman across from him violently objected. "That isn't true. I knew Rita and she never did that. She wasn't a whore. You don't know anything about it."

The man with the goatee jumped in. "If they won't have sex with him, he does it to them after he kills them."

This was met with stony silence, and I for one lost the courage to go on with my soup. I sipped coffee and looked around the large room. There were many older people here, but the majority seemed to be young women with toddlers and children. There was one young white woman at the next table who couldn't have been more than fifteen with a bi-racial baby on her lap. The baby was swaddled in what looked like several layers, but the young mother had only a sweater and a windbreaker.

Sitting across from her was a white woman in her thirties who was wrapped warmly, including a white silk scarf. Something about her looked familiar, but I couldn't place it. She looked up, so I had to move my gaze to another table. Soon the teenager with the baby got up to leave, and I got up to follow her. I picked up my tray and followed her to the table set up in front of the kitchen door where two volunteers were scraping the leftovers into the trash. We put our trays down at the same time, and I let her step ahead of me toward the door. When we hit the sidewalk, I asked her if she wanted a cigarette. She narrowed her blue eyes at me but nodded. I opened a pack of cigarettes and offered one to her. Silently I offered her a light, and she juggled the baby to light up. When her cigarette was lit, she waved the smoke away from the baby and looked back at me.

"That's a cute baby you have. How old is it?"

"He's three months. Be four next week."

"Have you got a place to go tonight?"

"Sure, I haven't slept outside since I had the baby. I got to take care of him, don't I?" It sounded like bluff to me, but I pressed on.

"Have you heard anything about the cemetery murders?'

"Those women who got killed in the cemetery?" She squinted through a trail of smoke.

"Yes, I was wondering if you were afraid he might try to get you."

"Nah, those were all old ladies. I was at a shelter one night with that Lubbie. She was a crazy old coot. They probably all were.

Crazy to go off to a cemetery."

"They weren't killed at the cemetery, they were just dumped there."

"Well, anyway they were crazy to go off with somebody they didn't know. Probably comes from sleeping in the park. I don't do that no more." She shifted the infant to her other hip. Small delicate flakes of snow began to fall around us.

"Can you get a place when your next AFDC check comes?"

She looked at the sidewalk and scuffed the side of her tennis shoe against the concrete as if she were scraping something off. "They cut me off last month."

"Why?"

"'Cause somebody told them I wasn't living there no more. You got to have an address to get a check. So, I gotta sign up again as soon as I get a place." She looked into the distance as if she could see the home she hoped to find. "Look, thanks for the cigarette, but I gotta get on the next bus. It's too cold out here for Jamal." I offered her bus fare, but she shook her head. I held out the pack of cigarettes and she took them and walked up to the corner. I watched as she sat herself inside the plexiglass structure.

I stuck my hands in my pockets and trudged toward the opposite corner. Where had I seen the white woman in the scarf before? She was familiar, but I couldn't place her. I stood at the corner debating whether to go back and try to question her. Gradually, the previously innocuous flakes were growing larger, and the wind was picking up.

I turned and walked back into the mission. The woman that looked familiar was just sitting, sipping coffee and gazing into space. I pulled out the chair beside her and sat down.

"Hi, my name's Meg."

She glanced at me and nodded. I couldn't place her. And now that I was closer, I wasn't sure I had really ever seen her before. But I figured I'd never find out unless I asked. "I'm a private investigator. My client has hired me to find out about the cemetery murders. I was wondering if you'd heard anything about them."

She sniffed and pulled at the neck of her sweater. "You don't look like no cop."

"I'm not a cop. I'm a private investigator." I tried to think of some way to describe it, but for some reason, I was at a loss to explain my job.

"Edna was a friend of mine," she said.

I leaned forward in my chair. "When was the last time you saw her?"

She thought for a moment. "Wednesday. The day she was

killed. It was after noon. Edna had some money, and we both had a hot dog from the cart across from the park. She went back to sit awhile on the bench. Her bones were aching. I was scrounging around trying to find some cans." The woman shook her head. "The last thing I said to her was 'That was good, but we'll both have the heart burn tonight.'" She again shook her head, this time at the ordinariness of this last communication with her friend.

"Wasn't she still on the bench when you came back?"

"No, last I saw, she was talking to her friend."

"Someone you know?"

"No, but they were laughing together, so I guess Edna knew him." Her fingers reached up to touch her scarf. At once I knew: it wasn't the woman that was familiar; it was that scarf. I had seen it, or one like it, somewhere recently.

"Have the police talked to you about this?"

She shook her head.

"So, you think she went somewhere with this friend?"

"I don't know. We didn't exactly keep that close tabs. She might have just gotten on a bus to get out of the cold. Her arthritis was bothering her that day."

"What did the man look like?"

"Oh, just an ordinary guy. Sorta young."

"White? Black?"

"White guy."

"How was he dressed?"

"Overcoat. Jeans. He wasn't scroungy."

"May I ask where you got that scarf?"

She touched it again and looked away. There was a long pause while she considered. "Do you think that man killed her?"

"He might have. Or he might know where she was or who she was with right before she died."

"I think it's his. It was on the bench after they were gone."

"Would you let me buy it from you?"

She sighed and looked down into her coffee cup. "It sort of reminds me of Edna." I waited. She jerked it off and laid it on the table in front of me, pushed back her chair, and started for the door. I reached out to grab her sleeve but wasn't fast enough. "Wait! Do you know Leanna?"

"I've seen her around. Don't worry. None of us are old enough. Yet." With that she headed for the door at top speed. Every head turned. It seemed that chasing her would be an unpopular move. I sat quietly a moment staring at the scarf, urging my brain to dredge up the connection. I stuffed the scarf into my pocket.

It was snowing with a grim purpose when I got back outside.

Edna's friend was nowhere to be seen. I willed the universe to make a warm and safe space for her and Jamal and his mother tonight. I glanced at my watch as I stepped off the curb. I heard a roar and felt a mild vibration on the street and looked up into the front grill of a black utility vehicle. I leapt to the left, but there was no where to go. I felt the hood hit my right shoulder and something cracked.

Chapter Seventeen

I woke up and dozed, woke up and dozed in great sweeping loops. Each waking loop grew wider, longer. Then the weight of my eyelids pulled me back down each time into some mushy consciousness where I heard murmurs, felt my body as a solid ache, finally slipped deeper into letting go. Gradually each loop upward toward the surface brought sharper pains.

I woke up to the sharp smell of alcohol, the dry-throated hoarseness of mouth-breathing, and mellow brown eyes peering into mine.

"Are you back?" she asked with a smile. Her hands were clasping my right hand.

I couldn't find my words or my voice. I sent her a mental smile; I couldn't make my lips move either. I fell off that edge and back into a loop.

Then the brown eyes were back. I could pry my eyes open and see them peering into mine sympathetically. The brown face was oval and lovely with just the lightest touch of lipstick emphasizing the particularly lovely mouth. A nurse. No. The white lab coat, the stethoscope. A doctor.

She was talking, confirming this. "Blink if you're hearing me."

"I hear you," I croaked. I wasn't showing off. I didn't know how to coordinate a blink yet. My reception was still blurry.

The lovely lips stretched into a truly beautiful smile. "I'm Dr. Moore. You're a lucky woman. Nothing's broken. And you're alive."

She took my hand into hers: cool, smooth, gentle hands holding mine in a gentle, reassuring clasp. I was rocking atop easy waves.

"Do you remember what happened last night?"

I started to shake my head; all the rocks and pebbles lumbered forward in a great landslide. I think I frowned.

"Your head hurts?"

"Yes."

"You've got a nasty knot on your head from hitting the concrete. We had to relocate your shoulder. You have serious bruises that go deep on your legs. You have several ugly abrasions. You are going to hurt like hell tomorrow."

She said that in the way doctors have. Now you've got yourself in a fine pickle, and it's only right that you hurt like hell. She was so lovely I forgave her. I have always been afraid that I wasn't up to the requirements of an interracial relationship, but I was pretty seriously in love.

"You're going to be all right. You need plenty of rest. We're going to send you home with your brother."

My brother? How did they get my brother's number? Had he flown in from Savannah?

"What happened?"

She frowned for the first time. The lovely light of smiling faded from her face. But she was still wonderful. I was ready to pledge my troth. "A car hit you."

A flutter started in the corner of my brain. A car.

"Can I get you anything?"

"A date." It came out in a harsh croak. My eyes closed. I forced them open.

She was looking at me calmly. "My, my. I can see how you might get yourself in trouble from time to time."

The next time I opened my eyes I was looking into familiar blue eyes. Well, recognizable blue eyes. Lindstrom was peering down into my face.

Her own face looked sober, as though she were attending my funeral. I felt like Huck Finn and Tom Sawyer, seeing my own demise and the reaction to it. She was a striking figure, tall and straight-spined, even at a sickbed. She was not clasping my hand or murmuring sympathetically.

She said, "Ah, you're awake. How do you feel, Darcy?"

"Not at my best, Lindstrom." But my lids weren't as heavy, and I felt that I had a good idea where the several abrasions were.

A half-smile tugged at one side of her mouth. The well-chiseled mouth residing above the well-chiseled chin. All very Nordic and perfect. "I can't stay long."

"That's too bad."

"They won't let me."

"Tell 'em who's boss."

The other side of the mouth tugged. The two parts together made a complete smile. "You're feeling better."

"No, I'm not." I was disappointed that she hadn't grasped the situation.

"Do you remember what happened?"

"A car came up fast. I think it hit me."

"Did you see it?"

"Black."

"Did you see the license plate?"

I tried to call it up. I couldn't retrieve it. I remembered not to shake my head. "No."

"The driver?"

"No."

"Anything else you can recall that would help us?"

"No." I lifted a hand. "Sorry."

She took my hand and placed it back down on the scratchy sheet. "Don't worry." She patted the hand and let it go. The doctor had a better bedside manner.

"There was a homeless man who saw it happen. You were lucky. The car aimed for you, but didn't get a clean swipe," she said.

"Too bad."

Lindstrom didn't smile. "You didn't listen to me about letting us do the job of interviewing the homeless."

"You should not scold an injured party."

She looked at me sternly. No smiles. "Do you have any other case going that might have provoked this attack?"

"No. Wait a minute." I needed to think and thinking hurt. The woman with the scarf. "Where are my clothes and stuff?"

"In the closet, why?"

"Get them out. Is there a white scarf there?"

She rummaged a minute, then pulled the scarf out of the narrow closet. "This?"

I sighed. I hadn't lost it after all. I explained to Lindstrom how I had gotten the scarf and what the woman who had worn it had said to me. Lindstrom held the scarf tenderly. "I'll take this. Anything else? Are you holding out on me?"

"No. Don't browbeat me. I'm an ailing woman."

"You're a lucky woman." She looked at me sternly some more. Then she patted my hand again and said, "I'll be back later today."

Instead, later, I woke up to a truly familiar pair of blue eyes. He was perched on the other bed, which was otherwise empty. His blond hair and clean-shaven face were reassuring; I smelled his cologne cutting through the alcohol. "Patrick."

"Hi, sis," he said softly.

I thought about it. "How'd you find me?"

"Don't you remember? In your billfold you have my name and number in case they can't reach Betty."

I thought about that. How had he explained our different surnames? "Are you my step-brother?"

"No. I told them about your short, unhappy marriage."

"I see." I turned it over. "I'm sorry they had to know about that.

170

I've kept it secret so long."

"I know. I thought even you might have forgotten about it." He scooted his rear off the bed and came over to my side. "Will it hurt if I give you a kiss?"

"Are you getting mushy on me?" I reached up and grabbed a hand and tugged him down. He kissed my forehead gently, a perfect brotherly kiss that my brother never would have given me.

"You didn't look so great the first hours, but now they say you're going to be fine. They're going to send you home this evening. In my care. You'll have to promise to behave."

"Help me sit up."

He had had practice with hospital beds, and he wasn't one to run away. He cranked the head of the bed up, fluffed my pillows behind me, making sure my head still rested in its nest. "How's that?"

"Terrific. Will you stay?"

"I've already called in sick."

Patrick was perfect; he didn't once turn on the television. We chatted in a desultory way, and I napped again, but only in five and ten minute bouts. He didn't ask about the case, and I didn't ask either. I knew thinking about it would make my head hurt. Besides, I suspected my thinker wasn't up to my usual perspicacious conclusions. We were actually chatting about our planned Christmas Eve at Betty's house when Lindstrom came in again.

"Hi, Darcy, remember anything yet?"

"Good afternoon, Detective Lindstrom. I'm feeling a bit better, but not at my best yet."

She grinned. "Okay, what still hurts?"

"Every fiber of my being hurts. Getting hit by a car is not recommended."

Patrick got up and pulled the chair from the other bed over for her.

"Thanks." She perched on the edge of the seat.

"I think it was a Jeep, or a Jeep-like thing. Maybe a Bronco or an Explorer. The grill and bumper were definitely chrome. Not dirty."

"Nothing on the plate?"

"It was a Missouri tag."

She frowned but managed to restrain herself from scolding me for not jotting down the license plate just before it hit me. "They're letting you go tonight?"

"So they say. The doctor is supposed to see me one more time."

"Have you got someone to stay with you?"

"Yes, she has." Patrick answered before I got a chance. Clearly he saw the question as an insult to one of us.

"We'll have a patrol car by as often as we can. Just to keep an eye out. Don't do anything more on this case. And I'll need whatever notes you have written up."

The sheer effrontery of it had me speechless. It was times like this that PIs need quick and cutting replies to domineering cops. Unfortunately, my riposte department was closed down for repairs. I just said, "Huh?"

She looked at me without a blink. "You heard me, and you know I'm right as well. I'll stop by your apartment tonight." She pushed the chair back and turned to leave.

"Bye, Detective Lindstrom, thanks for stopping in," Patrick said. I don't know what I'd do without the boy.

So it looked like Lindstrom was just going to pretend our little foray into the personal hadn't happened. I could pretend, too. Or try to get her to see the error of her ways. Or slap her. Or get drunk and trash her to all my friends. For now I figured pretending was a pretty good choice.

About forty-five minutes later my fiancee, alluring in her white physician's coat, opened the door, and flashed her famous smile.

"How are you feeling?"

"Awful. Are you going to give me something for the pain?"

"Yes, you should take acetaminophen or ibuprofen every four hours. That's a Tylenol or Advil."

"That's all?"

"Yes, that will do it. The pain is your body's way of telling you to lie still and rest. You should listen to it. Nothing more athletic than walking slowly to the bathroom for the next forty-eight hours. Make a follow-up appointment with your physician within the next seventy-two hours."

"I think I should see you. I don't really have a doctor."

She smiled again. "Sorry, I'm an intern here at the hospital, I don't have a practice yet."

"I could come back here to see you."

She shook her head and glanced at Patrick, then looked directly at me. "Listen, girl, I'm happily married, and you'd better think about your head and not your hormones for the next couple of days. Let that policewoman catch the bad guys. You go home and rest." She used that thing-a-ma-bob to look into my eyes one more time and patted my shoulder on her way out. The end of another great romance.

Patrick took me home and tucked me into bed. He must have stayed, but you couldn't prove it by me. I slept straight through the night.

The next morning, Monday, I stretched my limbs tenderly. I tried to turn my head to look at the clock on my bedside table. That was a mistake. I eased my torso upward and shifted my hips gently back toward the headboard. With a few shifts and a couple deep breaths I was able to turn and look at the clock—ten a.m. I knew I couldn't go back to sleep. But getting up in this much pain was not quite thinkable. So I sat quietly and thought about a youngish man talking to Edna Haley hours before she was murdered. What were the probabilities that he was a friend of Edna's and this was an innocent encounter?

I concluded that I'd better get up and stretch a bit before I stiffened completely. I swung my legs over the edge of the bed. Harvey finally stirred and came over to rub against me. Together we shuffled from bed to bathroom to kitchen.

In the kitchen I found a note from Patrick saying he had to go into work that morning. He also explained that Lindstrom had stopped by about nine o'clock last night for my notes on the case, but he had shooed her away saying he didn't know where my notes were and refusing to wake me. I made a mental note to do something really lovely for him when my head hurt less.

I made a pot of coffee and pondered the fact that several deep scrapes and a few dozen bruises had increased my appetite. I ate and retired to the couch to watch CNN's news. I fell into a doze till four when my phone rang. I let the machine answer it. A woman's voice identified itself as Rudy's girlfriend Nikki Dial. She left a number and asked me to call. I started sitting up as soon as she said her name, but as I picked it up, the dial tone buzzed in my ear. I replayed the message and punched out the number she'd left.

"Hello, Nikki. This is Meg Darcy."

"Hang on a second, here she is." There was a longish pause and then Nikki picked up.

"Hi, Meg. I didn't expect you to call right back."

"Yeah, I was just a little slow getting to the phone. What's up?"

"This probably isn't anything, but I thought maybe you'd want to know."

"Sure, what is it?"

"I found this scrap of paper in the pocket of Rudy's jacket. It's a phone number."

I pulled a note pad close to me but couldn't see a pen anywhere. Harvey finds it amusing to bat them around and then abandon them under the couch or behind the bookcases. "Hang on a minute, Nikki, I need a pen." I found one in my desk drawer, and after a few scribbles it was in working order. "Okay, read it to me." She read me a number whose prefix was unfamiliar to me. "Is there an area code?"

"No. I tried it a couple of times, but there was no answer."

"Did you try during the day or evening?"

"Once at ten in the morning, then last night about nine-thirty."

"Will you do me a favor and not try anymore? I think I can track it down pretty quickly. I promise I'll let you know, okay?"

"Okay, Meg. Have you found out anything new?"

"Nothing that sheds much light. But I'm following up some promising leads. Listen, since I have you, do you remember if Rudy ever met Dr. Rolfing outside work, or talked about conversations with him?"

"Dr. Rolfing?"

"He's the owner and house doctor at Gateway."

"No, I don't think so."

"Thanks anyway. If you find any written reference to Rolfing, will you let me know right away?"

"Sure, Meg. I hope the phone number helps somehow."

"I do, too. We could use a break."

I looked at Harvey and wished I could get him to fetch my city directory. I started by looking up the list of St. Louis prefixes in the front of the phone book. This prefix wasn't listed. I picked up the phone and called information. The prefix was for a cellular phone. I stared at the number. It was four-fifteen. Would he or she be on the way home from work? Only one way to find out. It rang only once.

"Greg Brooks here."

Chapter Eighteen

Dr. Moore had said to stay quiet, but I found myself leaving the couch to pace or to stare out the window. The snow was melting, and I could look into the street and see rivulets of water tunneling down from the snow mounds along the curb.

My head was still hurting—not steadily but with spells of throbbing.

Getting Greg Brooks on the line had so startled me that I'd cut the connection without speaking.

For several moments I'd spun my wheels wildly. Had Greg and Rudy had a drug connection? Had Rudy supplied drugs while Greg squandered money to pay for his habit? My first reaction was visceral. At some level Greg was still Ann's cousin to me—someone I knew slightly and wanted to create excuses for.

But only for a few moments. What broke the spell was the image of the black utility vehicle barreling out of the shadows. The driver had not wished me well.

I wandered back to the kitchen and popped a cup of water into the microwave. I was pouring the water over a tea bag when the scarf the woman at the shelter had given me floated back into view. This time it was hanging on the coat rack in Greg Brooks's office.

Suppose it was not drugs. Just greed. Getting in too deep with bad stock buys. Borrowing from Aunt M's account. Fearing disclosure. Maybe just wanting faster access to three million dollars he could call his own.

I squeezed the tea bag hard. How had he crossed the line to kill a relative he seemed so genuinely fond of? Every day I heard myself and others thinking somebody like Aunt M would be better off dead. He'd persuaded himself. That left four other old women, helpless and harmless, as victims. Well, our society treated old women as though they were as disposable as tissues. Why would Greg treat them better?

But how? He'd paid Rudy to lead Aunt M out. Then Rudy would have to be killed simply to make sure Greg's secret was safe and sound. By now Greg was enjoying the elaborate game and feeling superior to us all. He liked risk. He was a stock broker. A spelunker. Spelunkers carry rope. I was on a roll.

I walked back to the couch and addressed Harvey. "I bet he drives something besides a BMW to get to those caves. Damn, Harvey, how am I going to tell Ann? How am I going to convince Lindstrom?"

To me all the little pieces fell into place, but Lindstrom had been burned by arresting William Bishop. Arresting Greg Brooks of Brooks Brewery lineage would require more evidence than I had to offer her. But she had the means to look for rope and to get answers about his whereabouts on the six nights he'd been committing murder.

Start at the beginning Walter always says. I placed the call only to hit my first wall of frustration. Lindstrom was in court testifying. I asked for Neely. He was in another courtroom doing the same. I left a message I begged the police clerk to mark urgent.

I went back to the sofa for a good think.

My phone rang. Lindstrom.

I moved so quickly my stomach went queasy from the pain in my head.

"Meg? This is Ann."

"Ann," I acknowledged a bit feebly. I sat down hard on the phone end of the couch.

"I just got a call from Greg. He says Bill Curtis wants to meet us at Aunt M's grave site. To place a wreath and bury the hatchet." She gave a nervous laugh. "It sounds fishy to me. What's Curtis up to?"

I couldn't keep up with the thoughts that flew by. Instead I blurted, "Don't go, Ann."

She laughed again. "I thought you'd take the other side. Greg says Curtis is making a heal-the-wounds gesture." Her voice abandoned irony. "But I'm worried. Greg sounds too wound up. I'm afraid he may punch out Curtis if Curtis says the wrong thing."

"Ann, I can't tell you all my reasons over the phone. I've talked with Lindstrom. I think it's dangerous for you to go." I was thinking I needed to see her face-to-face to accuse Greg of serial murder.

A silence. "Do they have something on Curtis?" I'll give her credit. She wasn't gloating.

I skipped that. "What does Greg drive when he's not in the BMW?" I asked.

"What—"

"What kind of vehicle?"

"I heard you. I just can't figure out what it has to do with this conversation." But she could. I heard it in her voice.

"I'm just tying down loose ends, Ann. Does he have a black utility vehicle?"

I don't know if she detected the fib. But after a short pause she answered. "The Jeep he uses for spelunking. You don't suspect Greg."

But the protest sounded pro forma. Under it I heard worry.

"Ann, I don't have a right to ask for promises. But, as a friend, I'm asking you. Don't go to this meeting. And don't tell Greg or Curtis why you aren't if they call you." I kept my voice low and even, but I still sounded over-the-top in my own ears.

"What are you afraid of?"

"Just what you said—that things will get out of hand."

"Sometimes I can calm Greg down," she said. "Maybe I could be the peacemaker."

"Not between those two. Why are you being so stubborn?"

"I feel silly being afraid to go." Another nervous laugh.

I understood. The suspicions she had didn't fit the world view from Ladue and UMSL. The ones I'd planted about Greg were worse.

"Blame it on Philip," I said, meaning for her to use him as an excuse if Greg called her. "Promise me?"

"All right. When will you tell me about this new police information?"

"I'll call you tomorrow. I promise."

We hung up. I propelled myself up and into the kitchen. I filled a glass from the spigot and gulped four Advil.

Harvey came into the kitchen to make his own inquiries. I rubbed him absent-mindedly while he pranced and purred.

I hadn't begun to tell Ann all my theories.

Greg Brooks must be stretched to the snapping point. To conceal the motive for Aunt M's killing, he had killed four homeless women, making Aunt M's death looked connected to serial murders. To conceal that plot, he'd killed Rudy. He'd created a surface of killing from madness to hide his narrow personal greed.

But killing six people in this calculating, cold-blooded way must have destroyed whatever sanity he started with. I thought Greg Brooks was now out of control. Maybe he'd killed Edna Marie Haley after Bishop was released to cast more suspicion on Bishop. Certainly the media had gone wild. But it was dumb, a stupid risk. Because the cops were watching Bishop. A smart man would have predicted that unless something overrode his caution.

I tried Lindstrom's office again; the patient clerk promised to deliver my message. I rang up Curtis.

"Ah, Ms. Darcy, how are you today?"

Without preliminaries, I asked, "You're meeting with Greg Brooks today?"

"Yes. At four-thirty in Bellefountaine." He was his usual arch self.

"Why did you ask for this meeting, Mr. Curtis?"

"Oh, but I didn't. Greg called and suggested we meet there. A kind of ritual to bury the hatchet. Reading between the lines, I gather Ann thought we might get past the tensions that surfaced at the reading of the will."

"You didn't suggest the meeting?"

"Oh, my dear, no. I wish I could take credit for it. Linda and Aunt M were so close. It's tragic their families are at odds."

For a moment I wavered. Curtis had the gift of making the truth sound like a lie. But something rang a bell. A too-clever-by-half scheme to tell first Curtis, then Ann—or vice versa—that the other had asked for this grave side gathering.

"Skip the appointment, Mr. Curtis. Have a flat tire."

"I wouldn't miss it for the world. Ann will be there. It's our chance to become a happy family."

I could see it now. Bill Curtis climbs the social rungs to join the Brooks family.

"Ann won't be there."

"A pity." He sounded genuinely regretful.

"Look, Mr. Curtis, I don't know how to say this, but I'm afraid you might be in danger."

A longish pause. "From Mr. Brooks?"

"Possibly." I hated myself for sounding as coy as Curtis, but I didn't trust him enough to tell him the truth. I wasn't sure he wouldn't put himself into more danger by talking too much.

Another pause. "Interesting. I never go anywhere unescorted." What did that mean? Before I could ask, he added, "Will you be joining us?"

"No, I'm calling the police."

"Delicious. Shall we save that as a surprise for Mr. Brooks?"

"Look, Curtis, this meeting is not a smart move."

"Please, Ms. Darcy, you have forewarned me. I'll go prepared. Now do forgive me. I have to leave if I'm to be on time." He rang off.

I redialed, but he wasn't answering. Damn fool.

Next I tried calling Greg Brooks, not sure what I'd say if I reached him. But his secretary said he was out of his office. No answer on his cellular phone either. I looked at the clock.

I was just buckling my shoulder holster when Patrick returned from work.

"Whoa! What's this? Are we playing cops and robbers?"

"Stuff it, Patrick." Quickly I recounted both the deductions and the conversations of the afternoon.

"Have you heard—they've invented telephones. Call the cops."

I explained how I'd tried.

"That gun doesn't look like you're anticipating the sort of restful evening the doctor recommended."

"The gun is just to make me feel better. Probably I'm wrong about Greg's thinking, and he won't be foolish enough to attack Bill Curtis."

"Meg, this can wait one more day."

"But it can't. If I'm wrong about Greg's foolishness, Bill Curtis is in danger, and he's arrogant enough to think he can handle it." I was zipping up my jacket.

"Then I'm going with you."

I drew myself up. "Whatever for?"

"In case you faint and fall face down in a pile of snow. To run for help if someone drives over you. To plot your next move on Lindstrom." He was moving out my doorway. "Back in one."

We met in the hallway and began a debate about which car to take. I won. Even if the snow was melting, it might get slick by nightfall, and I preferred the Plymouth's front-wheel drive to the MG's lightness.

The late afternoon light was already dimming as we drove east on 44 and north on 70 toward Bellefountaine. Rush hour traffic started slowing us down. "Let's take the side streets," I said, and Patrick peeled off at the next exit. The fog Ben Able had predicted was hanging low in wispy curls.

Patrick said, "How about on the way home I stop for some Chinese takeout or something? Maybe we'll rent a movie. I'll put an afghan over your feet and tuck you in."

I didn't protest. Now that I was out and about, venturing into the great outdoors was rapidly losing its appeal. I tried to concentrate on the scene ahead, scripting scenarios, then discarding them.

Rush hour had hit West Florissant by the time we turned onto it. From there Patrick made a fast and flashy left into the cemetery to honked complaints. Within yards of the gate the entrance drive branches off into a half dozen asphalt choices; these lanes twist and wind through the cemetery, subdividing and doubling back on themselves. Down here the fog was speed crawling across the snow. The lanes were slickly black, wet from the melt, ready to refreeze by midnight.

Patrick looked at me. "Now what?"

"Can you see to drive with your lights off—going very, very slowly, of course?"

"Why would I want to do that?"

"So that someone won't see you coming."

"I thought a major point of headlights was to get someone to see you coming." But he flicked them off and began to creep forward.

I unzipped my jacket and reached in to touch the thirty-eight in its holster.

"Are you taking out that gun?" Patrick asked.

"No, just making sure I can."

"Shouldn't we go for the cops?"

"Love to. But we don't have time."

"Meg, Chinese. I'll rub your feet."

"Patrick, watch out. You're nearly off the asphalt."

Fog disorients. It takes twice as long to drive even on a familiar street. I had attended Aunt M's grave side service and in theory knew where she had been buried, but our hope of finding it again seemed slim; it would be so easy to drive past the right turnoff. I dug around in the map pocket and found the cemetery map Lindstrom had marked for me, but there wasn't enough light to make it readable.

"Take it easy. Whatever he is going to do is going to take a little time," I said.

"Why do you think Greg is going to do anything? If he killed all those women to cover up his killing of Ann's aunt, won't making moves against Curtis—and Ann, too—reveal his connections to those crimes? It's undoing all the work he's done."

"Spoken like someone who's rational."

"You think Greg's a nut case?" Patrick grimaced. "Beyond what you'd have to be to kill five women and Rudy Carr."

"Rational is elastic, isn't it? Think of people who believe they're Napoleon, but then deduce logically from that fact."

"But he can't believe the police won't look suspiciously at the only one left standing after this is over—if he kills Curtis and goes after Ann."

"Maybe he's compelled to play the game through to the end just because he has this vision of himself as the only one left standing when it's all over." I snatched at another idea that bobbed up. "Maybe he has a scheme to kill Ann and Curtis and plant evidence to make Curtis look guilty. Like Greg himself came to the rescue too late to save Ann but in time to catch Curtis red-handed."

"Now that's convoluted."

"Not for a control freak. He's got to line up his ducks."

"Are you sure it's not Curtis? He sounds weird enough."

"Don't stereotype," I snapped. Then I reached out to touch his arm. "Sorry. I'm almost one-hundred percent sure."

"Ninety-nine point six?" He said it with a smile to show he forgave my testiness.

"At least."

We fell silent.

Strands of fog drifted over our hood, thick as blankets. Patrick rolled down his window and stuck his head out; I did the same on my side. We were looking at the ground, trying to see just ahead of our wheels. The Plymouth was not exactly silent as it strained forward, but the fog would muffle some sounds. The hills around us still had a layer of snow. White on white. My headache returned. I felt it in my eyes. As we climbed, the fog would part, then drape over us again. I looked at my watch. It was five. Whoever was inside now, including us, was locked inside. I didn't tell Patrick. He seemed tense enough.

"Damnit!" Patrick so seldom swears that his outburst seemed as shocking as whatever we hit.

I looked out. We were off the road and had run up against a low-lying tombstone. It looked like we hadn't damaged anything too seriously.

"Sorry. Lost my concentration," I said. He put it in reverse. We heard the spin. We got out of the car. We were off the road and onto a patch of ice.

"You take the wheel. I think I can shove it back on the asphalt. The Plymouth is light," he said.

"Wait. Let's go ahead on foot. I think we're pretty close."

He blew a little puff of air. "Shouldn't we have the car ready to roll in case we have to leave fast?"

"I don't want to make a lot of noise."

"Get in the car, Meg. Just put it in neutral and let me push it back."

Patrick doesn't use that tone often; I decided compromise was in order. "Let's both push it back; it doesn't require much steering."

We got in front and pushed. The snow was slippery with a layer of melt on top. We braced against the headstone that marked the grave, lifted the bumper a fraction, and, on the count of three, shoved. The car slid in the right direction. We were back on asphalt. Patrick got in the car and slipped it back into gear.

"Meg, I think it's time to get in and go home," he whispered.

"Follow me, Patrick," I said in my most forceful whisper. "Stay with me."

He climbed out, and we set off walking single file. Patrick grabbed the tail of my jacket. I wasn't moving quickly. I wanted off the asphalt path. Which might have been a mistake. The branches above were dripping cold water down our necks, except when we hit a low-hanging one which dumped snow. The ground snow was mushy, and we sank into it. Except for those spots which were still frozen. Then we slipped or skidded. We were gradually moving uphill. My heart was thudding, and my breaths came in noisy heaves. As we climbed, the fog thinned a bit, but night had closed in.

I fell twice, once dragging Patrick on top of me. I scuffed my shins against low-lying tombstones, and once just walked right into a tree. Patrick hung onto my coat and didn't complain. Maybe his own lungs were rasping too painfully. I was starting to wonder if we would spend the night wandering in circles around the huge cemetery. Not what the doctor ordered.

Then ahead and above me I saw two yellow pools of light, diffused and blurred by the fog. Headlights. I saw a dark figure pacing back and forth by a squat rectangular building. A mausoleum. I signaled Patrick to be quiet, not that he had much control. But we stopped moving, and I pulled him over behind the tallest, broadest tombstone we could find in the vicinity. Just stopping helped us to quiet our breathing. The figure in the dark overcoat had an aureole around his head. Bill Curtis with his wispy hair. His hands were jammed into his pockets. The temperature was in the high thirties still, but all the dampness in the air made a cutting chill. I was glad the recent exercise up the hill was warming my blood, but if I had to stand still long, I'd be shivering.

Then another, taller figure stepped out of the fog. This man was dressed in coveralls and a Greek fisherman's cap. There was a muffled exchange.

I pressed my lips to Patrick's ear. "I'm moving closer; you stay here."

I moved away, bending down and duck waddling to a nearer but lower tombstone. When I reached it, I flopped down on my belly. I had on thick layers, but I could feel the cold seeping up. I eased out my thirty-eight. Just in case.

"Where's your car? Surely you didn't hike in like a Boy Scout working on a merit badge." This was vintage Bill Curtis. Though his timbre seemed less secure than his mocking banter would suggest.

"I thought you could give me a lift out," Greg Brooks replied, his hands in the front pockets of his coveralls.

"But where is your Jeep?" Curtis persisted. He sounded peevish.

"That's not important, is it?" Greg sat down nonchalantly on a nearby tombstone.

"But it puzzles me. I like solving puzzles," Curtis said. He found a tombstone of similar height and perched on its edge, keeping his hands in his pockets. The two were now facing each other, perhaps two yards apart.

Curtis continued. "Well, Greg, Meg Darcy seems to think you're the cemetery murderer. Could that be true?"

"What do you think, Curtis? Did I kill my own aunt, helpless and insensible as she was?"

"Two million dollars is a considerable sum."

Greg laughed, not a pleasant sound at all. "Not for me. I make and lose millions before lunch."

"You don't get to take those home, however. This money would belong to you."

"What did Darcy say?"

"Not much. Just that you might be thinking about killing me next."

Greg pulled his hands slowly from his pockets, and I caught Bill's movement from the corner of my eye a moment too late.

"Drop it," Curtis yelled as he pulled out a tiny pistol from his belt.

"Drop what, Bill? You've been giving too much credence to the dyke detective. I don't have a gun."

He turned his palms up so Curtis could see.

Then Brooks moved again, slowly, deliberately toward the asphalt road. After two steps he just turned, giving Curtis a broad back to aim at.

Curtis jumped up. So did I, heedlessly.

"Wait!" he said. Then the headlights shut down. We'd both been looking toward them. I was blinded by the sudden dark, and so no doubt was Curtis. "Wait!" he called again. I heard the engine stop, the thunk of the door. Silence.

I remembered a trick I'd read about and closed my eyes, willed them shut a painfully long minute, opened them. I could see better. Curtis was moving toward his Bronco, but slowly, stopping, turning. I glanced behind me to see if I could see Patrick, but I couldn't. Curtis shuffled forward. I circled out in an arc away from him, but moving faster in the same direction. I got to the asphalt a step before he did. He tried the car door. It was locked. Curtis sank into the door, kicked the tire. Brooks had the keys. And where was Brooks?

I glanced toward the grounds off the asphalt. With the fog drifting through trees and monuments I could see only looming shadows, their size and shape distorted. The cemetery had many tall, ornate monuments with crosses or angels at their pinnacles. Some were slender enough to look like a standing figure. The fog moved. Was that tree moving?

It was time to locate Patrick, round up Curtis, and get the hell out of there. But even as I turned my eyes back toward the Bronco, I saw Curtis disappearing back into the fog. He had a gun. Maybe he assumed he was safe. Maybe he thought Brooks intended to garrote him as he had the women and his gun would trump that piece of rope Brooks was likely to conceal in his coveralls pocket. But Brooks had used a gun on Rudy. If Brooks shot Curtis and used the Bronco to cart the body away to another spot, then maybe there'd be a chance for him to separate this killing from the others, or, as I'd suggested to Patrick, plant evidence to incriminate Curtis.

But did Brooks really think the police wouldn't scour over every detail of another coincidentally related death? That I wouldn't? But then, he'd already made one move on me. He was, I had no doubt, waiting in the fog for Curtis. Greg Brooks was more desperate and reckless with every hour, but he surely kidded himself that he was maintaining control. Though he didn't know it yet, to survive this night, he would have to kill three more people.

I needed to round up the other two. I had missed my moment to call out to Curtis without attracting Brooks's attention. I didn't want to make myself an easy target for the gun he was undoubtedly carrying. I really needed to find Patrick.

There was no help for it. I stepped off the asphalt back into the little wooded area at the top of the knoll where the mausoleum was. In daylight, the trees looked farther apart; tonight, the fog filled in the space. I moved forward slowly, a finger of fear running up my spine. At the moment, I didn't feel a single throb of pain. I was moving slowly, straining to see past tree and stone, straining to see *through* tree and stone and fog. I wasn't so much walking as sliding my feet forward in a slow, gingerly shuffle. I stubbed my toes against the low headstones, but I kept moving forward, trying to penetrate the fog before me, trying not to think about the fog and trees closing behind me, trying to breathe very shallowly and quietly.

My left foot slid. For a beat I lost control of my left leg, the one that was already stiff from Saturday's collision with Brooks's Jeep. The leg skidded out without my will, and I pitched forward and threw out my left hand, still skinned, and slapped it against an icy obelisk and stopped my fall. I stood there a moment, feeling especially vulnerable, while my heart thumped and I tried to regain control of my breathing. If anyone wanted a shot at me now—

I didn't have time to dwell on it. Somewhere ahead I heard a crack, its sharpness softened by the fog. It sounded like a muffled gunshot or the snapping of a branch. There were plenty of old limbs lying on the ground. Maybe someone else had misstepped.

But the noise was not a clear directional signal in this night of smoke and mirrors. I tightened my grip on the thirty-eight and peered around the obelisk. Again, I saw too much movement, although it may have been swirls of fog. I listened so intently my ears ached. I blinked just to relieve the stress on my eyes and new configurations formed. I wasn't sure where I was in relation to the obelisk near Aunt M's grave or to the spot where I'd left Patrick.

I scooted a foot forward, letting my fingers lightly touch the obelisk I was standing by. I reluctantly left that behind and moved toward the next, another obelisk, this one with a cross on top. I reached out for it when a hand grabbed at my face from behind, a heavy arm around my neck. I didn't hesitate. The ground was too slippery to set myself for a good over the shoulder flip. I grappled with the hand seeking my mouth, thinking a bite might do it. A swing backward with my elbow, aiming for the groin area, was nearly reflexive.

"Meg!" The whisper was husky and urgent. The slim body sidestepped the blow to the crotch, though I hit his hip hard enough to send a jar through all my sore muscles.

"Patrick!" I whispered back. I was both annoyed and glad to see him.

I pulled his head down and pressed my lips to his ear and whispered hurriedly, just catching him up on the essentials: that Greg Brooks and Bill Curtis were out there, both armed I was sure, and both nervous with itchy trigger fingers.

Patrick leaned forward and put his lips to my ear. "Meg, lets—"

Then the bullet zinged by. Without ceremony I grabbed his fleecy coat and let my body weight pull us down. He didn't need many hints. We fell in a scramble, and I slithered away from the spot, guiding him by pulling his sleeve. We kept our heads down.

"Wish I knew who that was," I said.

"What difference does it make?"

"Slide over there, behind that tombstone," I said, pointing to a waist-high stone a little to our left. He made a face but did as he was told, using his elbows to propel him across the snow like an army-trained boy.

I fired in the general direction of the shot, aiming a little lower than I thought I should. Then I quickly slithered over to Patrick, landing on top of him and pushing his head down. I heard another bullet zing by. It hit something, a tree from the sound of it. But the shooter was off, aiming toward where we had been.

I slid off Patrick. I put a finger to his lips, then motioned him to follow. We scooted forward on our stomachs. In a way it's terrible to be lying down—there's a horrible feeling of vulnerability. On the other hand, I had a hunch that no one would be looking for us down there. It would be quieter to leave Patrick behind, but I didn't want to lose him again. He was my responsibility, and he was unarmed.

Probably I ought to have pointed us both downhill to my car and out of there. But I had a notion that it was also my responsibility to get Curtis out. Or maybe, more honestly, to prevent Greg from killing again. I was angry that it had taken so long for all the pieces to fall into place.

We inched forward slowly, and all the forgotten places on my body started to deliver reminders of how much I could still hurt. My coat and jeans were getting soppy with a wet cold. None of that was as important as someone's taking shots at us, but it all added together.

Then I heard several noises, less a series than a blend. Grunts and thuds and breath torn out of the lungs. I scrambled onto my feet and heard Patrick doing the same.

"Stay here!" I called as I moved toward the sounds.

"No way!" he answered.

I hadn't forgotten to be careful, but I figured it takes two to scuffle. I couldn't run, but I managed a little trot, still skidding once or twice. I heard a shot go off, a male voice say, "Fuck!", more thuds, and then I saw the two—like one thick blob in the fog.

I heard Patrick come to a skidding halt behind me. I moved forward, dropped to one knee, took a firing position, and yelled, "Stop!"

One figure pulled away, fired a shot toward me that I returned in the instant. We both missed, but I flopped down to offer less target area. The man who fired turned and ran. The other figure was sinking toward the ground.

I scrambled up and ran toward him. It was Curtis. He was breathing raggedly. "Are you shot?"

"No, get him," he rasped out. I saw his small pistol on the ground beside him and scooped it up.

Patrick had come up behind me. I handed him the pistol. "Stay here."

I started off in the direction Brooks had gone. We were headed downhill. I couldn't see him, but he was making enough noise to carry, snapping though some twigs and branches on the ground. I heard Patrick still behind me and didn't have the time or breath to scold him. I heard a 'wompf'—the sound of Brooks falling I thought. I kept going, skidding myself into an unplanned downhill slalom. For a yard or two there were no monuments as I careened down the slope.

I kept my footing till the end. Just as I thought I was home free, my feet swooped up ahead of me and once more I took a flyer. I landed with such a thud the breath whooshed out of me and the thirty-eight flew. Patrick damn near fell over me.

"Meg?" His voice held so much concern I nearly cried.

"Where's my gun?" I said, trying to scramble up. I saw it just a few feet away and clumsily retrieved it. "Come on," I said, my voice hoarse in my ears.

We were still headed downward. He was trying to provide escort services and ease me down the slippery slope.

I shook him off. I can't run as fast as he can—he was good at track—but I shoot a damn sight better. I didn't want him in the line of fire if Brooks shot back. My sides were burning now—sore ribs, cold air raking my lungs, a stitch from running.

Then in the mysterious way of fog we got a rent in the veil. I looked down and saw the slope turning gentle, and in the distance ahead of us Greg Brooks was making a clumsy run toward a section of fence where the pickets were down. It opened onto the street—Calvary, I think—that bisects the two cemeteries. It would lead back to Broadway. He could flag down a ride or find a phone to call a cab or retrieve his Jeep or whatever.

"Get down," I snapped to Patrick. I slid to a kneeling position, yelled "Stop!" and fired a warning shot in the air.

Brooks kept running.

I aimed low and fired again.

"Jesus," Patrick said as the man ahead of us stumbled and fell forward, then rolled onto his side and onto his back. He lay very still.

"You stay behind me and keep your pistol on him," I said. We moved down the gentle slope rapidly.

I approached the supine figure with my gun in firing position. I've seen all the movies where the downed bad guy springs back into life.

From under his body a black puddle was spreading in the snow. I have seen few scarier sights in my life, but I moved forward, still keeping the gun aimed at his torso.

He was alive and able to lift his head. The blood was coming from his leg. He was going to need first aid and soon; his whole thigh area was saturated in black.

Our eyes met. His in this light were black pools that reflected hate.

I waved Patrick forward and handed him my gun. I walked closer to Greg Brooks. I reached down and pulled the plaid wool scarf that he'd tucked under his coveralls from around his neck to use for a tourniquet.

In one of my college classes we'd worked on a problem about how to get six people across a river full of crocodiles when three of the six can't trust the other three. It's not exactly a logic problem; it was to invite us to be creative.

Patrick and I had to juggle how to get the cops and an ambulance, plus round up Bill Curtis. I finally sent Patrick down toward Broadway to find a phone while I stayed with Brooks—not that he was going anywhere. I figured we could round up Curtis when the police arrived. I told Patrick to insist that they send Lindstrom. After all, it was her case.

The wait seemed even longer than it was because the wet spots on my clothing were starting to freeze, and I was afraid I might go into shock. But all the little abrasions and big bruises I had acquired from Greg's vehicular attack on me were hurting full steam which was probably a good sign I wasn't. I had to loosen the scarf now and then so Brooks's blood could continue to circulate. I was too tired to fantasize much about tying it around his neck and pulling it tight.

I asked him some questions while we waited. Some of the big and obvious ones: Had he paid Rudy? Where had he killed Mary Margaret? How had he lured his other female victims to their deaths?

And some of the lesser ones: Had it been he or Curtis who had shot at us the first time this evening? Where had he lost his gun?

He saved his breath.

The ambulance and Patrick arrived about five minutes before the police. He had cleverly directed the paramedics to the convenience store he was calling from, rightly figuring that he could more easily lead them personally to the spot, especially in the fog.

The paramedics had Brooks in the ambulance and hooked to an IV by the time Lindstrom arrived with Neely. They had an extra patrol car with them.

Patrick and I just stood there, shoulder to shoulder and thoroughly tuckered, and watched her walking toward us.

"You two!" she said when she got close enough to recognize us. She kept on walking till she was near to the amoeba-shaped blotch on the snow. She stared down at it as though reading tea leaves. Then she looked up, and said, "You were right."

"Yep," I agreed modestly.

Chapter Nineteen

It wasn't over. We had a long night ahead. Lindstrom and Neely called for more uniformed reinforcements who were put in charge of packing Patrick, me and Curtis into three separate patrol cars to Clark Street Station and then into separate interrogation rooms—as dull and stale as their TV imitators. Lindstrom and Neely followed Greg Books to the hospital where his only statements were a profane version of 'ouch' and a call for his lawyer.

Lindstrom and Neely returned and took turns taking me over the evening's events after they gave up on Brooks. They'd go through everything very carefully, and I'd think, whew, that's over. Then they'd leave me alone while they questioned Patrick or Curtis. The waiting was the hard part.

On their third visitation, I asked, "Can I see my lawyer?"

Neely looked amused. Lindstrom said, "Very funny" in a tone which indicated she was not.

She looked tired under the cold fluorescent lights, her hair and face not just pale, but leeched of color. I hated to think what I looked like. All the thumps and thuds of the chase had been hidden by an adrenaline rush that had worn off. Now my body was reminded of not only my earlier injuries but of fresh bruises as well.

I tried an appeal to pity. "My doctor said I should rest. In my very own bed," I added.

"Where you were supposed to stay," Lindstrom said sourly.

"Lucky I didn't," I said. So far I'd resisted any crowing about catching the cemetery murderer. I could tell that Lindstrom and Neely thought I had the right culprit, and to give them credit, they were relieved. Of course, they'd still get the collar. But lesser cops wouldn't get over being bested.

"Yes, tell us again how you happened to be on the scene," Lindstrom said.

Neely looked understanding, something he was good at. "We want to be very careful about how we proceed, to make sure the case stands up," he said.

I nodded and started over.

At three a.m., after another interval of my waiting while they questioned someone else, Lindstrom reappeared by herself. She looked a little perkier, as though she'd got her second wind.

"You can go now. We'd like you to stop in later today and sign your statement after it's typed." Her official tone put a big distance between us.

I hopped from my chair and stretched hugely, only to feel the red creep up my cheeks as I realized she was watching my breasts move.

Her eyes met mine without apology.

She shrugged. "We're getting a warrant to search Greg's home and Jeep. Rope fibers, mud on his shoes—any links to the bodies."

"Don't forget Aunt M's coat."

She looked puzzled.

"It wasn't hers. Greg must have dressed her in it. Fibers. Plus, where did he get it?"

She nodded, comprehending my tired shorthand.

"What about Curtis? Did he help?" I asked.

She hesitated because I was a civilian, but then answered. "Somehow he got the idea we might be charging him with extortion. He became quite cooperative. He corroborates everything you've said—and more." She looked pleased.

Even so, she and Neely would still have to tie the knots to make the case. I could see their work wouldn't be easy.

"I was lucky," I volunteered.

She knew what I was talking about. She nodded. "But persistent, too. You wouldn't give up on your notion that Aunt M's death was crucial." Her tone was detached, judicial; the effect needled me. I might have been any civilian who'd given the police a tip.

It was my turn to shrug.

"Which is what surprises me," she added in a different tone, the voice I heard as the Ice Queen.

I looked into her blue eyes.

"That you aren't more persistent in other areas. That you go off in a huff."

"It wasn't a huff."

"A huff." No give there.

"You are so arrogant."

She shrugged again. Lovely shoulders. I wanted to remove the corduroy and oxford cloth.

"Maybe," she said. "I am sorry I was so neglectful afterwards. The case absorbed everything. My ex couldn't understand that."

Trickery. Trickery.

"Sure. I get involved in cases, too," I said. I couldn't help it. The blue eyes? No, the etched mouth. Body memories.

"I can give you a ride home," she said.

I was caught off guard. I resented that. "Where's Patrick? Where's my car?" Even to my ears, I sounded suspicious, as though the cops were hiding my friend and my Plymouth.

Lindstrom looked amused, which irritated me. "I sent him on with assurances that you would arrive home safely."

Was there no end to her arrogance? She must think riding home with her was some great honor or something. I had been looking forward to debriefing with Patrick. Maybe over a greasy breakfast. at Irv's Good Food. Now I was stuck with the Ice Queen, who had been growing steadily less attractive as this long night wore on. Surely she wasn't counting on another celebration of the sort she'd held after arresting Bishop. I wasn't up to that. Although the thought that I might get to be the top since I had caught the bad guy did bring a flutter. I shook my head. No, one thing was clear. Lindstrom's Ice Queen neurosis went too deep for me. I wasn't willing to put up with the high-handedness, even if the sex was great. She'd just have to go push some other unsuspecting dyke around. But still I needed a ride home. "Okay, let's go, I'm beat."

We climbed into her department-issue beige, Crown Victoria, and she headed southwest toward my neighborhood. The city was quiet, traffic light, with almost no one on the streets. Not where we could see them, anyway. The night was colder now, but still foggy. I hoped Jamal and his mother and Leanna and Edna's friend with the scarf were someplace safe and warm. Stopping Greg's killing spree wouldn't make their lives safe. And it would certainly lose me a friend. Even if Ann could forgive me for bringing Greg's crimes to light, she would never forget it. It isn't the kind of thing that even lifelong friends could get around; I was sure our friendship didn't have a solid enough base to rise above it. I yawned. My mouth had middle of the night sourness and my head was pounding again. I needed my tooth brush, three ibuprofen, and a good night's sleep. And maybe a new career that wouldn't limit me to the sad and the evil and the arrogant. I would definitely work on it.

"The end is always disappointing, isn't it?"

I looked at Lindstrom. "What do you mean?"

"The end of a case. It isn't really a moment of glory, is it? It feels more like shoveling shit than hitting a home run."

"Yeah. Especially when you know the asshole's family."

"She'll be glad you stopped him. Eventually." She paused. "Or maybe she won't. Either way you did your job. Did what you needed to do."

She obviously couldn't imagine what it felt like to have a loved one exposed as a murderer. I wondered if there were any situations in which she felt empathy, or if her imagination were so limited, she never knew what it was like to be someone else. I glanced upward as she pulled into the parking area behind my building. Patrick's lights were still on. Good. He had waited up for me. Maybe I'd get that greasy breakfast after all.

"I need to go back to the station to finish the paperwork, but I'd like to walk you up if that's okay."

"You've never bothered to ask if you could come in before." In answer her gaze was steady, but her eyes narrowed just a bit. I finally said, "You can come up for a minute, but I'm headed to bed as soon as I've fed Harvey and brushed my teeth."

We climbed the stairs in silence. In my kitchen she turned toward me. "Darcy, you know you should give me a break. I'm not as bad as you think."

"What did you have in mind?"

"Just don't assume the worst of me, okay?" She put her hand on my cheek and then pulled me into her arms. She leaned into me, and I felt her shoulders relax. "You know we might take a chance. Just a chance to get to know one another. As women. Apart from work."

"What does that mean?"

She put her cheek against mine and asked, "What do you want it to mean?"

Crafty. Implying I had choices.

I ran my hand up her back and tried to sort the jumbled reactions of mind and body. She pulled me to her tight for an instant and then let go. "Sleep well. Call me when you wake up."

She strode out.

Two seconds later Patrick was standing in my kitchen with a grin and a question, "Irv's Good Food?"